PRAI

A DROWN

'A duo that might just come to rival the *Thursday Murder Club*.'
DAILY MAIL

'This intriguing mystery combines the perils of the thriller
genre with the meticulous, slow craft of detection.'
CRIME TIME REVIEW

'A gripping story of toxic families, dangerous secrets
and the past catching up with the present.'
ISLE OF WIGHT OBSERVER

'The novel is an unputdownable brainteaser.'
ON THE WIGHT

'Every character plays a game of hide-and-seek with the truth'
WALTHAM FOREST ECHO, SARAH FAIRBAIRN

'It is thrilling to navigate Merry's journey.'
SHOTS MAGAZINE, JUDITH SULLIVAN

'An irresistible brainteaser.'
PLATINUM MAGAZINE

'I found it – like Merry's daily saltwater swims – sharply compulsive.
In fact in many ways, the story brought to mind the ocean –
seemingly calm or ominous on top, with all sorts of currents and
debris beneath the surface, ready to snag the unwary . . .'
JM HALL, author of *A Spoonful of Murder*

'A kooky protagonist. A missing person. Dark secrets resurfacing.
What's not to love in this perfectly plotted, gripping mystery?'
MEERA SHAH

'An engrossing, twisty mystery, so richly evoked you'll be booking your Isle of Wight holiday before you turn the last page.'
TAMMY COHEN, author of *They All Fall Down*

'Beautifully written, gorgeously twisty and a complete page-turner ... full of brackish, stony, loamy Isle of Wight authenticity.'
FIONA WALKER, author of *The Art of Murder*

'A standout mystery crime thriller.'
FRAN TAYLOR, author of *Wind in My Wings*

'I fell in love with Merry, foibles and all.'
KATHERINE ADAMS, author of *Tonight, I Burn*

'In this beautifully written book of cryptic clues, doubts and suspense, we are swept up in a current of uncertainty and fear.'
ROSIE SANDLER, author of *Murder Takes Root*

'A brilliantly crafted story with captivating mystery and a wonderfully unique main character at its center – I couldn't put this down.'
SOPHIE FLYNN, author of *What Stays Unsaid*

'An addictive, beautifully written whodunnit that will stay with you long after you've raced to the final page.'
LEAH PITT, author of *The Beach Hut*

'A beguilingly atmospheric, tensely mysterious story with a warm, beating heart.'
GYTHA LODGE, author of *DCI Jonah Sheens series*

'Unique, enthralling, unputdownable. Hugely engrossing, quirky and beautifully written.'
LIZ WEBB, author of *The Daughter & The Saved*

A DROWNING TIDE

A DROWNING TIDE

SARAH LAWTON

Black&White

First published in the UK in 2024.

This edition first published in the UK in 2025 by Black & White Publishing.

An imprint of Bonnier Books UK
5th Floor, HYLO, 103–105 Bunhill Row,
London, EC1Y 8LZ
Owned by Bonnier Books
Sveavägen 56, Stockholm, Sweden

Copyright © Sarah Lawton 2024

All rights reserved.
No part of this publication may be reproduced,
stored or transmitted in any form by any means, electronic,
mechanical, photocopying or otherwise, without the
prior written permission of the publisher.

The right of Sarah Lawton to be identified as Author of this
work has been asserted by her in accordance with the
Copyright, Designs and Patents Act, 1988.

This is a work of fiction. Names, places, events and incidents are either the products of the author's imagination or used fictitiously. Any resemblance to actual persons, living or dead, or actual events is purely coincidental.

A CIP catalogue record for this book is available from the British Library.

ISBN: 978 1 78530 675 4

1 3 5 7 9 10 8 6 4 2

Typeset by Data Connection
Printed and bound in Great Britain by Clays Ltd, Elcograf S.p.A.

www.blackandwhitepublishing.com

*For Liz, Katherine, Jo, Marija,
and all the Tuesdays.*

Author's Note

Eagle-eyed residents of the Isle of Wight may notice that I have taken some liberties with small parts of our geography for artistic purposes. For the main part though, all the places I have described within this novel are real and beautiful and well worth a visit.

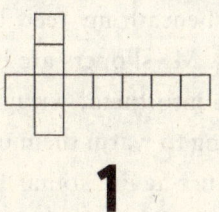

1

ACROSS: 17. False information is undesirable (3,4)

THE BIG HOUSE IS ENTIRELY lit up, which seems odd for five in the morning. I didn't hear a party, and I'm a light sleeper. It looks cold out there, the grass of my small patch of lawn and theirs beyond is silver tipped and probably delightfully crunchy. I wonder if I should go over and check up on them, but I haven't been particularly welcome recently, and it's five in the morning.

Instead, I crawl back into bed and pick up my notebook. I still have four crossword puzzles to submit on a deadline this week, which is not like me. I'm usually more organised. I should stop noseying at the neighbours and keep working. Maybe they're going on holiday. Lucas would usually tell me though, ask me to keep an eye on the place while they're away. I don't know. Maybe it's the moon distracting me, shining in my window all night, making me dream of things I'd rather forget, even though it's only at first quarter. It's no good.

Thinking of the moon makes me think of tides and that pulls me again from my bed, downstairs, to the kitchen. The smooth tiles are cold beneath my feet, but the familiarity is as steadying as always. My slippers are by the back door and I slide my chilled feet into them, wriggling my toes against the woolly fabric, trying to warm them up. As the kettle boils I look over at their house again, so much bigger and grander than my tiny cottage. Still all the lights on. What a waste of electric.

I take the tea into the front room and tell my contraption to play me Classic FM. It's nice this time of the morning, they don't play the louder pieces until later, for now it's small and soothing for those of us who are awake at ungodly hours. The tide chart is in the neat little drawer of my coffee table, well worn. It's nearly the end of October, I'll need to order next year's soon. The tide was up at 3.53 a.m., only an hour ago. If I hurry, I could still catch a decent depth at Appley, or I'll have to wait until four this afternoon. I quite like swimming in the dark on a clear night. Though I got a face full of weeds last time, which put paid to my pretensions of being a selkie, all shiny and secretive, slipping through the water. Later then, and only if I've finished a whole puzzle and sent it off.

With thoughts now full of seawater and mythical creatures, seal-women dancing on lonely beaches in remote places, I settle on a theme for my crossword, raiding the bookshelf for my *Lore of Land* and my dictionary. I'll start, I think, with Selkie, two e's and an s, it's a good central word to spread out from. *Skin-shedding mythical creature (6)*. I start by mapping the grid, a rough shape at first, plotting out some words and phrases. Dredging up older clues I've used before to tweak, leaving new ones for later. I find the absorption I need as dawn melts away the dark night. My tea has gone cold.

I'm boiling the kettle again and pondering breakfast – Marmite or jam on toast, trying to remember what I had yesterday or if I even ate anything – when there's a knock at the door. It's a rather loud knock for barely half past eight, though I suppose my front room light suggests that I am up and about, even though I am still in my dressing gown and slippers. Maybe it's my new book. It's not. It's two policemen. At least that's my assumption. There's a man in uniform and a woman in a suit with a long, slim-fitting wool coat over the top, both looking stern.

We stand staring at each other for a long stomach-swooping moment while my mind trips and scatters to the winds of bad memories, of a scene like this played out once before, but I gather myself and my voice is firm when I speak.

'Yes? Can I help you?'

The young man talks while the woman watches on. 'Sorry to bother you so early,' he says, his accent catching on a nerve. Why do all young people want to sound like they're from London these days? I recognise this nipper, he's a look of his mother about him, as local as I am.

'I'm an early riser,' I interrupt. 'What do you need?'

'We're here about your neighbour, Lucas Manning,' he says, and my innards lurch again. 'His wife Alison has reported him missing.'

'Missing?' I parrot back stupidly.

'She hasn't seen him since Sunday evening.' This time the woman speaks, a silky Scottish burr, words as smooth as her shiny black hair. She's a long way from home. *Selkie*. 'D'you mind if we come in for a wee minute? It's cold out here. It won't take long.' She takes out a black leather wallet from her pocket and flips it open, showing me her warrant card. There's a braille plaque on it beneath the shiny crest which glints in the morning sun.

'Okay,' I say, stepping back into the narrow hallway. 'You'll have to excuse the mess. Kettle's just boiled; do you want a hot drink?' There isn't a mess but that's what people say, isn't it? They follow me through to the kitchen. The young man – is he a Harding, or was that his mother, I can't recall – waits for his superior to assent before he also agrees. It is very cold this morning. I make them both tea, use the time to gather my thoughts. *Missing?*

They settle themselves around my small kitchen table and I feel slightly embarrassed at its scruffy and scratched surface and scattered collection of notebooks and pots of chewed-on pens. The boy takes out his own notepad and I could almost picture him licking the end of a pencil before starting to write. I don't know why silly things like that pop into my head when I'm nervous.

'Here you go.' They both take the mugs I offer them and draw them across the table where they've sat, cupping them for warmth. A slim band of silver gleams from the woman's wedding finger. Maybe she married an islander; I can't think why anyone would move so far from home to end up here otherwise.

'When did you last see Mr Manning, Mrs . .?'

'Ms. Ms Merriweather. Or just Merry, if you like.'

'Merry,' she says with a small smile as my name rolls in her mouth, a flash of teeth showing past unadorned lips. No make-up at all it looks like, which is unusual. I thought I was fairly alone in my eschewing of powders and pastes. 'Merry, when did you last see your neighbour? How did he seem?'

I have to think for a minute. I don't see Lucas as much as I used to or would like to, really, apart from the little jobs he does for me. 'A few days ago. I saw them going off for a walk, Sunday afternoon maybe, but it could have been Saturday. I don't think I've seen either of them since then.'

She makes a note in green loops on a scruffy pad of paper. I hate green ink. 'Where did you see them walking? Do you know where they were going?'

'I'm not psychic, they could have been going anywhere. But they were next to the woods just over the back, so either through there or maybe down to the beach.'

'How well do you know them?' She doesn't look at me as she asks but I hear the interest, and wonder what Alison has said about me, to send them straight over to me like this.

'I've always lived here,' I tell her. 'I've known Lucas his whole life, his parents lived there before he did and his grandparents before that. They're all gone now.'

The boy flickers his eyebrows, and I curse inwardly. Always so blunt. 'I don't know Alison so much though, she's a quiet girl. Not from the island. Not like you, I think I know your mother. Catherine, isn't it?'

'Yeah,' he says, with a surprised smile. 'I live on the mainland now though, come over on the boat. Mum and Dad still live in Ashey.'

'Thought so. Do they like you being in the police?'

'I think so. I mean, Dad worked at Parkhurst; it's not too much of a stretch.'

'Quite,' says the woman, not approving of our detour. She must be used to this, everyone knowing everyone's business, or who they're related to, or who they've been with. It's not a

5

small place by any means, the Isle of Wight, but it's surprisingly hard to keep secrets. Most secrets, anyway. 'So, you saw Mr Manning on Sunday. Did you speak to him?'

'No, I just saw them through the window when I was washing up.' I incline my head towards the window above the sink which looks out over their drive and the front of the house, only separated by the long stretch of lawn. The border of the woods runs alongside part of their back garden and mine.

'You get a good view of their house from here. You can't see much from the road,' she says.

'No, it used to be open though. His father planted those ridiculous trees. Lucas keeps saying he is going to get them cut down. They block the light on the side of my house. But he was funny about privacy, David. Lucas's father. This house was a staff cottage, back in the old days. For their house. The big house.'

She smiles over the mug, which she's lifted to drink from. 'You must know him well then?'

'As well as you can know a neighbour, I suppose. He's a lovely man.' Though I've been trying to ignore it, the word missing is pulsing in my head like a migraine. Where would he go? He would never worry Alison like this deliberately. It's making me feel a bit faint. I need some toast and wish they would leave.

'So, Sunday, Saturday afternoon, you didn't speak to him, and he's seemed normal to you recently?'

'I haven't seen him so much lately. They've been busy. They've just finished building one of those silly garden offices and re-landscaping the garden. It's been very noisy.' I sound petulant, but it's true. It's probably why I'm so behind on my work, all the thudding and drilling and hammering. Like the house isn't big enough already without outside spaces too. 'Is there anything else? Only I have lots of work to do today. I'm on a deadline.'

That gets an eyebrow raise out of them both. I wonder if they know they mirror each other. Not much of a poker face between them.

'We might have some more general questions. Would it be okay to pop in later in the week if we do? At a more convenient time, maybe?'

'Mornings are okay this week,' I tell her, taking away their mugs and putting them in the sink noisily. 'You should ask his boss; now I think about it, maybe he has seemed a bit stressed these past months. Not like himself at all. Keeping his nose to the grindstone at all hours I expect.'

'We've a few lines of enquiry, Ms Merriweather, don't worry. People usually turn up. Maybe he's just taken a breather.'

This ridiculous statement from the Harding boy. What is his father called? It will annoy me all day if I can't remember. I'll have to go through the alphabet, *Adam, Allan, Andrew* . . . ugh.

'Here,' the woman says as she holds out a card towards me, sharp edges looming from her small, fine-boned hand. Pale pink nails, no polish, neatly trimmed. That's a good word for her, neat. I take the card, read the name. *Cora Macaulay*. Detective Inspector. Must be a slow news day to have come out for a non-suspicious – presumably – missing person case. But this is the Isle of Wight, not many exciting headlines here. This is probably the most interesting case to crop up in months. An actual mystery. I wonder again why she's come.

They bustle out of my house, leaving silence behind them. I don't get many visitors these days, nor do I court them. Life's easier with only yourself to think about. I manage the rest of the crossword and send it off to my editor, promising another tomorrow. The focus helped me ignore my worry over Lucas, little right that I have to worry over him really, now that we aren't close anymore, but now the afternoon and evening yawn ahead without it. He can't really be missing, can he? This is a mistake of some sort I'm sure.

At three I decide to head to the beach. I wriggle into my suit and brush back my hair, twisting it into a tight plait, though half of it will have escaped again on the ride down I don't doubt. It's pure vanity: I should just cut it all off. A 'crowning glory', someone told me long ago. Indeed. It's more grey than copper these days. I check the bike tyres and then set off with my towel in the handlebar basket. I must look very odd, a skinny ginger stick in a wetsuit on a bicycle, but I don't really care. People have been thinking I'm weird for nearly fifty years.

It's getting colder after a warm September, a stiff north easterly blowing in. When the sea comes into view, I turn to ride down Union Street, and see that the waves are white tipped. I like it a little wild and anticipation bubbles as I whizz down the steep hill and round the roundabout at the bottom. It's quiet, not many lurkers or day-trippers today, though there are a few people smoking outside The Marine. Rain starts to spit as I pass the canoe lake, but I'll be as wet as I can get in a minute, so the rain's no fuss.

I chain my bike on the lamppost nearest the café on the corner, where the road ends and the beach and promenade start, and run in.

'Afternoon, Merry,' says Nicky behind the counter, giving me the usual impish grin that crinkles her eyes. 'What time today?'

'About forty minutes please, you're not closing early or anything?'

'Nah, you're alright. Put your towel on the rad if you like.

See you in a bit.'

'Thanks, Nicky.'

I do put my towel on the radiator, and I leave my trainers under it too. A solitary customer sat by the window looks at me curiously, and then looks outside at the sea and gives a discernible shudder as they pick up their coffee. I hold in the laugh, hurrying out the door and down the steps over the path and promenade onto the beach. The waves are crashing on the shore, and spray glimmers. I can never resist for long, running into the crashing water, gasping as the cold envelops me, holding frigid air in my lungs and diving in.

Underwater all I can hear is the roaring motion of the sea, rushing like a heartbeat in my head, roiling all around me. It's so cold but it makes me feel invigorated; the salt stings against my tightly closed eyelids, the current tugs at my loose strands of hair like it's weeds and I'm stone. I let it pull at me, take me where it will, before finding the rippled sand again with my feet and pushing out until I burst through the surface, and gasp again for air, feeling the rush of adrenaline that forces everything else out of me, all I am in this moment is alive.

There's such a comfort in swimming, the same motions each time, arms powering, legs scissoring and turning my face out to the air for breath before returning it to the water, streamlining. It's focus, and blots everything else out. I power back and forth in line with the shore, swimming between the café and the tower, eventually feeling the deep ache begin in my muscles and my limbs start to lose their sharp form. I roll over onto my back and find the shape that lets me float and see the pale grey sky, cold needling my scalp. I could almost fall asleep, but then a wave slaps over my face so I stand up and walk out of the surf, wringing my plait into a coil to try and get some of the water out.

My legs are wobbling a bit as I head up the steps to the seawall promenade to rinse the sand from my feet. I know the water from the rusty old push tap is cold but it feels almost warm on my frozen toes. When I drag myself into the café Nicky is just finishing my hot chocolate. I grab my now toasty towel and scrub my face and hands before wrapping it around my hair. It's quiet at this hour after lunch time, the wicker-back chairs all empty after that last customer, but she must have been busy earlier. I can tell because all the delicious-looking cakes in the display have been reduced to the odd slice. They won't last either, because the afternoon tranche of dog walkers will be in soon enough, but for now the café is all mine.

'You've got this one covered I think, Merry,' says Nicky as she brings my drink over. I pay for three hot chocolates per week on a Monday so I don't have to bring anything but myself and my towel when I come for a swim.

'Thanks, lovely,' I tell her, taking the hot cup gratefully and holding it in such a way that as much skin as possible is touching it, feeling the warmth leach into my hands, driving out the painful tingling I get after a very cold swim. The exhilaration and mental clarity it gives me is well worth any small discomfort, and a hot chocolate after an October swim might be the very definition of heaven, especially if Nicky has made it. I'm sure she puts an extra spoonful in just for me.

'What's new with you then, Merry? Any goss?' she asks me as she's polishing the glass teacups that line up behind the counter. Nicky's tall and well-built but her movements are always nimble and darting, attracting to the eye.

'Not so much. Well, I had the police round earlier.'

Her big brown eyes widen even further as she looks at me. 'What have you been doing?' She laughs.

'Not me, my neighbour. Don't know if you know him, Lucas Manning?'

'I know the name, I used to knock about with a Manning at school.' She frowns briefly as if she's trying to remember, pushing her thick brown fringe off her face. 'Definitely wasn't called Lucas though. What happened?'

'His wife reported him missing, she hasn't seen him since Sunday night.'

'Oh shit, that's not good. She must be really worried. I'd go spare if my Steve went missing. Are you close?'

'Not really, but it's very strange. He's not the sort to do a runner.'

'Do you think something bad has happened?'

I haven't been letting myself think about this. *Do I think something bad has happened?* Not now, surely. It was different before, but that was a long time ago. No, I can't think anything bad has happened, but there must be something odd going on with him, and I can't help wanting to find out what it is.

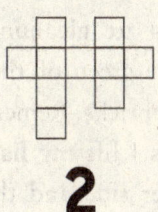

2

ACROSS: 21. The ways in which He works, or the ways in which she moves, perhaps (10)

THERE WAS A VERY INTERESTING programme about sea creatures with bioluminescence on the television last night, so today's puzzle also had a distinctly fishy theme. It's a bit too easy by my standards, but the last few have been especially difficult. My editor complained she didn't know what a selkie was yesterday. Personally, I feel that's part of the attraction of a puzzle, having to learn the occasional new thing. I'm sure everyone will get jellyfish though.

The morning's work done, my mind strays to Lucas again. It's been straying there a lot. Surely, he must have come home by now. I should check, really. It's a neighbourly thing to do, and I'm still their neighbour, despite everything. I pull on my boots and coat and check in the narrow mirror in the hallway that I don't have anything on my face that's not supposed to be there, before going out through the kitchen and the back door.

The early frost has gone to dewdrops, and I spoil the sheen on the lawn with my footprints as I trog up to the big house.

The large bay windows are gleaming in the crisp morning light, reflecting back the green of the gardens, standing out against the yellow stone bricks. Remembered arguments make my heart rate stutter as I lift my hand, make a fist, knock. Feet scurry on the other side and the oversized green door swings open. Alison looks awful, her usually serenely pretty face all red and blotched, her long hair unbrushed. It takes her a moment, it seems, to recognise me, that she's expecting someone else, but when she focuses it's only for another second before she flings her arms around me, almost knocking me backwards off the step.

'Merry!' she sobs, her breath hot in the space between my neck and coat. 'I don't know where he is.'

It's quite a job to manoeuvre her into the front room, where I manage to disengage and place her onto the long raspberry-coloured sofa. At a loss, faced with violent emotion, I go to the kitchen and make tea. Everything is still in the same place, bar the view. Sullied as it is by the strange glass and plank building at the end of the garden where it dips away. Scruffy rolls of mismatched turf have been rolled down where there used to be lovely flowerbeds. But I can still see the sea, and it's not so bad I suppose. Seems a foolish thing to have fallen out about now.

Alison receives the drink mutely, staring into it a while before putting it down on the side table without a coaster. She pulls her skinny legs up against her, resting her chin on her knees like a child, her full bottom lip even more of a pout than normal. I don't know how to offer help, now I'm here, so I just perch on the low-backed chair that matches the sofa and gabble like a silly gossipy turkey instead.

'Have the police found anything? They came to see me yesterday.'

Alison shakes her head, and grimaces. 'No. He's a grown up, people go missing all the time. They were just asking if he was stressed or seemed depressed.'

'Did he? Seem depressed?' I feel like a ghoul for asking, but some people say talking helps.

'No, not at all. At least, I don't think so. Bit stressed at work, but that's always stressful. He didn't say anything unusual. We were making plans for our anniversary next month. And it's not like him, is it? To disappear. To not tell me where he is. I just don't understand.' She begins to cry again, squeezing herself into a little ball. I watch her for a long while as her tea gets cold, cast around the rest of the room. It used to be homely but now it's like something out of a house magazine with nothing interesting to dust, just posh furniture that makes your arse ache, and the telly. She looks up eventually, the end of her nose a damp pink. She rubs her cheeks dry with her fingers and I see she's been pulling at her funny false nails, two are gone and the others are cut right down. They look sore and worried and fit to bleed, and it makes the bottom of my back cringe. Poor Alison.

'Did he say anything to you?' she asks as she starts picking at her nailbeds, lifting the edges of the acrylics that are left, not looking at me.

'No,' I tell her. I've been wracking my brains since I found out, trying to think if there could have been any undertones in the last conversations we had, but they were quite rare over the last few weeks, and the thought of that makes my stomach hurt a bit. If we hadn't fallen out, he might have come to me. He used to talk to me all the time.

'No,' I repeat again, shaking my head. 'I haven't spoken to him much recently, not after . . . well. No. I think the last thing we talked about was how cold it might get. He was teasing me about riding my bike in my wetsuit.' His laughing face flashes in my mind. I'd hoped it meant he was going to forgive me after the argument and the scene I'd caused.

'He is a wind-up,' says Alison, gulping down another sob, putting a hand up to her stringy, honey-coloured hair, which looks like it needs a good wash as well as a comb. I've never seen her with so much as a strand out of place in the two years I've known her, always caught between a jealous kind of admiration mixed with derision at how long it must take just to get ready every morning to face the world. Her frailty now makes me feel bad about being so judgemental about silly things and not trying more to be nice. I want to help.

'Did the police search the house? Lucas might have left something here, a clue, maybe.'

'Oh, you and your clues,' she says crossly, looking up and scrubbing her cheeks with the back of her arm this time. 'Yes, they looked, and no, they didn't find anything. He's just gone.'

I didn't make myself a drink and wish I had because my hands are wringing for want of something to do and it's making me feel useless. 'Shall we have a look together, anyway? They don't know Lucas. They might have missed something.'

'Merry, no offence, but I don't particularly want you poking around through Lucas's underwear drawer.' Her face is sour now, she looks like she did when we had the falling out about the garden office they built, and my sympathy flickers weakly. I make a huffing noise as I stand, which further irritates me.

'You're right, Alison, I'm sorry. It was a silly thing to suggest. I'm sure Lucas will turn up very soon.' I wait a millisecond for her to apologise but she doesn't. 'Just call me if you need anything, I'll let myself out.'

I try my hardest not to be cross with her for being so rude as I head back to my house and shut myself inside it. She's having a tough time and must be very worried. A mean part of me thinks that Lucy, Lucas's ex-girlfriend, would have let me look round. But Lucy actually liked me and I don't think Alison ever has, really. So I tell myself very sternly to not get caught up in it as well, to focus on other things. I distract myself with dusting, which is my least favourite chore after putting clothes away – I don't understand how I create so much washing on my own – and spend some time carefully wiping down the covers of all my books. I get further distracted by thinking I'll rearrange them by colours like the nice pictures I saw in the magazine in the dentists' waiting room, but now I just have several enormous piles of books on the floor instead of dusted on the shelves. I wonder how much I've spent on books over the years. At least I've never had to worry too much about money after inheriting the cottage from my aunt. That and the other money.

Deserting the teetering towers of tomes, I make a cup of tea and sit down at the little table in the kitchen, pulling my laptop towards me and opening the lid. Idly, I google Lucas's name. Nothing comes up on the local news, so I assume that his disappearing hasn't raised too much notice yet, which seems odd. Surely social media acolytes should be sharing the news in Manchester, Moldova and Outer Mongolia by now. His name doesn't show up anywhere else at all – well, lots of other Lucas

Mannings show up, but none are the Lucas Manning I'm looking for – and I know all those putting things in quote mark tricks from the college course I did last year on computing. I like to keep up with technology, makes me feel younger. Not that fifty odd is ancient these days, but the kids probably think we're decrepit by thirty-seven.

Lucas is very good with computers; I'd sometimes pretend I didn't know what I was doing so I could ask him to help me. Sad old woman alert, but it worked a treat. He helped me set up my phone with applications even though I knew I could have done it in about five minutes. I wonder if the police can find him through his phone, like a tracker? He always had it. I keep leaving mine in cardigan pockets, but most people are glued to theirs. I would ask Alison, but she's probably had enough of me for today. It seems strange that he's not on the internet anyway. Even I'm on the internet – there's an online article about solving cryptic crosswords that I contributed to a few years ago that pops up when I search up my name. He doesn't even have any social media or anything, and I know he used to. I find some pages for Alison, but everything is locked up private so I can't see if he's linked there. How annoying.

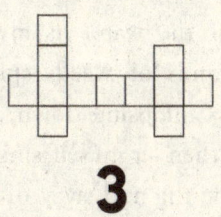

3

DOWN: 4. Air intake (that one may want to save?) (6)

I GIVE MYSELF A TERRIBLE headache looking at the screen for too long, so I have a sleep on the sofa. By the time I wake up, it's almost three and I know the tides are good at Seaview in an hour, so I get all my stuff together and head down to the beach, cycling past the café and along the sea wall past the Tower and Puckpool. The cold air clears out my head, the tang of salt a delight. It smells better in autumn without the undertone of sun-baked rotting weeds.

The beach that makes Seagrove Bay is empty, which is just the way I like it. Not that I'm bothered by people seeing me in my wetsuit, scampering down the sand and over the pebbles to launch myself with an ungraceful splash into the water, but there's just something so calming about a silent shore. And it is almost silent today, the sea calm, a millpond some might say, though you can never tell what's going on in the greens beneath the placid surface. The tides here can be strong if you come at the wrong time.

But now is fine, the sea will be up for another forty-five minutes before the moon continues her work. I walk out slowly, feeling the pressure of the water as my thighs cut through the surface, small strands of weeds spiralling away, caught in the wake I create. Collapsing down, I swim until I can't touch the bottom and then let myself sink until I'm suspended in the water, feeling the tug and sway of the current spinning me gently, a cold womb.

Breaking the surface to take an icy breath is the invigoration I need to swim, from the point of Priory Bay back to the wall in front of The Old Fort pub, and back again. Dog walkers make their way on to the beach, going obliviously about their business, but one small hound barks as it sees me. At least it doesn't leap in, there's sometimes a Labrador here who wants to swim out and sink us both in an attempt to lick my face off, but not today.

It's always so much harder getting out, tired limbs, the pull of the water, the tide on the turn and beginning to retreat away down the beach. I read somewhere that the salinity of seawater is similar to that in blood. It's not precisely true, but I do feel rather primordial swimming in the sea, like we're old kin. It would never do to get too friendly though, not if you want to keep air in your lungs; the salted siren can be a wicked creature if your senses lack judgement.

The beach is silent once more, so I sit on the sand for a moment, where it's still firm but beginning to dry, forming a crackled crust of tiny grains and pebbles, dotted with the odd piece of smoothed wood, decaying plastics. There used to be sea glass all along here, but not anymore. Litter doesn't turn into anything beautiful these days. It's getting dark, so I head home with my head clear and ready to begin looking again for Lucas. I've remembered something.

The cycle up George Street nearly does me in, and by the time I get in my front door I'm almost ready to pass out, but the thought that's been scurrying around my head drives me into the kitchen, pulling out drawers and rifling through the detritus of ages. I end up pulling most of it out onto the table. Takeaway leaflets for restaurants that are closed now – I still miss Mr B's pizza – batteries, a lump of rock solid blu-tack, old pennies, charger cords . . . dear God, this needs a proper sort out. I spot the spare keys to the big house, tucked away at the back of the drawer. I forgot I had these. I wonder how many people move into a new house and don't change the locks? All and any number of people could have keys to your home. I've never given anyone a key to here, though there is one buried underneath the ugly gnome in the garden. I should give them back at some point. Then finally, yes, here. A business card. Lucas's business card. It's from a few years ago, in case I needed to call him at work in an emergency if the house was blowing up or if something happened to Julia. He was away quite a lot then, just before he met Alison and just after all that awful business with Sean, so I kept an eye on things for him.

I put the card I'd found next to the laptop, realising that my fingers are blue around the edges, and that there's sand all over the floor from standing here in my wetsuit.

I pull it off and chuck it in the shed outside, cursing myself for an idiot, before going upstairs for a very long hot shower. Afterwards I dress in my fleecy pyjamas and dressing gown and pad back down to the kitchen, where the white square of the business card shines on the dark wood of the table like light coming in through a small window. I'm not sure what I'm thinking of doing with it, really, but the mystery of Lucas leaving like this is taking up more and more space in my head with each hour that passes. I don't have any friends, but I do care so very much for him – impossible not to when you've watched someone grow, unravel, from a small, frightfully loud baby into a tall, kind man. I suppose he would consider us friends as well as neighbours. Maybe even an honorary auntie, of sorts. It's hard to remember now as I don't see him so much.

But I do know this is horribly out of character. And it wouldn't hurt, would it, to try and find out where he is myself? I do know him, after all. And if there's anything I'm good at, it's solving a puzzle. But I need some dinner first, so I open the freezer and pull out the bottom drawer where I keep frozen leftovers. It's half stuck; I need to get the hairdryer and wooden spoon out to defrost the buggery thing again. There's a hefty wodge of lasagne lurking in the back beneath several bags of peas and the rest of those whim-bought gyoza that taste like wallpaper paste. That will do very nicely for tonight.

I put the chunk of pasta on a plate and sling it in the microwave. What is it Alison insists the Welsh call them? Popty-pings. I think she was teasing me. But she doesn't have much of a sense of humour, so maybe that's right. I watch as the turntable revolves, and the lasagne redistributes itself all over the plate. I'll have to make another one to batch freeze. It takes forever, according to my tummy, for the machine to do its business and for the food to reach a suitably volcanic temperature. I grate some extra cheese on the top because what is life without extra cheese, and I take it into the sitting room.

The first mouthful is far too hot and I do that inelegant thing of attempting to blow on it to cool it down when it's already in my mouth. Not for the first time I think it's a good thing that I live alone. It's tasty though, better once I've ignored my greed and let it cool down. Savoury tomato flavours merge with the piquant Cheddar, and there's enough sauce. Dry lasagne is deeply disappointing, like chewing cardboard and mince. I wish that I had some garlic bread to mop up the plate with, but I have to settle for sneakily licking it like a child. Or a dog. Manners are a social construct anyway, who needs them.

Dinner done, cleaned away, digested, I let myself pick up the card once again. It's a very nice card, thick paper with a pleasant feeling grain, sharp embossed lettering. He's done well for himself, considering. There's his number, and the work website and office number. It's too late to call now, but at least I can look up where he was working. I put the website into my search engine. Sentient Security Systems. That's a mouthful. Too many s's. I do like the word sentient, but it makes me think of that terrifying robot film, what is it, with the Skynet taking over. *Terminator*. I hope he hasn't been making those.

I'm being silly. The website is very smart, not a lot of text, clouds that sweep over the screen as you scroll. There's no list of people who work there, which is maybe why Lucas didn't show up online earlier. It says they make large-scale facial recognition systems, bespoke projects for companies and governments and the like. That sounds important. They must be missing him if he's not there. I always knew he was very clever. On a whim I click on 'contact us' and rattle off an email saying I'm looking for Lucas. It feels a bit wrong, as I'm sure that sleek detective would already have been in touch, but I don't want to waste their time asking if they have; they'd think I was strange, butting in. I just want to know where he is.

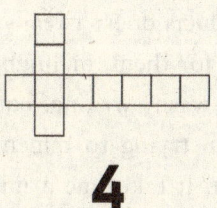

4

ACROSS: 31. If Charlotte made her home in a book (3,4)

I WAKE UP ON THE sofa with an extremely stiff neck. It's getting light outside, silvery fingers of dawn reaching underneath the curtains and creeping across the floor, and the birds have started up their usual cacophony. It's a good thing I'm not one for lie-ins, I'd have to get earplugs to block the noisy buggers' twerping out and I just don't fancy the idea of sticking bits of foam in my lugholes.

Armed with a herby-smelling microwave beanbag thing I got from one of the short-lived artsy-fartsy shops in town, and my first cup of tea, I sit down again at the table. Holding the heated bag between my head and shoulder, pressing it against my neck, I have to breathe as I stretch out the seized muscle. This never used to happen. I'm still the same size I was at twenty, but I was all lithe and bendy back then and could spring out of bed. Maybe I should start doing yoga.

Rolling my head gently starts to do the trick and I check my emails. Nothing yet from Terminator Inc., but it is only seven. Inspecting their website again and reading all the frankly boring blogs about their products doesn't really get me any closer to what it is Lucas does for them, or might do. At first, I think it's just terrible wishy-washy writing, but then I wonder if it's deliberately vague. I'm trying to remember a time when he talked about his work. It takes me a minute, but I do recall. Christmas, a few years back. I dropped by with a card, and we had a glass of wine. It was red wine, which I don't like as it gives me a headache, but it was nice to be invited, so I drank it anyway. It tasted like earth and berries and made my teeth pink. I only noticed afterwards.

If I close my eyes, I can picture him, his lean face with its sharp cheekbones and strong but slightly unruly brows. He was wearing a butter-coloured shirt and he needed his hair trimmed, thick dark strands of it were brushing over his collar. His father wouldn't have approved. We'd talked about my puzzles, his expressive eyes glinting as he told me how he'd managed half of one on the train to work and felt smart all day. I told him it wasn't about being smart, it was about figuring out the nature of the clue, knowing the tricks. And he'd told me his work felt like that sometimes, that he made puzzles too, only that other people weren't supposed to be able to figure them out. People or other computers.

So he must have been a programmer of sorts, I assume. I don't know a lot about the subject. My course didn't go much further than research and anti-virus and email, and I already knew how to do that. I'm not even twenty years older than Lucas, though I feel much older in spirit, and he would probably think I was at least as old as his own mother.

As always when I think of Julia, sadness washes over me. Such a lovely woman. A good friend. My only one, really.

The only person who saw who I was or could have been maybe, in different circumstances. I didn't have the easiest of childhoods.

I spend the next few hours working on today's crossword, then I cheat and amalgamate lots of clues from last year to make another one. I usually write new ones, but I feel dull and lackadaisical today, and my neck still hurts. Just as I'm making my ten o'clock coffee – I only have one a day to keep everything regular – the doorbell shrills. It's that policewoman again, with the lovely name. Cora the selkie, with her slippery looking black hair.

'Did you hear me switch the kettle on?' I ask her. She is rubbing her fingers together briskly; it's bitter again today, the parsnips will be liking these early frosts. November soon. She should be wearing gloves; her hands are all ruddy, she'll get chilblains if she's not careful. 'Come in. Would you like a drink? I'm making coffee.'

She would, again, so I make her one using one of my guest mugs for the guests I don't have, which doesn't have a silly picture or slogan on it. Just a plain crackled green, a kiln-fired one. I think it's from the same shop I got my beanbag, which is slumped on the table looking sorry for itself. I see her glance at my laptop. She must have moved it as the screen has come back to life; it's on the homepage of Lucas's website. I close it as I put her coffee down.

'How have you been, Ms Merriweather?' she asks me in that burr of hers.

'Merry, please. I'm okay. But I'm worried about Lucas.'

'We're concerned too,' she says. 'Though most missing people do show up again fairly shortly.'

I make a distinctly dubious noise, remembering the poor boy who went missing one night in Cowes. There's never been a trace of him since, but I suppose that Lucas is a grown man with means. 'Why are you here, then?' Her mouth curves slightly at my tone. I don't think this one is easily moved.

'I was just hoping you could tell me a little more about Mr Manning,' she says. 'What your relationship with him was. To get a clearer picture, you understand.'

I don't understand. 'We were neighbours. I told you that, and it's obvious. He's always lived there, and I've always lived here. I've known him his whole life. So, I can tell you that he would never just disappear and not tell Alison where he was or why. It's not normal for him. Something must be wrong. I have already told you this.'

She looks down at her coffee before looking up and straight at me. 'What was your dispute about last month?' Trying to catch me off guard. That won't work on me.

'It was silly, really. Nothing to do with this.'

'Tell me anyway. It sounded stressful.'

It was stressful, at the time. 'It's nothing now. They just did some work on the garden, built an outbuilding. It spoilt the view.'

'It's not a view you can see though, is it?' says DI Macauley tapping a slender fingertip against the rim of her mug. 'Seems strange you'd be bothered what they do with their own garden.'

'It was noisy, I told you this as well, you know, the other day. And it wasn't their garden I was worried about, it was Julia's.'

'Julia?'

'Lucas's mother. She spent years on that garden, choosing the plants, digging the beds. It was beautiful, a whole lifetime of work, and Alison wanted it ploughed under and turfed to have that silly glorified shed they don't need. It just didn't sit right with me.' I don't know why she wanted it anyway considering she doesn't even work.

'Did you fall out over it?'

'Not really. Like you said, it's not my business what they do with their garden. It's just a shame.'

'So, you didn't have a shouting match about it with Mr Manning a few weeks back?' She's still looking at me with her clear pool-grey eyes. There's no insinuation in her voice, but it echoes around the room regardless.

'I might have got a little bit carried away when I saw them digging everything up. They didn't warn me. It was just a bit of a shock.'

'Were you close with Lucas's mother? Julia?'

We could be having a normal conversation from her cool tone. I can imagine her prising secrets out of people with little effort this one, taking full advantage of her placid expression and soft words. I think I would not like to see her lose her temper. It takes me a moment to answer, because of her thinking of Julia always hurts. 'Quite close. Closer than I am to Lucas, anyway.'

'When did she pass?' asks the detective, though I don't see why she needs to know. Nosy by nature this lot.

'Eighteen months, give or take. Just after Lucas and Alison got married. They'd just gone on their honeymoon. They had to come back. It was awful.' That was the last time I used those spare keys. I just don't remember putting them back in the drawer, must have been the shock. I'd gone to call, we were going for a walk, and she didn't answer. I won't think of her face.

'Did you know Mr Manning senior well?' she says, shifting back on the chair as she shifts the subject.

The change rocks me. This time she has caught me off guard and my mouth feels dry, so I drink some tepid coffee before I answer. 'Only as a neighbour.'

'He went missing too, didn't he? In 1985. Do you think that's strange, both of them vanishing like this?'

I don't like to think about this. 'David was a complicated man. There was a lot going on in his life that his family didn't know anything about.'

'That's one way of putting it. Quite the file that one's got. Still open, you know. Were you questioned about his disappearance at the time?'

'It was a long time ago. I can't really remember.' I feel sweat start to prickle under my arms and around my waistband. Poor Julia. I don't want to think of how horrendous that was for her, David going like that. 'I don't think it's a similar situation to this though, do you? Lucas couldn't be more different. He wasn't even eight when all that happened. And I told you, he wouldn't worry Alison like this.'

'Perhaps not,' says DI Macauley. She looks at me for another long moment, expressionless, and then she pushes away from the table, the chair legs screeching on the tiles. 'Thank you, Merry, for your time.'

I stand and follow her down the hallway. She plucks her nice wool coat off the newel post where she left it and shrugs back into it. Turning as she opens the door she says, 'You will call me, won't you? If you remember anything to do with either of the Mr Mannings?'

A tight smile creaks on my face and I manage a nod as she goes.

5

DOWN: 34. Does Alisha still live here? (5)

IT TAKES ME A LONG time to push away the blurry memories of when David disappeared, to try and replace them with happier ones. I hate thinking of the past, it's nothing but pain. I shove all my books back on the shelves, regardless of colour, and I sweep the kitchen floor, watching as small piles of sand build up in the corners beneath the cabinets. I wish for the first time in a long time that I had someone to talk to. In the front room tucked away in a drawer there's a photo in a frame of me, Julia and Lucas when he was a toddler that she gave to me. She was always so kind like that, dropping in with small gifts or things she thought I might like that she didn't need or had extra of. I think she would buy extra on purpose, for an excuse to come round and spend some quiet time here away from her rambunctious menfolk. Or just to be kind.

She'd been a good person to me for a long time. I was sixteen when I moved here properly, though I'd come and stay regularly before, when Mum was off with one of her men. My whole childhood was just one long episode of her being drunk, being gone, of there never being any money for food or clean clothes. It was no wonder I was bullied; I must have stuck out like a sore thumb and schools didn't really interfere back then with neglected children. It stays with you though, the mistrust and the hard shell you must develop to survive it.

And at least I had Auntie Rosie. It was such a relief to get to be old enough to escape and move here. Not that we had long together – I can't believe it's more than thirty years ago now, when she died and left me this place. My mum never spoke to me again when I wouldn't let her move in to my 'free house' and Julia kind of stepped in exactly when I needed someone the most. She always could see past my thorns. I pull open the drawer at the bottom of the bookshelves and take out the picture, polishing the glass with my cuff. I put it away when she died because it hurt to look at it. It doesn't hurt so much now, though I don't know if that's the passage of time or my worrying about what's happened to Lucas. Holding it to my chest for a moment, I make a promise to Julia that I'm not going to rest until I find out what's happened to the boy in the picture, and then I put it back on the shelf where it belongs.

I spend the rest of the afternoon making a ginger cake. It makes the cottage smell delicious, like spice and hot sugar, and I have to force myself to wait until it's cooled before carving off a slice to test. It's a good one, and I cut the rest of the cake in half, wrapping one end in foil.

With the warm parcel in my hands, I walk up to the big house and stand on the doorstep, taking a breath before shuffling the cake so I can knock. I hear Alison come down the stairs and sense that she's looking out through the little peephole glass in the door, at my face in a distorted bubble. The door swings open, and she doesn't speak but I see her sigh.

'I brought you some cake,' I tell her, proffering it.

Her mouth curls at the edge. 'What type?'

'Ginger. It's the only one I can make that turns out like it's supposed to. Not flat.'

'Thank you,' she says, smiling properly. 'Come in and have some with me.'

She looks better today, though her hair still needs a wash, I notice, as I follow her into the kitchen. Her talons are back at least, all shiny and beige and pointed. I always find myself wondering about how she goes about certain things with those before giving myself a stern mental telling-off.

The sink is full of plates, and she fishes two small ones out, rinsing them and drying them on a sorry-looking tea towel. It's not very clean in here, which is unusual: it's normally spotless. Gemma mustn't have been in for a while. I was surprised when Lucas kept Gem and her husband Jack on to keep the house and garden; I thought maybe Alison would have wanted to do it herself, having such a lot of free time, but no. Maybe they're on holiday.

'This is yum, thanks,' says Alison, who has demolished her slice of cake while I've been wandering in my thoughts. I wonder if she's been eating properly. 'I saw that detective was at your house again yesterday. What did she want?'

Well, I would have thought that was obvious. 'She was asking about Lucas again. And David.' A shiver passes over me, sweeping down from my neck and around my ribs. If she notices, she doesn't enquire.

'Lucas's dad?' she asks. She licks a fingertip and uses it to pick up errant crumbs and puts them in her mouth.

'Yes. Did Lucas ever talk much about him?' I watch her intently, but when she looks up her face bears its usual guileless expression, all big blue eyes and fair skin.

'Not really,' she says. 'Bit of a touchy subject. What was he like?'

'Bit of a touchy subject,' I reply. 'She was asking me if I thought it could be connected, the two of them going missing.'

Alison frowns. 'Do you think David is still alive somewhere? I always figured he'd run off to Spain or something and changed his name. Do you think that's what Lucas has done? Do you think they might be together?' She leans forward, intent. Hopeful.

'I don't know,' I tell her, feeling like a bit of cake is lodged in my throat, absorbing all liquid, swallowing compulsively against the dryness. I can feel the sweat starting again. 'Do you think he's run away for some reason? Why?'

'It's the only explanation, isn't it?' she says, sitting back again. 'Something happened, and he had to leave. He'll come back; I know he will.' Her face is shining now with an odd fervour. 'There are a few things missing, you see. After you left the other day, I had a proper look. His passport is gone, and there were some envelopes in the safe, they're gone too. I think he's just gone somewhere, like David.'

'David never came back though,' I say without thinking, the words almost falling out of my stupid mouth. I may as well have slapped her for the flinch she makes, and I bite my lip, not that it stops me gabbering. 'I'm sorry, that just came out, I didn't mean to say that.'

'Lucas isn't his father,' is all she says. 'And I'm sorry too.' Her hands are never still, and she begins to twist her wedding and engagement rings around her finger as if winding herself up to continue. 'About everything, Merry, the stupid garden, being so rude to you when you came over yesterday. I was upset.'

'You don't have to apologise for anything,' I tell her, feeling sick with guilt, and confused about her thinking Lucas would have disappeared like this without contact. But what if she's right? Could he have got mixed up in the old awfulness? It's not like the family doesn't have a track record for it. Could it have reached out with its oily tentacles and snared him too? The thought of it makes me feel worse. Lucas is the good one.

'I haven't looked everywhere yet,' she carries on, her voice quick and almost panicked. 'Would you still be up for helping me? Maybe you know more about this old house than me. You must have been here a lot over the years, with Julia? Are there hiding places?'

'I don't know, maybe.' I'm a bit confused by her change of heart, but my inquisitiveness isn't going to pass this up. I think of the promise I made to Julia this morning, that I will find out what's happened to her son, somehow. This is a good start. 'Shall we start at the top and work our way down?'

Alison makes a funny little moue of disgust with her mouth. 'I'm not going in the attic with the spiders,' she says, shuddering. 'You can look up there while I have some more cake if you like. I'll help in the other rooms upstairs, apart from our room. I've already looked a hundred times in our room.' She sighs and then starts unwrapping the foil again.

I've been in the attic of this house before, a long time ago. I think I was helping Julia put Christmas decorations away: she'd had one of her falls and broken her arm. The hatch is in the top-floor corridor. It's changed since then, the hatch, there's a metal catch on it now and a quick look into the bedroom directly next to me reveals a stick with a hook propped behind the door.

It pushes up and back on a mechanism now, and there's a ladder to pull down. This is much more convenient than clambering up off a dilapidated stepladder and getting my fingers slammed in the dropping board that sealed the loft. The switch is on the nearest beam and light floods the space when I flick it, an unnatural yellow glow that fails to reach the corners. The ladder makes a creaking noise as I ascend. Someone's tidied up since the last time I was here: everything is packed away neatly into boxes except for a pile of assorted chairs and other bits of furniture in the corner. I see the outlines of bars against a dark wall, a deconstructed cot, and my heart hurts.

Brushing away useless feelings, I move to the back of the loft, ducking beams. I have a disagreeable incident with a cobweb and my face on the way, but it didn't appear to have an inhabitant and it's foolish to be scared of spiders in a country where they can't hurt you anyway. The boxes against the back wall are all labelled. I look in them regardless. There is a box full of 'Granny's china' carefully packed in brown paper. Each piece has writing on it I recognise as Julia's and for a moment I have to close my eyes and breathe slowly through the hurt of missing her so much. It's poignantly funny too, her having written carefully on each piece what it is. Side plate, blue edged. Teacup, daisies. Always so organised.

The box next to it is old clothes, baby and small boy clothes to be precise, and that feeling of nostalgia washes over me again. They smell a bit fusty, and old, but the material is still kitten-soft, tiny cotton garments washed and loved and kept in the hope of grandchildren no doubt. She would have been the most wonderful grandmother. But I'm here to find Lucas, not Julia, so I close the box and move through several others. I'm digging through all sorts. There's an especially lovely one full of artwork, crumpling sugar paper with blue stripes for sky and always a sun with rays in the corners, names with backwards letters in them along the bottom. I love how innocent they are. But these aren't my memories to pore over.

Closer to the hatch, I find men's things, but I don't think they're Lucas's. I didn't know they'd kept all this, though I suppose I can see why. I close the boxes quicker than I open them, almost afraid of what might escape. There's nothing else, no papers, no files. I don't think Lucas has even put anything of his own up here except that enormous faux Christmas tree, which must be an Alison addition. They always used to get a real one when Lucy lived here, same as when Lucas was younger, the whole house would smell of pine the day they brought it in. It feels a bit pointless to even be looking around like this.

I clamber back down the shuddering ladder, finding the noise it makes quite offensive as I'm not that heavy, until my feet are back safely on the carpet. As I'm pushing the ladder back up into the hatch, I hear Alison come up the stairs behind me. I turn to tell her I didn't find anything, but she pulls a face and pushes me into the bathroom, where I see the cobweb has left its mark all over my cheek.

'That's why I don't go up there,' she says, sitting on the edge of the bath as I wash my face and dry it. 'That's Lucas's job; he gets the decorations and things down.'

There's a glaze on her face as she's talking, like part of her has gone somewhere else. I can hear that she's trying to convince herself he'll be back soon like nothing's happened.

'Lucas loves Christmas,' she tells me as we leave the room, trailing me like a little girl. 'If you look in the spare rooms, I'll look in our bedroom again. And he uses that other bathroom, the en-suite in there, but I didn't notice anything when I looked.'

She shuffles off into the bedroom down the corridor that has always been Lucas's. He mustn't have wanted to move into the master that his parents had shared. All these rooms are huge anyway, I could fit my whole ground floor into this one. The tall windows let in the dimming light from outside and I walk over to admire the view. I can feel the cold coming through and have to wrap my cardigan tightly around me as I look out. The garden drops away and I can see up over the roofs of houses down West Street, and past the crenellations of St Thomas' church tower there's the wide stretch of dark green sea speared by the pier. The sky is becoming coral colours, the sort of sunset you only get when the year is drawing in and it's getting cold, purple at the edges. It's a shame it's too late for a swim.

There's nothing in this room anymore of Julia's. There's a painting on the wall that I don't recognise, or particularly like, one of those generic close-ups of a flower that looks more labia than petals. Fannies on the wall do not interest me. The bed has too many cushions on it and a shiny quilt that looks like it would slide off all night, and there's a frankly tacky ornate silver frame on the bedside table containing a black and white image of Lucas and Alison dancing at their wedding. They got married in London, a small, short-notice affair like the rest of their relationship. I wasn't invited. It looked nice though, from the photos scattered around. This soul-stripped room annoys me more than it should. I look in the drawers and underneath the bed, but all spaces are empty bar a solitary dust bunny and a white charger of some description in one of the drawers.

The bathroom is more interesting, there are actual possessions in here. A dressing gown, heavy quilted cotton, like from a posh hotel, hangs on the back of the door. Nothing in the pockets. Men's shampoo and bodywash sit on a little chrome shelf in the shower cubicle. There's a rubber window cleaner on the floor, to scrape off the steam I suppose. So very neat and orderly. Someone who could disappear without a trace, tidying up behind themselves. I need to look harder. He must have left something, anything.

The cabinet reveals Lucas's taste in expensive face creams. I open one to smell it, but it's not much different to the pound shop stuff I slather on to combat the salt water. Maybe a hint of something green, sandalwood maybe. I wouldn't know. I put it back. There are a couple of rings on the shelf that don't have the corresponding items that made them, and then I realise there isn't a toothbrush in here, or toothpaste. My heart flutters a bit. If he's got toiletries with him, he must have gone somewhere on purpose, planned to be away. Maybe he did just leave.

It's like a smothering pillow being lifted away from my face, a dangerous weight I didn't realise was there, slowly suffocating. I've been ignoring it resolutely, but the fear was there, that something terrible might have happened, but this has made me reassess. I still believe that Lucas wouldn't just walk out on Alison. He's a faithful person. Something must have happened to make him go and thinking about what it could be curdles the cake in my stomach. If he had somehow gotten mixed up in all the bad things that were forever hovering around this family. Could someone have found something to hold over him? Threaten him? Surely, he wouldn't have gone down the same path, not after what happened to his father. He wouldn't have done that to Julia.

But then, Julia's dead.

I find Alison in their room, sitting on the bed looking out of the window at the same view I was admiring just before. The sky is darkening now, the coral gone to a freshly bruised mauve. Her face is unnervingly blank, and when she speaks, it makes me jump.

'There's nothing here,' she says softly, still staring. 'Well, there are things. Most of his clothes, except the things he left in and took for work.' I glance around the room, which has been entirely redecorated since I last glimpsed it, but I can understand that, seeing as another woman had lived in it. There's not a lot of personality here though, and I find it odd that Alison hasn't really made her mark here. Except that godawful plastic tree and shed, anyway.

'How did it happen?' I ask her, uncertain of how to be in this blank room with her, my fidgeting at odds with her stillness. 'Was it a normal day, did you . . .' I trail off, my voice hanging in the air.

'Did we argue? Not really. We never argue. I told the police everything was normal, but I've been thinking about nothing else since and it's made me wonder. If I was just being blind.'

'I told the police I thought he'd seemed stressed about work,' I venture, hoping to draw her out further. 'But he always was a bit.'

'It was a pressured job. All very secretive; he never really told me anything about his projects, just that his boss was being a fucking prick about stuff.'

This is the first time I've heard Alison swear while she's known I was there, and I'm faintly surprised at how casually she's spoken. I heard her cursing in the garden once and was impressed with her range. There's no slipping into that now though, her words as modulated as ever.

'You think there might have been something else, not just work?'

'Maybe. I just wish he'd come home.'

Frustration bubbles up in me. Maybe doesn't solve anything. You need specifics to work things out. 'When did he leave? Was he going to work?'

She sighs, and looks up at me, her pale blue eyes insipid and watery, the most boring of all the shades eyes come in. A spot is working its way up on her chin near her bottom lip, and the skin is red where she must have been rubbing at it. 'He packed his bag and left as usual on Monday morning to catch the five-fifteen. I was asleep when he left. He usually sleeps in the other room on a Sunday if he's getting the early boat; he doesn't like to wake me up because I can't ever get back to sleep again.'

'And what, he didn't come home? Did you hear from him at all?'

Alison shakes her head and sniffs, watery eyes progressing to teary. 'He usually calls me when he gets into work to let me know he's there. We always speak a few times a day on the phone. This is the longest we've ever gone without talking.' She stands up and her face blanches into a very peculiar colour, as she almost stumbles into me. I put out my hands and she clasps them for a minute.

'Sorry, sorry,' she mumbles, breathing heavily through her nose. 'I feel a bit faint.'

I push her back onto the bed and make her put her head down over her knees.

'Have you been eating properly?'

Her hair swishes as she shakes her head. 'Not hungry.'

She looks up again slowly, a bit better, and I help her up.

'You must make yourself a proper meal tonight. Or get a takeaway, something you like. I don't like the thought of you passing out over here and banging your head on something.'

'Thanks for that, Merry,' she says as we head down the stairs. 'Just what I need to think about.'

I'm about to head into the kitchen when she makes a shift with her body that tells me my welcome may have come to an end. I don't think I'll be searching anywhere down here. Not that there seems to be anything to find. Lucas has vanished.

As I walk back to my cottage past the woods that back on to the side of our gardens, I see a large shape moving in the trees. The golf course is the other side, but this stretch is private property. I could go and complain at them, but it's getting dark. Back in my home, I go up the stairs and I watch from the landing window as a man emerges on the edge of the trees by the low wall which he hops over, getting into a dirty white minivan that's parked illegally in the layby. It doesn't move for a while, though eventually it pulls away. I hope he wasn't going to the toilet in there: it's where I like to go and find mushrooms when they're in season.

After the only dinner I can scramble together – beans on defrosted and toasted bread, with cheese, obviously – I check my laptop again. There's an email from Lucas's company, and I hold my breath as I click it open and read it quickly. It doesn't take long.

Dear Mrs Merriweather
Thank you for your email. Mr Manning is no longer an employee at Sentient Security Systems. However, if you happen to get in touch with him, please could you ask him to contact us.
Regards,
SSS

Well, that's very strange. How long has he not been working for them? Is that a recent thing – did he get fired? Did he get the sack and not tell Alison because he was embarrassed? But it's not like they need the money, surely. Saying that, they might. I don't know how much all the awfulness might have cost him. He never said. But it's not polite to talk about money, is it. No one has ever asked me about mine.

6

DOWN: 10. I might wear an undergarment if I weren't so scaly (12)

I'M UP EARLY AGAIN, AND not in the mood for working on my crosswords. My real-life mystery is taking up all the room in my head. But I need to be busy, I can't just sit around trying to think. If you make space for things in your head by doing the menial tasks of day-to-day life, inspiration can creep in. So, I stock take, and make my shopping list. I loathe the big Tesco, especially this time of year when they get all the festive stuff out ridiculously early, all the people elbowing each other for mince pies that will go off before Christmas anyway, but needs must at least once a month for the tins and big packets of rice and whatnot.

The early bus gets me up to Brading Road before the madding crowds arrive and I wander around fairly contentedly trying to avoid the bargains that aren't and the things I don't need. I didn't have breakfast, which was a mistake because now I want to buy all the things in the bakery. I'm checking the salt content on the value range cannellini beans when a voice in my ear makes me jump fit to shed my skin.

'Sorry, Merry,' she says. It takes me a minute to place her, hair all waves, thick framed glasses, in her civvies. It's the detective again, in Clark Kent mode.

'Are you in disguise?' I ask her before I can stop myself.

She laughs loudly, the noise unexpectedly joyful. 'No, just out shopping, like you. An early bird too, is it?'

'I don't like it when it's busy. It gives me the heebie jeebies,' I tell her, not sure why I'm sharing so much. She's got that sort of face, that you could talk, and she would listen. Warm but cool all at the same time. Her trolley has a lot of fruit in it, and vegetables. My tins and packets must look very unhealthy, but I go to the greengrocers and butchers for fresh things.

'I know what you mean. I was going to come and see you again this week if you don't mind?'

'Do I have a choice?' I ask her. 'I only saw you yesterday and I still don't know any more about anything.'

'Ah, you'd be surprised at what people think they don't know,' she says with a small smile. 'Sometimes you just need to ask the right questions. You'd know that, surely?'

I have that feeling I get, when I don't know if someone is teasing me or mocking me, and have to swallow it and pull a long breath through my nose. 'Well, if you must. I'm busy though, tomorrow and the day after. It's the weekend. And I can't do Monday morning.' I'm not busy, but I want to prepare myself for whatever it is she wants to ask me. I can hazard a guess.

'That's okay. I'll come see you Monday afternoon then, if nothing changes in the investigation. Chances are I'll come anyway, to talk about the other case. We've reopened it.'

She looks at me intently, but I keep my face straight, despite the swooping feeling in my head. She doesn't want to get herself mixed up with all that. It's not safe, it never has been. Julia thought they were safe, but they weren't. Now Lucas is gone too, and there's always a chance it's all the same black cloud that haunts his family. I watch her as she wheels her trolley away up the aisle, small and lithe, defenceless.

My appetite has disappeared, but I robotically manage the rest of the shop, the mundanity a good way of trying to keep all the boxes in my head firmly closed. For a solitary person, I seem to have accumulated an awful lot of things I want to forget.

As always, getting everything home is a monumental pain in my arse. The two fold-up trollies I use are stuffed to the gills and it feels like I'm pulling two baby elephants up the hill from the bus stop to my cottage. I stop for a breather on the pavement outside before the final push over the ten feet of gravel path that leads up to my door. My swimming keeps me fit, but I'm starting to feel my joints when it's cold, and I forgot my gloves, so my fingers are like ice. I'm rubbing my hands together and thinking of inventive swear words to mutter under my breath when a flash of colour catches my eye. Just down the road, tucked into the layby, is that same scruffy van I saw yesterday.

I pull the bags into my hallway and run up the stairs to the landing so I can look out of the window again. It's definitely the same vehicle, and the same man sitting inside. Does he think this is a toilet pit stop he can make on his way home or something? Various repressed emotions seem to bubble up and coalesce into anger, and I whirl to run back down the stairs and out of the door, storming up the road with my arms back and forthing like pistons. I make a fist and rap on the window, hard. The man inside, who is writing in a notebook, jumps so violently his head hits the roof of the van, and I have to bite back a mean laugh. He leans back with his hand on his chest for a second before pressing a button to wind down the window.

'You aren't allowed to park here,' I tell him. 'And you aren't allowed in those woods either. I saw you there yesterday.'

'Sorry, love,' he says in an annoyingly calm voice. 'I wasn't staying.'

I'm turning to leave when he calls again through the window. 'Do you live there then?'

As I turn back, he's looking across the hedge to my house, and I frown. 'None of your business, pal.'

He ignores this. 'How well do you know your neighbours?'

'What?'

'Don't say what say pardon. Do you know them? The Mannings?'

'Why are you asking?'

'Well, that could be a long conversation. Maybe you could invite me in for a coffee?'

'Eh, I don't think so!' The affront is shocking. Like I'm going to let a strange man into my house. Even if he does look quite non-threatening. They're the worst ones.

'It's too cold to talk out there, do you want to jump in here?' He pats the seat next to him and smiles with teeth that are white but not quite straight.

'No, I certainly do not—who even are you? Why are you here?' I can almost feel myself bristling like a cat.

'I'm a private investigator,' he says. 'And I want to ask you some questions, but if you're not getting in here, and I'm not getting in your house, we'll be getting a bit cold, won't we?' He unlocks his door and gets out. He's tall, at least four inches on my five seven, and broad across the shoulders, though a bit of that could be the beaten-up leather coat he's wearing.

There are far too many people asking questions around here recently, and I don't want to answer any of them. If there are questions, I want to be the one asking them. But my curiosity has been kindled. *A private investigator?*

'Not here. And you can't park here. If you want to ask me questions, I'll meet you later, in the café at Appley. Do you know it? I'll be in there around five o'clock.'

'I'll find it,' he says, looking at me in a rude way before climbing back in his van. What a horrible man.

7

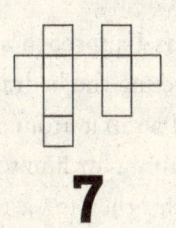

DOWN: 2. Yesterday or long ago, depending on the winner (7)

I SWIM VIGOROUSLY, TRYING TO push out the many intrusive thoughts that are rearing their ugly little heads. The pounding of the surf and the spray of the salt water aren't having quite the soporific effect on my brain that they usually do, but I thrash up and down anyway, feeling put out and angry that all these people are pushing me off balance when I just want to be left alone.

My clever wristband tells me the time and how many calories I have burnt and how far I have swum, which isn't as much as usual because of this person who wants to quiz me. Alison must have hired him, God knows why he keeps hiding around the back and pissing in the woods. I'm sure she wouldn't mind him using her bathroom. I haul myself out of the sea and up to the café, rinsing my feet off before I walk in. Smiling, Nicky nods and turns to the hot drink machine. I see that the man is already here, scribbling again, his greying head bent down over the table, a steaming drink at his side and a packet of open crisps.

He looks up sharply as I approach and does a double take. I assume he wasn't expecting the bedraggled hair and wetsuit. Snatching up my towel, I wrap it around my head and sit down heavily opposite him, waiting for him to comment. He doesn't, and we just look at each other for a minute. If he thinks he can psyche me out, he's got another think coming. Nicky brings over my hot chocolate and puts it down.

'Thanks, Nicky.' I ignore her intrigued expression. I hope she doesn't think this is some sort of date.

'Regular here then?' asks the man, smiling. He has very unusual eyes, a clear dark brown with funny depths: they remind me of how slowly poured milk clouds into tea the moment before you stir it. They're framed with thick black lashes, which annoys me further. Men always seem to get the best eyelashes. Some of his hair is also brown and the rest of it is grey, but I imagine he was quite handsome when he was younger. No wedding ring though, or even a dent of one recently removed.

'I come in a few times a week, yes. I pay for some drinks up front; I don't have any pockets for change.'

He glances down at my wetsuit-clad body and actually goes a little red. 'I'd imagine not,' he says with a half-laugh, as if embarrassed that he's accidentally looked at my completely flattened chest. 'I haven't introduced myself properly, have I? My name's Gareth Jones.' He reaches out a large hand over the table, which now I have to shake. It feels weird and awkward, but warm at least. His hand completely envelops mine. I have very small hands.

'Your fingers are freezing,' he says as he draws his own back. 'I already know your name, I'm afraid, comes with the job—'

'Merry,' I interrupt. 'I tend to go by Merry. No one ever calls me anything else.'

I can see he's holding in another laugh by the way he compresses his lips for a second, and I really dislike him. Nosy bastard.

'Did Alison hire you to find Lucas?' I ask him, picking up my drink to warm my freezing hands.

'Actually, no. Sentient Security Systems hired me.'

'What? Why? And don't tell me to say pardon again unless you want this drink down you.'

'I wouldn't dream of it,' he says, leaning back slightly.

There's a moment where he's sizing me up again before deciding on whatever it is that's going through his head.

'They hired me because it appears Mr Manning may have absconded with a rather expensive project he'd been working on. I don't think I should be telling you this, really, but you look trustworthy enough.'

Considering I'm sat here in a wetsuit with a ratty old towel wrapped around my head and what feels distinctly like a glowing Rudolph nose on my face I think this is mocking me. Part of me just wants to leave, but curiosity as ever is my driving force, so I stay, questions brewing up and fighting each other for priority in my mouth.

'What sort of project? Why would he steal it? Why would he steal it and run away but leave his wife behind?'

'I have no idea of the answers to any of those questions. I've just been tasked with finding him. It's not been very easy researching him these past few years. There's a fair bit before that though, before he worked for my client. Do you know much about that?'

'I don't like to talk about that, thank you. It was none of my business.'

'Quite the family though, don't you think? David Manning pulled a disappearing act too, didn't he?'

This man is as bad as that bloody policewoman. I feel like I'm getting it from all sides. Though speaking to Gareth might be good practice for speaking to her, for keeping the story straight. Some secrets aren't mine to share. It also occurs to me that he could find Lucas much more quickly than the police, who probably don't have the manpower, and judging by Cora's helpmate, the brain power either. 'He did, yes. In 'eighty-five. Long time ago. I expect he's dead by now.'

'You think he left, then? Changed his identity?' Gareth leans forward, an intent look on his face as he sweeps his hand across the table, feeling for his pen.

'He had the means. He moved in those circles, not that we – his family I mean, not me – knew anything about that. They thought he worked in shipping.'

'Well, I suppose it was shipping of a sort,' he jokes, but it's not funny and I don't laugh. He notices and the humour is erased from his expression. 'I'm sorry, I can't imagine it was an easy thing for them to find out.'

'He'd already been gone by then. The police had been closing in on him for a while, but we didn't know anything about that. Looking back with hindsight, it was obvious something was going on with him, his temper . . . it wasn't a good time for Julia. Lucas's mum.'

'You were close.' It's not a question, and I realise that the person opposite is perceptive indeed. It won't be easy to lie to him if he asks the right questions. But I have spent a lifetime lying, so much that sometimes lies even seem to become the truth.

'She was my best friend,' I tell him. My eyes prickle, so I look down into the creamy depths of my drink and take a long sip to gather myself. I don't do tears.

'Do you think his father disappearing is relevant to Lucas doing the same?' Gareth asks gently, damn him.

'I couldn't say. I don't see how. Lucas was quite little when he went off. And he wasn't always the best father, if they did things he didn't approve of. He was very domineering over them, the man of the house. My way or the highway sort of thing. I don't think Lucas would leave Alison like this for him, anyway.'

'Tell me about Alison. I haven't spoken to her yet.'

'But you've been watching, haven't you? I saw you creeping about in the woods.'

'You make me sound like a bogeyman. But yes. I tend to watch for a while before I approach someone. I've seen you a few times this week flitting about on your bike with your Boudica hair flying about.'

This makes me frown and put my hand up to resettle my towel which is slipping loose. 'Hardly that,' I tell him. 'It's more grey than red now.'

'I think it's very striking,' he says with a small curve of his lips. 'Got the reference though?'

'Was it a test? Does the local idiot know who the Queen of the Iceni was? It's pretty well known; I'd need a harder one than that. If you want a new fact, I could tell you that there's evidence that the Durotriges were the tribe that lived here at that time. It was Ynes Weith, back then. They found artefacts in Shalfleet.'

The small curve turns broad, a wide smile that lights up his face. 'I didn't know. I don't actually know much about the Isle of Wight at all.' He takes a breath as if to ask me something, but then shakes his head slightly. 'Sorry, I'm digressing. I haven't spoken to Alison yet. I was asking you about her, wasn't I?'

'Can't tell you much. I don't know her that well, really. Keeps to herself mainly. Doesn't have a job, so I don't know what she does to keep herself busy. Nice enough girl. She's worried though, about Lucas. All over the place, bless her.' I do not add that I am similarly concerned.

'How long have they been together?' he asks, not put off by my vague answer. I suppose you need specifics in his line of work.

'Around two years. They got married pretty quickly. Lucas told me he just knew when they met, that he'd never met anyone he had so much in common with. He'd been in a long-term relationship before that from school with an island girl, Lucy.'

'Did his mother approve of the shotgun wedding?' Gareth tips an eyebrow at this and I nearly smile.

'Hardly that. She was happy for him. Anyone with eyes can see that they're well suited and happy. I've never known them to row, or Lucas never mentioned they had. People seem to moan about their partners, don't they?' Not that I'd know really, never having had one to complain about. I don't let him ask the next question; I want a turn.

'When did Lucas's work realise that he had taken the project?'

Gareth leans back and twirls his pen between his fingers like a small parade baton. 'It wasn't that – he resigned without leave, and they haven't heard from him since.'

'When though?'

'Monday week.'

'That was the same day he went missing.'

'So it appears. He sent them a curt email, claiming enough was enough and that he had his mental health to think about, and they've not heard a word since, despite requests to return work equipment. His laptop, mainly. It's expensive kit, regardless of what's on it.'

'But there is something on it too? And they can't track it, or him? People have all sorts of gadgets these days, plus banking records, and CCTV. I'm surprised people even need you. Can't they charge him with something and get the police to find him, if he has deliberately stolen something? Do they think he's going to sell it to someone else? It can't be that important.'

'It's worth a lot of money, if it works. It's new tech, and there's a lot of industrial espionage in that industry. But they don't want to get the police involved at this stage until things are clearer. I get the impression this has come as a real surprise.'

They aren't the only ones surprised or confused. Maybe this has nothing to do with Lucas's family then. Maybe he's just done a runner with software worth a fortune. Maybe he did need the money after everything. Or the pressure has caught up with him and given him some sort of breakdown.

'Do you think she's in on it?' asks Gareth, snapping me from my reverie.

'What? Alison? No, definitely not. She's a complete mess. She had me looking in her attic the other day for clues.'

'Clues? Like your crosswords?'

I would reply but there's an indignant noise in the way, and my mouth just hangs open instead.

'I did say I already knew your name. I looked you up. I'm a fan, as it turns out.' He grins again as if I should somehow be pleased by this, but the intrusion into my life is infuriating. He has no right to do this, to watch me, to know things about me. I'm not involved in whatever situation my idiot neighbour has gotten himself caught up in. Almost too cross to speak, I stand up and take my empty cup back to the counter, where Nicky is watching with what appears to be bated breath, before striding back.

'I think I've told you everything I know. I'd rather not see you lurking around my house again if you please.' He looks bewildered as I turn on my heel and stalk away.

8

DOWN: 8. A doe's vision, perhaps (9)

WHEN I GET HOME, STILL in a fury, my heart is absolutely pounding from the rage-fuelled cycling up the hill and I'm not really thinking straight. I throw my bike on the gravel in the drive and storm straight over to Alison, using the knocker to rap repeatedly on the door.

She answers dressed in her coat, her face bright and windswept. I must have just caught her coming home. It's not like her to be out early evening, but I ignore my note-making brain and simply blurt out, 'I thought you should know there's a man digging about.'

Her face goes dreadfully pale, and I realise what she could be thinking with a horrifying wash of shame. 'A detective, a private detective. He's looking for Lucas as well, from his work. Sentient. Apparently, he has a laptop or a project or something that they want back. Did he leave it here?'

'I . . . I don't think so . . .' she says, breathing deeply. 'Do you think this man might find him sooner than the police?' She looks distracted now. I've overloaded her and feel horrible.

I shouldn't have come over here like this and surprised her. Every time the door goes, she probably fears the worst and hopes for the best at the same time. No wonder she looks ill again, which she does, still pale with high spots of colour on her cheeks, like she might faint. 'Thank you for letting me know', she manages, before closing the door in my face.

I'm not sure how I get back to my cottage; one minute I'm on their doorstep then I'm sitting on my sofa, still in my sodding wetsuit. Alison must think I'm completely mad turning up like that and shouting at her about private detectives. Why would it even matter to forewarn her – she'd likely know soon enough. He's probably on his way there next before he buggers off. It's not like I was much use to him.

There are crunching footsteps outside and I freeze as they approach the door, but the letterbox clangs and the footsteps retreat with a flash of orange past the window. Just the postman on the afternoon run of junk mail. It should be banned; imagine all the trees they'd save if they just outlawed unsolicited junk mail and those terrible catalogues full of weird sleeveless jackets and stepladders. The interlude is enough to snap me out of my mood and I get up to go get out of my wetsuit, which is starting to itch me. As I'm leaving the room, I glance down the hallway and the only thing on the mat is another one of those slips that arrive with sickening regularity. All the emotions and thoughts of the day bubble up in me again and I just pull off my suit where I stand, run past the offending article on the doormat and upstairs to the bathroom where I shower until my hot water runs out.

I ignore it again on the way downstairs, though I'm aware of its malevolent presence as I pass. I sit in the uncomfortable armchair in my lounge which I usually reserve for people I don't like, but liked or otherwise, no one has visited me in years except Lucas. He knew better than to sit here. This one lets me see the big house, half of it anyway. The front door is in view, and the large windows on the far side. It's the noise that alerts me after I become distracted trying to think of a clue for a word that begins with 's' and ends with 'l', eight letters, to fit in this puzzle or I'll have to rewrite half the poxy thing. Crunching gravel, an engine slowly growling past my house.

As I look out at the house I see a pale flash in the window, Alison, then the van obscures my view briefly, parking further up so I can see the door opening as that man approaches. Alison stands in the doorway, wrapping her cardigan tightly around her body against the chill. Even from a distance she still looks ill. He walks up to her and they shake hands. I wonder if his hands cover the whole of hers too, if they're still as warm. Then they go into the house, and I feel as if I could erupt with inquisitiveness. Does Alison hold a key to Lucas's whereabouts, without knowing it? For all they know, the police might already be on his tail. She'll be here tomorrow, that detective with her shiny hair and secretive eyes. Maybe I should have thought about being a copper, solving crimes all day, but then I don't think I could cope with all the idiots and drunks.

They're in the house a long time. My back is starting to ache from the upright chair, and I've chewed my nails down again, picking at a hangnail until it rips away, leaving a small crevice filling with blood at which point I stop, swearing. It's fully dark before the door opens again and he leaves. Alison watches him as he walks back to his van and he gets in it, making a U-turn on the drive. As he comes past, he looks right in through my window and our eyes meet, and a frisson of something causes me to jump right up out of my chair to the window, where I pull the curtains so hard one of the plastic rings pings off across the room.

I'm half under the sideboard trying to retrieve the stupid thing when I hear footsteps approaching again, and I shuffle myself back out across the floor, stand up and go to the hall. It must be Alison, and it is.

'We must stop meeting like this,' she ventures with a half-laugh. 'Can I come in for a bit?'

'Okay.' I stand back to let her in, and she walks through slowly.

'I think this is the first time I've ever been in your house, Merry. It's lovely.'

It is the first time she's been here. Lucas always used to drop by on his own for a cuppa and a catch up. 'The front room's just there. Do you want a drink of anything?'

'No, I'm okay. I just wanted to ask about that so-called detective bloke.'

'Ha. He didn't ask me much. I didn't really want to speak to him.'

She sits down in the uncomfortable chair, which she will regret if she's here for longer than ten minutes, and I sit down on the sofa opposite, tucking my feet up and pulling a cushion down on them because they're cold. My feet are always like ice blocks.

'Did he ask you about me?' says Alison, who is also picking at her fingernails. It must be catching. 'He wanted to know about me. I thought it was really weird, if he's supposed to be looking for my husband. I didn't know Lucas worked on anything that was worth anything like that much. I thought they just made creepy spying cameras.'

'I didn't really know much beyond computer stuff. He never really talked about his work much to me. And yes, that man did ask about you, but I didn't have anything to tell him. I didn't really want to, tell truth, it's not nice is it, talking about people behind their backs?'

Her eyes slide away, and I find myself suddenly picturing her and Lucas, sitting in their kitchen, laughing at me and talking about my meltdown over the garden works. I know I was awful, but it was really very upsetting.

'Well, hopefully he'll find him quicker than the police. I don't think they're even looking. Nothing is even suspicious to them. They just think he's a grown up and he's left me. Like I'm simply a hysterical scorned wife.'

'You can tell them that his work is looking for him too. Or I can tell her tomorrow, that Scottish woman.'

'Why are you seeing her?' Alison looks back to me again, a small frown making a crease between her eyebrows.

A sigh escapes me before I can answer, accompanied by a sicky feeling. 'I think she wants to talk to me about Lucas's father. She said they were reopening the case. If it ever actually closed.'

'It must have been infuriating him disappearing like that when they were about to arrest him.' She catches my look, quizzical, and shrugs. 'I looked it up on the internet. Lucas would never talk about it, but there's quite a lot online. Lots of theories. What was he like?'

'Lucas?'

'No, David. What was he like as a person? How did no one know what he was really up to?'

Now, there's a question I have absolutely no desire to answer. My memories of him are stark, a few jagged spears of pain that never seem to dull. He was a bad man. He tricked us all: he was a masterful liar, it came naturally to him. I had to learn how to lie to survive, to him to lie was to breathe. Alison's face though is sweetly expectant, and I realise she probably just wants to think of something, anything, else. So I swallow my apprehension, and tell her.

'He wasn't a good person, but he was charismatic, and that made him handsome. The pictures in the papers, none of them really look like him. It's hard to describe really. He wasn't classically good looking or anything, he just had this energy that lit him up and made people want to be his friend. Julia was completely under his spell. He had this way of speaking to you, seeming truly interested in what you had to say, like you were the only person in the world he wanted to talk to at that minute. He was like that with everyone.'

Even me, now I think about it. He wanted everyone to like him. I remember a New Year's Eve party they invited me to one year when Lucas was still very small. I didn't want to go, because I hate parties and people and small talk that makes me want to cut my ears off, so I was skulking at home. He'd turned up at the door at about nine o'clock and informed me that my absence was upsetting his wife. He ordered me to go and put on a dress and get my arse over to their house, waiting in the hallway with his arms folded until I did. He just expected people to do what he wanted, when he wanted, regardless of anything that had gone before.

Alison is looking at me expectantly, still intrigued. 'And no one suspected what he was really up to? He was basically a crime lord, for God's sake; how do you not notice something like that? Did no one wonder where all the money came from?'

'No, no one suspected. He told Julia it was an inheritance. They were already a rich family so it wasn't that far-fetched. And I don't think he got into that stuff, the drug running, until later after they married. She told me he had changed over the years, became . . . darker, I suppose. Especially after Lucas was born.'

'He looks a little bit like him, doesn't he? Lucas. Except across the eyes.'

I look down at my lap. He does look like him a bit, lots of people have dark hair and light eyes, all Celtic. But he's nothing like him inside. Surely he didn't stick around long enough to pollute him like that. I'm sure that whatever's happened, there's an innocent explanation. There has to be.

'What do you think even made him do it, if he was already well-off? They had the house didn't they, from his parents?'

Though this isn't a subject I ever want to even think about, let alone talk about, it's gratifying to see her distracted and interested, some colour and liveliness back in her face. It makes it easier to dredge through the darkness. 'I think he was attracted to danger. It was a challenge – he loved a challenge, to set his mind to something, to win things. He was a top sailor, won all sorts of cups. But he would get bored, move on to the next thing. Maybe it was just a perfect storm of things, or he met the wrong people. Was the wrong person.' A shiver tickles over my skin as I remember the intensity of his personality, how he could never stand not being the biggest person in the room. I have to rub my arms briskly to get the horrible goosebumpy feeling to go away.

'I never realised how much that stuff goes on down here,' says Alison, who doesn't seem to notice my efforts to compose myself. 'You think it's this innocent little holiday place with sandcastles and candyfloss, but then all this comes out.'

'It still is that place, it just has an underbelly like anywhere else. And it's easy for them, really. They bring the stuff in on yachts across the Channel, or yachts that have met bigger boats or container ships in the Atlantic, and then they can moor up off the coast here and bring the drugs through and just take it over on the car ferries. They bypass the ports and Customs entirely, if they're smart enough. And David was. He was bribing one of the harbourmasters to look the other way if boats went out at night, to not log their movements. They'd bring it in, load it all into vans with special hidden compartments and they'd just drive it onto the mainland. God knows how much death that man brought through here.'

'Did you see the story about the old boy walking his dog who found a big plastic-wrapped bale washed up down the back of the Wight? He cut into it with his penknife, and it was cocaine!' Alison looks shocked at this, but I've heard it all before. Bales over the sides of boats, bobbing drums full of ecstasy pills. All the filth you could imagine just pouring through.

'I did. They found a guy fully scuba-geared up too; he'd got washed away with the bale. They left him here and went. They come in and out on the night tides, like ghosts.'

'And David was what, a go-between?'

'I think he was the linchpin. He knew the coastlines; he knew the shipping routes; he knew the currents. He could get the boats in and out without being seen, he organised the transport, the storage here.'

'Storage?' Alison quirks her head to one side, her eyes narrowed.

'They used to bury stuff in the woods and out on the end of the sandbar island after it got cut off. There were massive holes all over the shop. Julia asked Lucas to get them filled in.' Feeling suddenly salacious, or more like blurting things out that I shouldn't because Alison is actually here talking to me for once, I can't help adding, 'He had people killed too, who'd threatened to talk. Maybe even did it himself.'

'Seriously?' Alison looks shocked. Not everything made the headlines.

'Yes. It's probably why they're reopening the case, with Lucas going like this. David had all the connections he needed to disappear, maybe they think he's helped Lucas do the same.'

'And he's got this thing from work. Do you think he's done it for the money? For his dad? I can't believe he would, but why else would he leave me?' Her eyes well up and she presses her lips between her teeth, sniffing hard, which makes me feel edgy again.

'I can't say, but I just don't think he would go to David, even if he was still alive.'

'You think David's dead?'

'I guess. He'd be quite old now if he wasn't. I don't think the crowds he mixed in would have led to a long, relaxed life somewhere abroad. I think the gangs he worked with knew the police had got onto him and wanted to make sure he couldn't talk.' I hate speaking about this. My wrist is sore and, looking down, I realise I've been rubbing at the same patch of skin with my thumb, near old scars, and I've taken the top layer of skin off with the friction of it.

'Will you speak to Gareth again?' says Alison suddenly, her voice clear of tears. 'He said he wanted to talk to you some more, that you might be able to help him figure out some things about Lucas that might give him a place to start looking. He said you left quite abruptly earlier. I told him that was just how you are all the time.'

Offended, I nod, feeling a sullen expression creep over my face which is humiliating given my age, and given that I know better. But all this reminds me of then, and I was young then, and different. Maybe I haven't buried that girl as deeply as I thought I had. She's just under the surface, even after all this time.

'I gave him your phone number, anyway,' she says as she stands up and then I walk her to the door and the waiting darkness outside. 'I know you want to find Lucas too, don't you? I knew you wouldn't mind.' She gives me a brief hug around my stiff body before she goes.

I do so bloody mind.

9

DOWN: 32. Eat something in a quick and eager way (5)

I CAN'T SLEEP. MY HEAD is full of painful memories and secrets, mine and not mine. The night is clear, and the moon is low on the horizon when I slip out of the back door into the chill air. I didn't hang up or rinse my suit, and it smells bad, but I don't care. If I don't swim, I think I might explode. The path through the woods behind our houses is dark and bumpy under the wheels of my bike, but I could ride it blindfold I've come so many times before. At the end of the trees, I carry my bike onto the gravelly shore, leaving it propped up against the bank. A scurry of pebbles behind me makes me startle, but when I look around it's just a skinny vixen looking at me curiously before turning and padding away, her burnished orange only a whisper of colour in the night.

There used to be sand here that curled right out to form a sort of cove, but this is where it washed away after they built the harbour; it's all built up on the Appley side now instead, and here it's just pebbly and rocky with a tiny spit of land left isolated out beyond. The moon's light is enough to see by though, and I tread carefully. The sea is like a pool of rippling silk gently shushing as it flows in and out, the most wonderful susurration. It's so cold, but the freeze pushes my frantic mind back into a clear scape where I can make things make sense again, where I can call back calm. I don't know how long I swim for, a slow, pulsing breaststroke that heats the muscles in my back and stretches the ligaments in my pelvis. I'm tempted to swim out to the sandbank island, but the channel is deep and I shouldn't go out of my depth at night so I don't go beyond the little jetty. I just swim until I ache, until my lungs feel salted, until I'm empty again.

It doesn't take me long to get home, shivering violently as I strip off and rinse my suit to hang it in the shed and slip back into my house for a quick shower. I collapse into bed with a towel wrapped around my wet hair and I sleep like I'm dead until the sun comes in.

I'm only just dressed by the time the door goes. I swear I've had more people knock on my door with the intention of communicating with me in the last week than I have in the last decade. It's exhausting. I want everything to go back to how it was.

It's the selkie again. She has two takeaway coffees in her hands, gloved this time, leather in an ivy green colour. I covet them immediately. 'Shall we walk and talk?' she says, holding a coffee out towards me. 'One sugar, and a little milk? I saw you make yours last week, I hope that I remembered right?'

'Mmm. Thanks. Let me get my coat and boots on then.' *What's wrong with my coffee?* Strange woman. I wrap myself up and pull on my boots, tucking a scarf that would match those gloves into my collar. My own gloves are just a woolly, stretchy, boring black. The cup I take is hot still, so I don't risk a sip yet.

We walk for a while, and I follow her lead as she turns off the pavement and down the public footpath that leads onto the golf course or splits off to the beach. It's quiet, still early, though a faint chink-noise of a golf ball being struck incorrectly echoes through the trees. The clear sky of the early hours has clouded over, it's grey and damp feeling, and I'm glad of the drink, which is really very nice post-volcanic heat. I don't buy takeaway coffees, but maybe I should.

'We've been looking into our files on David Manning,' says the detective. 'Tell me what you think happened to him. After Lucas you're the closest person left to the case that I can still speak to. Speak to easily, anyway.'

'He was just my neighbour.'

'Alison told me you and his wife were as thick as thieves,' says Macauley. A statement, no question. 'Seems odd that you don't have an opinion on him.'

'More after that, really. We weren't really friends before he went.' This is a lie and I'm pleased we're walking. It seems foolish of her to ask me to walk with her when she can't look at my face to try and work out if I'm lying. She is an odd policewoman. I was half expecting to be called into a station, into an interrogation room, maybe. Unless she thinks she can deliberately unsettle me by taking me out of my comfort zone.

'Did Julia talk about him, after that?'

'A bit. She missed him, despite everything. She hadn't known about any of the smuggling. She was a very innocent sort of person; he was quite a bit older than her. Charismatic, I suppose.'

'What was her theory on his whereabouts? I'd be very surprised if she didn't have one, or that he hadn't got in contact with his family somehow. No letters, no strange postcards?'

'Maybe. She didn't say.'

'Surely she would have expected him to get in touch in some way?'

'Maybe he did, and she just never told me.'

She makes a huff of breath that could be the beginning of a laugh. 'Perhaps. You know he was the main suspect in a double murder in Yarmouth, don't you? Two nights before he disappeared. Young men, not more than boys really. Both shot.'

'Yes, we knew that. We found out after he'd gone, your lot told us. I always guessed his own skin was more important to him than anything else and that he'd rather just leave everything behind than be caught and jailed. I've always pictured him on a beach, somewhere hot, drinking a silly drink. He loved being by the sea. And silly drinks. He'd always make a new one for the parties they had. I did go to a few; all the neighbours used to get invited, it would have been rude not to. They were a bit strong for me though, I don't really have a head for alcohol.'

We walk on silently for a bit down to the beach and along beneath the leaning trees. I spent a bit of time here when I was younger. This is where I learnt to swim, one good memory from my teenage years that I try and keep separate from afterwards. You have to compartmentalise when you don't have a lot of good times to remember, and those few weeks were special at the time. The branches of the trees are whipping about with the breeze that's coming in off the sea and the waves look choppy. I'm glad I went out last night because it looks like bad weather is blowing in, heavy clouds parting only occasionally to let down shafts of sunlight that create paler spots of colour on the dark green water.

'Is this beach part of the Mannings' land?' asks Macauley. 'There are some private beaches round here, aren't there?' She's looking up at the path I used last night that leads up to the big house, which ends here, working out the geography of the route we've just walked.

'They do own it, yes. That's their little jetty and boat there. But they've never made it off limits or anything, anyone can use the beach here.'

'Fancy having your own bit of beach,' she says, and I have to agree that it would be nice.

'What are your theories?' This time I ask the question, not really expecting an answer, just wanting to fill the space and deflect from myself.

'I don't think David Manning ever left this island. I'm not convinced that his son did, either.'

This stops me like a punch. I almost slip down a small bank of pebbles and she puts out a hand and catches my elbow. I'm glad of the moment to compose myself, my heart hammering fit to burst out of the cage of my ribs. She waits and she watches.

I look at her now. 'You think Lucas is still in town somewhere? Why? And what could the police even do about it if he just doesn't want to be found?' I feel like I'm gabbling, and pull in a tight breath, and another, trying to re-expand my clenching chest.

'Until we hear different, we'll continue with our missing person enquiries. We've checked CCTV footage at the ferry terminals on the date he went missing and he's not on it.'

'There are different ways off if you wanted to leave secretly. Other boats. I don't know why he would though. Unless he was scared or hiding. Should you be telling me this stuff? Why are you talking to me like this, all casual? It doesn't seem very professional of you.'

She doesn't seem to care that I'm being rude to her, changing the subject instead, 'I understand you've spoken to the private investigator that Sentient Security Systems hired?'

That bloody man is getting everywhere. 'I didn't think you would deal with an amateur.' My voice is snarky now, and I don't like it. I don't like him.

'Hardly that. He had some information that we found useful.'

I can't help pushing her again. 'Is this normal? Speaking to me like this, off the record? Shouldn't we be in a police station or something?'

An enigmatic smile is my only reply as she sets off again over the shingle, small pebbles scattering and sliding beneath her feet in tiny waves. Our walk takes us down the beach and back up to the sea wall steps. Macauley is chatting to me like we are friends, asking me things now that are nothing to do with Lucas or his father. I think she is trying to get me onside, trying to draw me out. It's a cold thought that shudders through me, that if she is playing this game, it's because she suspects that I know something that I'm not telling her.

We wind our way back up the hill towards the point where we could split – her to the station, me back home. She stops on the corner where she can turn off and I catch a whiff of chips from Tony's, the smack of vinegary scent making my stomach rumble beneath my layers.

'I'll leave you here, Merry,' she says, pulling at her collar so it stands against the wind, which is picking up. Wisps of escaped hair are brushing her softly flushed cheeks. 'Thank you for speaking to me. This is all very curious, don't you think?'

It really is most infuriatingly curious, among other ignored feelings. Selkie is like me, a seeker of answers. I'm about to leave when she speaks again.

'I meant to say, I like your scarf. Really brings out the colour of your eyes. You don't see many people with truly green eyes. Striking, really.' She flashes her small smile again, and turns away, leaving me shivering as the rain starts in.

10

ACROSS: 20. A child's toy, and another, and another, and another . . . (8)

I'M STILL IGNORING THE DOORMAT when I get in. It's always the same. What's worse, it being there on the floor or me having to pick it up and put it in the recycling without looking at it? Hopefully more junk mail will come and land on top of it so I can just bin all of it without touching the damned thing more than I have to.

It doesn't take long before my house smells like the packet I brought in with me, tucked tightly against me to preserve the warmth. Lovely, lovely chips for lunch, to help me forget about this morning. I unwrap the paper and steamy heat escapes from the golden pile. I don't need anything with them except the salt and vinegar already lavished on them by Jim at Tony's. I sit and eat them one at a time, each one fluffy perfection, until the paper is empty of even all the small crunchy bits. Which might actually be my favourite anyway.

The afternoon is whiled away productively on my puzzles. I've caught up with all the work I had to do, which gives me a little buzz, enough to see off the housework that needs doing as well. All thoughts of Manning men are pushed from my head until once again I hear the threatening crunch of a vehicle on the gravel outside my house. I peer out of my bedroom window and of course it's that man in his scruffy van again. As if I haven't had enough to deal with today. I hope he's here to see Alison, but I have no such luck. He parks next to my house and gets out and he's actually whistling, as if he could get any worse. I've almost decided to ignore his knocking, but he senses me watching him and looks up, giving me a cheery wave.

I do take my time getting down the stairs though and open the door as begrudgingly slowly as I can.

'Good evening,' he says, doing a theatrical 'brr' and rubbing the tops of his arms.

I don't want to ask him in. I can already feel the itchy edges of alarm scratching at me at even the thought of it. I don't understand why he has this effect on me. 'Do you want to come in?' The words feel stiff, like I'm turning into wood. Maybe a babushka doll, layers and layers of wooden Merrys, all full of things I don't want to let out.

'Thanks,' he says showing me his teeth again. 'I'll try not to keep you for too long.' He's wearing a longer coat today, a thick parka but without a hood, which he slings over my banister like he owns the place. I catch a scent from him, which isn't unpleasant, only male, but it puts me even more on edge. I tell myself if he can help find Lucas then everything can go back to normal, so I should assist him if I can. It's just hard.

I turn my back on him and walk back through to my lounge. He can have the armchair. It's an effort not to curl into myself as I sit down, to pull up my legs and wrap my arms around them, hide my face. This isn't something I do, but I don't trust this man. I don't know why. The reason scurries around my edges, I can't quite grasp anything but the discomfort. He takes up too much space when he walks through and does that strange tug up on his trouser legs that men do before they sit down.

He just looks at me for a while like he's about to smirk about something, but he doesn't.

'I need some more background on Lucas,' he says, leaning forward in his seat, clasping his hands and putting his elbows on his knees. 'Anything that could help me get a handle on where he might have gone, or even why he would go. He didn't need money; Alison went over their financials with me, there's no sign of him gambling or having an issue with spending, no unusual withdrawals or transactions. They own the house outright, there's still life insurance from his mother that's been invested.'

'Did that pay out?' I interrupt before I can stop myself.

'Why wouldn't it?' he asks, his eyes a lot sharper than his voice.

'They're tricky, aren't they, insurance companies. I just assumed they wouldn't, I don't know.' I can't hold contact with his eyes, looking out of the window instead, at the darkening wet slate sky.

'Well, they didn't have money troubles, far from it. Their lifestyle is enviously comfortable in that respect. So that's not a factor. His employers have said nothing was amiss, either personally or professionally as far as they were aware. He was highly regarded, and trusted. Completely trusted. He was the only employee allowed to work on the software offsite.' He frowns, his eyebrows coming together to form a thick line, the skin on his forehead crinkling in concentration. 'I hoped you might know people he was friends with, or people who knew him well. Alison makes them sound quite insular as a couple, but was that always the case?'

'No. He always had friends when he was younger at least. But his family, the things that have happened to them, they might as well be cursed. It doesn't surprise me that he withdrew as he got older, and he always seemed very happy to just be with Alison. She was very strong for him when Julia died. She organised everything.'

'Did he have many serious relationships before Alison? You mentioned a school girlfriend, was she the only one?'

I look back to him and he's rummaging behind his back, pulling out his tatty notebook from his rear pocket. 'Can I borrow a pen?' he asks me. There's one right in front of him on the table, and I nod to it, see him looking at my own notebook which accompanies it. There's nothing of note except half my latest puzzle. There's a good one for him there, *one who intrudes in other people's affairs (7)*. Meddler.

'She was the only one I knew,' I tell him. 'It wasn't too long before Alison, and I don't think he saw anyone else in between. Julia worried about him for a while, that he was lonely or a bit depressed about it. She was never sure why they'd broken up, he wouldn't say, and they'd been really solid before.'

'Is she still local? What was her name?'

'I don't see how it would help. What would she know?'

'You'd be surprised. The more you know about someone, the easier they are to find.'

'Macauley doesn't think he left the island. She thinks he's still here.'

'All the more reason to ask widely, my dear.'

I am not his dear. His grin is infuriating. 'I think she still lives in St Helens,' I tell him through gritted teeth. 'Her name's

Lucy. It was Baker, but she might have got married too since then or moved to the mainland. I haven't seen her for a long time, three, maybe even four years. But they were together a really long time; they met at school, like I said.'

He scribbles on his notepad, putting his nose close to the pad like he needs glasses. He has very thick hair for a man of his age. If it were longer it might curl.

'Is there anyone else I could speak to? Alison gave me some names of other school friends, a few university friends, but she says they aren't really in touch. There's no social media, which is frustrating. It's all I usually need these days if I want to find someone.' He flicks through the pages and reels off several names that I don't recognise, and a few I vaguely do, from a long time ago, during the summers. Teenage boys shouting in the garden, knocking on my door and running away, their laughter. It seems a very distant memory now, of a kinder time.

'I haven't seen any of those boys for a long time.'

He looks back to me, his expression soft, like he's pitying me for something. He doesn't have to pity me for anything. I hate people feeling sorry for me. I'm not defective.

'Tell me a bit more about Lucas, if you can. What sort of person he is, what sort of things he likes to do. I'd imagine you must know him fairly well if you've lived next to him all this time?'

A sting on my wrist makes me realise I've started rubbing at it again, an old habit I don't really want coming back. Julia used to tell me off when she saw me doing it, all the little friction burns I used to end up with. I sigh instead and tug the cuffs of my sweater down over my hands. 'He's clever,' I tell him, pleased when he stops eyeing me and goes back to his scribbling. 'He always worked hard at school, got on well. He wasn't sporty, but he loved being outside, especially sailing. David got him into that. He used to have a two-person dinghy, but I think they just have a little motorboat now. And he used to go shore fishing, with Lucy, but I don't think Alison liked it much. Can't say I blame her, she's not very outdoorsy.'

'Did you ever get the impression he was keeping secrets, or hiding things from people?'

'No, not him. He seemed the same as always. A bit tired, maybe, a bit stressed. It was hard after losing Julia, but he'd been more his old self again this past six months, back to laughing and teasing me when he saw me.' I don't bother to tell him about our falling out. It's so unimportant now and so foolish with the clear mirror of hindsight.

'Can you think of anything you've seen recently, that's stuck out in your mind or made you feel uneasy?'

'Only you,' I tell him, blurting it out before I can stop myself. He looks a bit hurt, and I feel bad, even though it's true. 'It's this whole thing. I really don't know why everyone thinks that I would know anything, or care. It's nothing to do with me, is it?'

'And you don't want to help?' he says, putting down my pen a bit too firmly on the table.

'Of course I want to help! I just can't. I don't *know* anything.'

He's still looking at me, a dubious expression hovering on his face. Then he stands, suddenly, taking up too much space again. I follow him as he leaves the room and grabs his coat, flicking it open and shoving his arms into the sleeves.

'Well, look,' he says. 'I'm really sorry I bothered you; I appreciate your time. It's been helpful even if you think it hasn't.'

He looks up at me from zipping up his coat, and I manage a smile at least, though it feels like it might be a bit wonky. There's one of those awkward frozen moments where people who don't know each other very well aren't sure how to say goodbye. Julia would have called it flapping.

A rush of relief runs through me as he turns to leave, but then he glances down at the doormat.

'Oh, you've got a letter,' he says and though I open my mouth to tell him to leave it, he swoops down and picks it up. 'Oh,' he says again.

I'm still gaping like a cod when turns back to me, his eyes trained on the envelope.

'Not to be presumptuous, but is this what I think it is?' His dark eyes meet mine and there's that frisson of something again, his sharp intelligence making itself known maybe. 'Merry, is this a visiting slip for Lucas's brother?'

I swallow and hold my hand out for the vile thing, careful not to touch the lettering emblazoned on it. HMP, glaring up at us. 'I don't know any other criminals, so yes,' I snap, tugging it out of his grasp, my emotions getting the better of me. 'I don't know why he sends them to me! I've never been to see him. I don't want to see him.'

Gareth doesn't look taken aback by my outburst. He's still intent. 'Do you think he might know anything about Lucas going missing?' He's watching my face now. I can tell what he's thinking, what he wants to ask.

'No,' I tell him as his lips purse with the question. 'Absolutely not.'

11

DOWN: 12. You might end up here if you steal (3,4)

PARKHURST LOOMS AGAINST THE SKYLINE as we turn off the Cowes Road, its floodlights lighting up the sky with a dirty yellow glow. Gareth's van rattles but it's surprisingly clean on the inside at least and it doesn't smell bad. I have no idea how he talked me into this. Not only talked me into it, but armed me with a list of questions, and driven me here to boot. Maybe he thought I would do a bunk if he didn't.

He'd be right.

I've spent the last day in a blur of misery, praying that Lucas would turn up. I've called him seventeen times, but it's just going through to a full voicemail. None of my texts have been answered. How can someone leave like that? The wrongness of it all is like the weighted blanket I bought on a whim, used once then consigned to the cupboard because I didn't like it stifling me. I woke up thrashing to get out. I want to get out of this.

'How long has he been inside now?' asks Gareth, breaking my reverie as we pull into the visitors' car park. I'm sure he knows perfectly well, the arse.

'Nearly three years.'

'And how long to go?'

'Not long, he'll be out soon enough. He should have got a much longer sentence.'

'Did he ever hurt you? Or Lucas?'

'Me, no, never. Lucas, sometimes. He was quite jealous when Lucas was a baby, Julia had to watch him like a hawk. And later as well. Lucas was poorly, and Sean definitely got left out.'

'Poorly?'

'He had leukaemia, when he was a toddler and later again. It was awful, they thought they were going to lose him. Sean would stay with me quite a bit because of the infection risk, so he could keep going to school while Julia kept Lucas isolated.'

'So you were close, then? When he was younger?'

I can only shrug and nod past the lump of emotion that might spill if I open my mouth. I feel bad for what I said before, Sean wasn't a bad child. Jealous, maybe, but sweet enough to me when I minded him. An image of him bringing me the delicate half-shell of a robin's egg, his eyes wide with wonder, flutters in my memory but I push it away. He's proved he's not that boy anymore.

We're early for visiting, and the windows to the van start to steam up with the condensation from our body heat and breath. I trace a small triangle on the passenger-side glass, and another to make it a star.

'Why do you think he wants you to visit him?'

'I have no idea. The letters started coming after Julia died, but I've always ignored them.'

'Why?'

Gareth isn't looking at me, he's looking at his fingernails on his right hand, turned away, but I hear a tension in his casual question.

'Why not? He's a criminal waste of space like his father, only worse at it,' I tell him, annoyed again even though it's me blabbering on. My sharp edges are back, bristling like spines, and it's all I can do not to fling open the door and run away screaming. I don't want to be here. I bounce my head back on the seat a couple of times and contemplate the colour of the sky. It looks like bad weather, but I might have time to get a swim in after this is all over; the tides are good later and the chill has gone, even if it is a bit blowy, it's going to be mild for the next few weeks. I'll need one to clear my head, chase the feelings away.

I get the list of my questions out of my pocket and unfold it, smoothing out the paper against my leg.

'Will I be allowed a pen?' I ask Gareth. 'He might try and steal it and stab someone with it.'

'I shouldn't think so,' he says with a laugh. 'But I think you'll remember the answers well enough. You seem very astute to me. Do you think he'll answer them?'

'He might. But it probably won't be the truth. He turned out to be a liar like his dad too.'

'People give away all sorts of things without saying them. Watch his body language. Most liars have the same tells. If he's lying about something, I think you'll know.'

'He'll lie about everything though. This is a waste of time.'

'Maybe. But it's important. He won't speak to the police, you know. Macauley's tried already to speak to him about Lucas and his father's disappearances, said he just sat there with a shit-eating grin on his face.'

'Delightful phrase,' I mutter, tracing over my fading star again.

'Thank you for doing this, Merry. I can see it's not easy for you.' I can see him looking contemplatively at me in my peripheral vision, judging me again with those warm eyes of his.

The clock on his dash moves inexorably towards the time I have to go in. I'm not afraid of Sean. I'm just so deeply disappointed in him that I couldn't bear to see him, or even think about him. He saw what David's actions did to his mother. But then he always blamed her for David leaving – as if she could have made that man leave. I just don't know what he wants from me.

I leave Gareth in the van. He doesn't say anything as I give him my best evil look, simply nods in encouragement. I feel his eyes on my back as I walk away.

Inside the prison everything seems dim and poorly lit, the walls in need of painting and covered with spots of old Blu-Tack. The hard plastic chairs for waiting on are filled mainly with tired-looking women, and a few children. Why would you bring your child here? I would never.

The process is interminable, forms, searches, ID checks, box ticking, pat downs, instructions from bored-sounding officers. They don't look like they'd know what to do if something kicked off, most of them are soft and doughy, though I know looks can be deceiving better than anyone.

Eventually we're ushered through clunking wire doors, buzzers going off, to a large room with tables, all with someone sat at them. My eyes scan the room almost of their own volition, flickering wildly back and forth. For a second, relief and hope bloom through me, that he isn't here, but of course he is. He's just different. His shock of black hair, the same as his dad's, is swept off his face. There's no softness to his figure anymore, his arms are hard sinew beneath the short sleeves of his t-shirt. I deliberately lift my chin as I walk over.

'Hello, Merry.' His voice is the same, gentle and sibilant. It sets the hairs on my arms on end even beneath my layers of clothes, though I can't say why. He looks so small somehow, reduced by his surroundings, like something vital has been leeched out of him.

'Sean.'

'I didn't think you would come. I've missed you.' He quirks his head to the side as he speaks. His new thinness makes his deep brown, almost black eyes look enormous and puppy-like in his face.

'I wouldn't have. But someone asked me if I would. So I could ask you some questions.'

'About Lucas.'

I don't trust myself to talk, so I just nod jerkily.

'How come you get all the fit birds, Manning?' yells another prisoner, making us both jump. 'This one ya mum?'

He glares at the interrupter then looks at me, but I can't meet his gaze. 'Merry, why didn't you come and speak for me at my trial? I thought we were friends.'

The change in subject puts me off kilter and a wash of guilt makes me angry. I shouldn't feel guilty about that, he didn't deserve my support. 'Because I didn't want to. I didn't want to defend you. Your behaviour was abhorrent, and illegal, and . . . you deserve to be here.'

His expression doesn't change, but his eyes seem darker, pools of pitch with no reflection. He leans forward, a snake-fast sudden movement, and I try to scoot back on my chair, but it's fixed to the floor, and he leans back and raises his palms. 'I'm sorry, Merry, I didn't mean to make you jump. I'm really happy to see you, finally.' He pushes his fingers back through his hair and squeezes his eyes shut for a second, biting his lip as if he doesn't want to keep talking. 'You don't know everything you should know. About what happened. It's why I've been trying to see you all this time. You need to know the truth. I had to tell you in person because you weren't answering my letters. I know you were just throwing them away, weren't you?'

'Sean, I already know the truth. Your mum told me about the trial. I know. You got caught trying to help smuggle drugs, you got sent to prison. I don't see what else there could be.'

He leans towards me again, his face earnest. 'But that isn't the truth! I need you to listen to me, please. Lucas isn't the person you think he is. He set me up for this, for everything. I never even met any of those other people I got sent down with. How exactly do you think I could have organised any sort of drug deal when I'd only just started living on the island again? When I didn't know anyone? Don't you think that was odd?'

His eyes are shining with zeal, like he really believes what he's saying. I can't formulate a reply to what must be lies, my mind feels foggy and reluctant.

'It's why he's gone!' Sean almost shouts, earning a glare from a guard. His hands shoot across the table, and I pull mine back and sit on them before he can touch me. A look I can only describe as devastation passes over his face. 'I thought this might happen, him running like this. No one believes me. But I'm up for parole next week, and he knows he set me up. Maybe he's afraid and done a bunk, like he thinks I would want revenge on him or something. But I don't, Merry. Life's too short. I just want to get out of here. But I've been wanting to speak to you for so long.'

The little boy he was swims in front of my mind's eye again and the image pulls at a deep thread of feeling that I thought I had cut off a long time ago. 'Why?'

'I wanted you to believe in me, Merry. You always believed in me. You should have known this was all some sort of mistake.'

'I'd hardly call being involved in trying to import half a metric tonne of cocaine a mistake, Sean.'

He shakes his head sadly. 'It wasn't me, Merry. You know the reason I got a shorter sentence is because Lucas gave me names of people to give up in exchange, like a plea deal? He told me he'd found them out, that it would help me and that a short sentence was the best I could hope for while he arranged an appeal. He said the police had too much evidence, although I didn't understand how. He said he'd visit me every week, but he's never come once. Not once. And there never was any appeal.'

He looks like he's about to cry and the little boy is back again, right in front of me, difficult to banish. 'Why was none of this mentioned in the trial? He wouldn't give you an alibi, if he was setting you up, so why didn't your solicitor challenge him about that. If you really were together?'

'Lucas told me I'd got the dates wrong for when we were together, that he couldn't perjure himself for me. He said the only way he could help was giving me the names for the shorter sentence. But the longer I was here the more I realised the only person who could have set me up was him. You must think I'm stupid.'

'I've never thought you were stupid. Foolish, maybe. But not stupid.'

He puts his forearms down to the table and laces his fingers together. There are small tattoos scattered across the back of his left hand. They're really quite beautiful, a line of music, a bird on the wing. A wave, a ship. They look like he's done them himself, and I remember how talented he was at drawing. David hadn't approved though, so he'd never developed it. He'd gone wrong instead.

'Okay, tell me one thing. Why on earth would your brother set you up like that? He loved you; he wouldn't have any reason to do something so awful.'

Sean gives me a level stare that makes me squirm uncomfortably again in my chair. 'Brother? Ha. He ruined my life when we were kids, maybe he wanted to ruin it again. I've never been able to work him out. You know Dad loved me more than him, don't you? I think it made Lucas jealous of me early on, and it never left him. It makes sense that he would be jealous of that, doesn't it? If you think about it. Or maybe it was because I was building bridges with Mum, and he didn't like me moving back home.'

I shake my head. 'No. He wasn't jealous, he idolised you. And that *was* an accident. There's no way he could have known you'd be injured like that; it was a silly little boy prank that went horribly wrong. It devastated him that you couldn't play football anymore. And you've always made your own choices since. I don't think you know anything about Lucas being missing now, so there's no point in me being here or asking you anything. You're just trying to torment me for some reason. Your brother had nothing to do with any of this. You deserve to be here.'

Sean looks at me silently and I can feel my heart booming in my chest, clenching and expanding fit to burst. His voice is soft, but his words are knives. 'Oh, Merry,' he whispers. 'I know you don't believe me, but I think you'll find out soon enough what sort of person Lucas really is. I might not know exactly why my brother fucked me over again, but I know more than you think. I know everything about you. *I know what you did.*'

12

ACROSS: 25. Rising water commonly associated with low pressure (5,4)

THERE'S AN ECHO IN MY head as I'm led out of the sweaty visitors' room and down through the bleak corridors. It's much darker when we all walk out, disorientating. Gareth waves from behind the wheel of his van and I stagger towards it, feeling jerky and uncoordinated, a twisting marionette on tangled strings.

He leans across to open the door and I clamber in, starting to shake. I want to go home. I want to swim.

'Merry? Are you okay?' Gareth puts out his hand, but I lurch away from it before he can touch me, and he withdraws it as quickly as if I had burnt him.

'Can you take me home please?' My voice clatters in my head like a magpie chased away from a nest.

Gareth doesn't say anything else; he has the sense to just start the van, make the smooth movements of gears and wheels and arms, turning and exiting the car park. Coppins Bridge is as horrific as always, cars nose to tail, and I think he's going to speak to me more than once, a hitch in his breathing that should precede words but doesn't. He must think I'm insane. I think I might be.

Rain begins to patter on the windscreen as we come down the hill in Wooton and the windscreen wipers make a *skreek-skreek* noise which drills into my head and makes me grit my teeth until pain begins to radiate through my jaw into my scalp. I deserve it.

He pulls up in the bloody layby again, and I don't speak to him. I jump out and slam the door, take off at a run towards my house. I don't go in, instead throwing open the door to the shed, hurling my bag into the corner, pulling off my coat, jumper, t-shirt. I throw them down too, unable to put enough force behind the actions to get rid of anything that I'm feeling, any of the rage, the guilt. The grief.

Trousers and shoes join the pile and I wrench my suit off the hanger. It's the wrong one, my spring short sleeve, but I don't care, I don't care. I pull it on over my underwear, force my feet into my wet-shoes and then stagger out to my bike, yanking it off the stand and swinging my leg over it, barely able to summon the coordination to make the pedals turn.

Scenery I usually admire rushes past me, rain hitting my face, chilling my arms and numbing my fingers on the handlebars. The rushing in my head won't stop, the only thing I know to do to make it stop is to swim. It's fully dark by the time I get to the beach, the café is shut up, the wind blowing the ice cream sign back and forth with a clatter that I can only just hear over the wind howling past my ears, the only light is pooled on the floor by the lamps along the seawall.

I leave the bike sprawled on the promenade, before running down over the sand towards the waves. They're enormous, pounding against the shore ferociously. But it looks smoother, further out. I just need to get past the breaking.

Forcing my way past the crashing waves sets off a burn in my muscles, and when I dive over and past them, I swim underwater, straight out until I feel my lungs spasm. Breaking the surface and my first breath is salt laced, a good hurt, and I wonder if this is what it's like to be born. I keep swimming with my back to shore, I don't care how deep I am, I don't care what happens, if I drown, if I disappear. I could just do this forever, arm over shoulder, kicking my legs. I swim. Eventually the repetition does what it always does, it smooths away everything in my mind, pushes away things I don't want to think about, gives me clarity. I stop to breathe, tread water. I'm very far out, and I realise how stupid I'm being. I could be hit by a boat here – how would someone feel if they killed me by accident? I'm being an idiot. I turn to look round, and the pinpricks of light on the shore seem very far away, and the sky is roaring and black. Not only that but the swell is huge, the lights appear then disappear as I dip and peak on the water. There's a current beneath the water that would pull me under the second I let it, and the realisation that I don't actually want to die tonight is like a razor slicing through everything else.

I put my head down, and begin to swim back, but my arms and legs feel leaden. I've burnt out, I wasn't pacing myself. Years of training in open water vanish in a second as my strength dissolves. I haven't eaten properly for days, and I can feel it now. All I can do is keep moving, even though it's more flailing than anything else, and hope that the tide is still on its way in. I have no idea what time it is, the sea's rhythm a sudden mystery. I stop to try and see where I am – I still can't feel the bottom – and a huge wave breaks over me, forcing my head down and catching my body in its looping power, twisting me upside down in the water. It's forced up my nose, stinging into my sinuses and I feel a moment of utter blind panic, trapped in the green, before I'm slammed hard onto the sand. I must be near the shore.

I let the wave move away before I push off and follow it, breaking the surface, pulling in a desperate gasp of air before another wave slams me down, holds me on the bottom as it roars over me, before I manage to catch the upside and ride it, choking and coughing as I come to the surface again. My arm is burning, but I can't check it because I'm slammed again, but this time as the wave presses me against the seabed, I know I'm not as deep, I know I'm almost safe if I can just stand. But my legs are completely gone, I have no strength left and I'm being tossed around like flotsam, barely able to grab the air that I need. And I'm cold. I'm so cold I can't move anymore. My eyes close as I'm spun again, and then it stops. Everything stops.

13

ACROSS: 14. In which you might find the number of the beast (10)

I HEAR A PATTERING SOUND, and then something presses hard against my mouth and air is forced into my chest. I twist sideways and seawater propels itself from me in a burst and a cough, once, twice, and then I breathe. The noise is rain pouring from the sky hitting the sand next to my head, fat drops of water, my cheek is pressed against the rough grains. Hands are slapping my back, from above my hips to between my shoulder blades as I choke out as much brine as I can, shivers wracking my whole body. My eyes are burning with salt, everything blurred and dark and confusing. Eventually I can take in air without coughing and I roll onto my back again taking deep, juddering breaths, enjoying the feeling of the rain on my face, of being alive.

When I open my eyes, the blurriness has been blinked away and Gareth is looking down at me. He's shivering too: he's drenched through.

'Are you fucking mad?' he half shouts, raising his voice above the weather. 'I thought you were dead! I couldn't see you out there . . .' He pushes a hand over his short hair, the gesture makes me think it must have been longer recently. It seems an errant thought, and I laugh, a jagged sound in my sore throat, and it turns to my horror into sobs. I don't even have the strength or will to struggle away when he pulls me to sitting and wraps his arms around me hard. I just cry hysterically into his shoulder. At least he is already wet.

After what feels like forever and a minute both, I take control of my breathing again, and he lets me go, but keeps hold of my arms.

'Come on, I'll get you home,' he says. He puts his arm under my shoulders and lifts me to my feet. My legs wobble, and before I can say anything, he sweeps me up, holding me against his chest and carrying me up the beach. For a moment I let him do it, feel like my body is melting into his, but then I remember who I am.

'Put me down!' I whack him on the head with my palm and he drops me.

'Ow! I'm only trying to help! I'm pretty sure you were *actually dead* a minute ago!'

'I'm fine, I can walk.' I manage to scramble to my feet again, fending off his attempts to support me. My legs are very shaky though and I lurch against him several times as we head up the beach. His stupid van is parked at an angle across the prom, the driver's door flung open. He nearly ran over my bike. When we get to it, he follows me round to my side and unceremoniously shoves me into the passenger seat.

'Shit – Merry – I think you're bleeding . . .' He looks down at his khaki trousers, which do seem to have a bit of claret on them, drops of red splatted and smeared. The sight of it is almost enough to send me into another tailspin, but I'm so exhausted all I can do is slump backwards and feel faint and screw my eyes up. I cannot look at blood, I just can't. My arm reminds me it is the probable cause of the mess, springing back into sensory life and stinging viciously, a pain that shoots like electricity up and down the inside of my forearm. I don't look but I feel Gareth's hand take mine and gently turn it over to expose the damage.

'This looks nasty but I don't think you need a stitch. It's just a deep graze. Have you got a decent first aid kit at home, or do I need to stop at a pharmacist? Will there be one open somewhere?'

'I've got one,' I gulp, shaking so much my teeth chatter. 'The b-boys were always g-getting themselves in scrapes in the garden. Always kept one after, habit like.'

'And you were Nurse Merry?' The warmth in his voice – the only warmth in my world at this freezing moment – makes me open my eyes and look at him. He's showing me those teeth again, so I frown and he disappears, opening the back of the van. He comes back with a tea towel, and a sleeping bag of all things, and wraps the first round my arm and the other round the rest of me so tightly I can barely breathe, and then does the seat belt up over the top. I feel more than faintly ridiculous, and utter shame begins an assault on me. This man has saved my life tonight. I'm going to have to be nicer to him now. *For fuck's sake, Merry.*

He grabs my bike from the ground in front of the van and wheels it to the back of the van. I watch him in the mirror – he puts it in a lot more carefully than he did me, slotting it in beside all sorts of stuff that I can't quite make out, including what looks very much like a bed. Does he actually live in this thing?

The drive back to my house is silent apart from my teeth clattering in a shuddering spasm now and again. I cannot get warm despite the cocoon I am wreathed in. Gareth is shivering as well; his fingers are white on the wheel. He must have come in after me. He could have died too. I swam to try and get rid of emotions, but now I have a whole new raft of them. Sean's face and his bladed words crowd back into my mind, but this time I accept them. It's time I accepted everything.

My cottage is dark but as welcoming as it always is. It is the big house looming beyond that seems ominous with dark windows like eyes, staring out in judgement. I feel like it's mocking me, that it knows I'm about to spill one of the biggest secrets of my life to a virtual stranger. I owe it to him, after all this. A secret in return for saving my life.

After Gareth de-cocoons me from his now damp and grubby sleeping bag I have to get my keys out of the pile of my belongings in the shed. He's polite enough not to comment, that or he's too cold to talk. We walk through into the kitchen, and the warmth of the room hitting my skin is as painful as it is pleasant. I pull out the first aid kit and pass it to him, and then hold out my wrapped arm, but he shakes his head.

'It needs cleaning first, there's a lot of sand in it. And you're freezing, you need to go and have a shower, or a bath. Let the water heat up slowly, don't scald yourself. Don't come down till you've warmed up, okay?'

'What about you? You're soaked.'

'I've got a towel in the van, I'll have a scrub with that and change clothes. I wasn't in there for long, it's your core temperature I'm worried about. You made a remarkably good job of trying to kill yourself tonight you know.'

I don't acknowledge his words because I'm still half trying to not think of what sent me to the water. 'You can use the shower, if you want. After me, obviously.'

'Obviously,' he says, and his lips make a funny little jig on his face, he must be trying not to laugh. I have to remind myself to be nice to him, so I just scowl before wobbling up the stairs. The hot water is glorious, I could almost give up its salted brethren for life to just stay here and let it pour over me, hot and clean. A sorry selkie I've made tonight, just a foolish woman peeling off a wetsuit, trying not to look at her arm. I do though, once I'm sure all the blood has washed away. It's a nasty, deep scrape and I have to use the shower head to really get all the sand out. It hurts like a bitch.

Eventually I feel like I could almost be warm again. I get out and dry and dress myself in fleecy things, rolling my sleeve up for Gareth and his first aid. In the kitchen, where he is taking up far too much room again, he's standing by the fridge, having lined up a selection of things from the box on the kitchen table, clearly in the order he intends to use them. I'm secretly quite impressed. I do like an organised mind. He gestures to one of the chairs and sits down opposite me. I put out my arm, the raw skin a hideous burnt pink. I look away.

He bends over and I can feel his breath on my palm as he inspects the wound slowly, turning my arm gently. He doesn't speak, but picks up a small bottle of disinfectant and a cotton pad, and liberally collides the contents of the bottle onto it. He'd already removed the lid. It stings unbelievably, but I don't move. If he's impressed by my stoicism, he doesn't say. Just dabs, gently, inspects. When he's finished with that, he picks up a tube of cream which he squeezes, a small blob of cream onto the tip of his finger, which he then sweeps up the graze with a touch as light as silk. I would barely feel it were it not for the infernal stinging. Satisfied with the unction, he picks up a large dressing and presses it the length of my forearm. I don't remember having one so big. He wraps a bandage around it to hold it in place and then makes a huff of contentment.

I think it is the single most erotic thing I have ever experienced.

When he looks up, I know I must be blushing, but he should think it's from the hot shower. 'You can use the shower, if you like. There's always plenty of hot water – I had to get a new boiler last year, cost me—'

'Soon,' he says. 'First I want you to tell me what on earth that man said to you that's caused all this.' He looks a bit cross.

'Yes, well, that.' Now he looks bemused that I've gone from drowning insanity to burbling nonsense. Well, that's me all over. I actually feel a lot better, knowing it's out, or about to be, somehow. 'He told me that he knows.'

'Knows what?'

'That I'm Lucas's birth mother.'

14

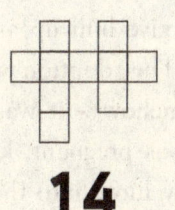

DOWN: 7. One who watches over (8)

HE DOESN'T LOOK PARTICULARLY SHOCKED.

'That picture in your front room, that's you with Lucas and Julia?'

'Yes.'

'I thought he might be your nephew or something. I didn't realise it was him and I'd not seen a picture of Julia. Green eyes, the both of you. So, he doesn't know?'

'No. I didn't want him to know. I was ashamed that I couldn't look after him. He doesn't look anything like me, except my eye colour. Even that looks different on us because of our hair and skin tones being so dissimilar. I don't think anyone would guess we were related.'

'How old were you when you had him?'

'Seventeen. Just. It still feels like yesterday, not thirty-four years ago.'

'How did it happen – the adoption? It doesn't seem like a very usual way of doing things, for you to be here and for him to be there, right next door. It must have been really hard for you.'

'It was agonising to give him up at first, but I'm good at putting things in boxes. The adoption was private, well, David's parents arranged it somehow – it was them who lived there then, so they knew I was pregnant, knew my history. David and Julia didn't actually move into the big house until a few years after they adopted Lucas, which made it a bit easier. Julia had wanted a sibling for Sean, she couldn't have another one. Put his nose right out of joint when Lucas arrived.' I could almost laugh at the memories of sweet Sean, so indignant that there was a baby not in my tummy anymore but on *his* mummy's lap. 'And it was lovely to see him grow up once they moved in, even though I wasn't doing anything.'

'Why has Sean told you this now? That he knows? Why did you react so . . .' He trails away but his face finishes the sentence for him. He thinks I'm mad.

'I stopped myself thinking about it. It's the only way I know how to cope anything – I lock bad memories away in my head and ignore them. He told me that Lucas was behind him being in prison, that he'd set him up for everything.'

'And you didn't believe him?'

'No, I just couldn't see why he would ever do that. Then . . . then he told me he knew what I had done.'

'Meaning the adoption?'

'Yes. When he threw it at me, he said he would tell Lucas, and that he was going to contest Julia's will as soon as he got out, take everything away from Lucas, that he wasn't his real brother, something just snapped. I couldn't bear the idea of Lucas finding out that I was his birth mother like that. Our relationship was already shaky after this summer when I ruined everything. I couldn't handle the idea of him hating me for a real reason. He adored Julia. She was such a brilliant mum.' I look at the bandage on my arm again, remember the dark water. 'All those years of pretending he was just my neighbour, never being able to tell him. I was too ashamed. And I loved him so much, but it didn't have anywhere to go. So I had to pretend, to lock it all away and try and forget that he was mine.'

Gareth looks like he has too many different questions in his head to know which one to choose. I befuddle everyone I ever meet. This is why I don't have any friends. I'm weird, prickly as a sea urchin. Too many secrets. My long speech has made my lungs ache. I can still taste salt on my breath.

'How would Sean have found out recently? Did he not remember his mum not being the one to actually have the baby?'

'He was really little, too young to remember. I have no idea how he found out. Maybe he's known for a while but never said anything.'

'Oh. So, he thought Lucas was his brother by natural means before?'

'Pretty much. Do you want a drink? I need a drink.' I stand up from the chair slowly, still feeling faint, and walk to the kettle. The familiar motions are soothing, cupboard doors opening and closing, the water roiling, the clink of the spoon. I don't take sugar normally, but I add two tonight. None for Gareth, who must be sweet enough.

I put the drink down and he excuses himself to nip out to his van. When he returns he has chocolate biscuits, my absolute favourite, which I don't buy as I'd eat them all in one go. He puts the pack between us and takes one to dip in his drink. I mirror him, and the melting treat in my mouth is almost enough to set me off crying again.

We munch in silent companionship for a minute and drink our tea.

'Is it okay to have that shower, Merry?' he asks, rolling his shoulders. He must still be cold, and stiff. And uncomfortable if the salt is drying all over him: I know from experience that seawater sets like scales if you don't rinse it away.

'Yes, it's the door nearest the top of the stairs. There're more towels in the airing cupboard.'

He leaves to pad up the stairs, picking up another bundle of clothes that he must have got out of his van with the biscuits. It feels very strange to have a man in my house, using my bathroom. It might be the first time, apart from the odd tradesman needing the loo, I suppose. I don't know if Auntie Rosie had many male guests, she was an oddbod loner like me, though I never asked her why. Maybe it's genetic.

I hear the water upstairs and let the hypnotic noise loosen some of the tough bonds of memory I've cultivated over the years, never wanting to think about the things that hurt. I didn't want to give him up, not really. But I was young, and alone, and afraid. My mother didn't raise me so much as drag me around behind her chaos until I was old enough to leave. I didn't want to do that to a baby and have the baby turn out like me, difficult and strange and lonely.

They had the big house, they already had Sean, money, security. I just had Aunt Rosie. I didn't know she'd leave me this little place, and I still harboured a small wish to go back to a different school and get some qualifications. I never did, in the end, but I taught myself a lot over the years. All you need is a book, and you can learn anything you want. And Lucas was just next door where I could watch from a safe distance. But it's never been easy, and I never wanted him to know what I'd done. Because it wasn't just a normal adoption. They paid me. I took money, for my baby. What sort of mother would sell her own child? And where had that money even come from? Blood money. Death money. It's another thing I don't want to think about, but it could all be connected, another piece of the puzzle, another letter in the crossword. You always think these things are separate, but nothing ever is. Everything leads into something else. You just need to understand the clues.

He's a long time washing, that man, but then I suppose there is rather a lot of him. When he eventually lopes down the stairs, I've made us another drink and eaten half his biscuits. He doesn't pause for thought.

'Do you think this is connected, Sean finding this out, and Lucas disappearing? Is there an angle here?'

'I don't know, I don't even know how he could have found out about the adoption for sure. Only six of us knew, and five of those are dead. It was all . . . it was all really dodgy, I think. I had him here, Lucas. In this house. They took him before I'd even looked at him. I didn't want to look at him, I just wanted it to be over. I didn't register the birth; David's mother was a retired midwife . . . I don't think I'm even on the birth certificate. I certainly never went to the registry office. There might have been other people around who thought I was pregnant, I guess. It was the reason I left school. The only thing I can think is someone was gossiping, and they've put it all together and told Sean somehow.' I can't meet his gaze. He must think I'm an evil person. He doesn't know the half of it.

'I can't imagine how difficult that was for you,' he says, and this time I do look up because his voice is kind. His hair is all fluffy from the shower, and I can smell the lemon from my body wash that I bought because it was a pound and then regretted. It's good on him though.

'Do you have children?' I ask him, not wanting to feel emotional again.

He smiles. 'I do, yes. One of each, all grown up now. I'll probably be a grandad before I know it.' He laughs at the thought, but I can see the delight it gives him sparkling in his eyes.

'So you're married? Where do you all live, when you aren't gallivanting round the country looking for missing people?'

'No, not married. We've been divorced for a long time. I was in the army, she didn't like the life, I did, so she found someone else. I can't blame her really, it's not easy.' He doesn't look particularly sad about this, but I don't want to probe too deeply because I wouldn't want him to think I was interested. I'm far too old for anything like that, even if he does have lovely hands and funny brown eyes.

'I think we need to speak to Sean again,' says Gareth, creasing his brow. 'I think he could know more about this.'

'I don't want to speak to him again. He just lies. And what could he know? Lucas resigned his job and disappeared. He wouldn't have resigned for no reason. How would Sean have gotten him to resign? He's in prison.'

'I just have a feeling this is a good lead. Did you say Lucas testified at the trial?'

'He did. He couldn't not, really. He didn't know anything incriminating but he wouldn't corroborate some of Sean's lies about his whereabouts.'

'And now Sean blames Lucas for his sentence.'

'Sean blames everyone but himself for his mistakes. I think maybe he just wanted to hurt me because I wouldn't visit him. He can't do anything from inside.'

'He'll be out soon though, if his parole is successful. Even next week.'

'Well, I'd rather not think about that.'

'I think you should. I'd like to know more about Sean's claims that Lucas was the one involved in the smuggling.'

'It's ridiculous. He said Lucas gave him names to give up so he could make a plea deal. I mean, it would be possible to find something like that out, I guess. But that would have helped Sean get the lighter sentence. It seems weird to get someone sent to jail but then help them get a shorter sentence.'

Gareth tents his fingers together and presses them against his lips, tapping them back and forth. 'There might be some elements of truth to it. If Lucas was involved in getting dangerous people sent down and word got out recently, he might well have decided to run. It's not something you want to get mixed up in.'

I don't know how to respond and he doesn't comment further. His eyes flick to the clock on the wall that doesn't work because I took the batteries out years ago because of the infernal ticking, and then to his watch instead. 'It's late. You can't stay on your own tonight; you had a lot of water in you earlier and I don't want you getting sick here on your own. If you can't call anyone, I'll stay here so I can keep an eye on you.'

I have no control over my jaw literally dropping at the thought of this. 'You can't stay here; I barely even know you!'

'Do you have someone else you can call?'

I don't. I don't have anyone. Lucas is gone, Alison is already under far too much stress and probably doesn't actually like me. Julia is dead. Who would I call? Nicky from the café? How utterly ridiculous. Gareth must see how pathetic I am, because he gets all bossy.

'Right then. It might be easier if you take the sofa in your front room, you don't want me creeping in and out of your bedroom all night, I'll just sit up in the chair. I've had worse beds in my time.'

He hasn't sat in my chair for more than ten minutes. The thought of him trying to spend the whole night in it almost makes up for my embarrassment about not having any friends. And at least he wasn't trying to get in my bed.

15

ACROSS: 16. The physical practice of ancient philosophy (4)

I'VE WOKEN UP ENOUGH TIMES on my sofa to not be too confused when I open my eyes. It is very comfortable, and I feel surprisingly rested. After all the revelations of yesterday, I thought I wouldn't sleep. I thought I wouldn't be able to sleep with a man in the house, let alone in the same room, but I went off as soon as I lay down, smothered by exhaustion. Near-death is obviously an excellent sleeping pill.

It hurts to sit up and all the muscles in my arms and legs and back scream in protest. It makes me squeak in pain and Gareth looks blearily at me from the armchair.

'I made it then?' I ask him, and he nods, wincing himself and rubbing at his neck. I hide my smirk and swing round to sit up, pushing away the covers. I stretch out each leg in turn, toes *en pointe*, turning my feet from side to side to loosen the muscle. It's not a bad hurt, and I roll my shoulders and neck too, taking stock. My arm seems okay, and there's no pain in my chest. I've been lucky.

'Thank you,' I tell him as he levers himself out of the

armchair, even stiffer looking than I feel. He edges around the coffee table and squats down in front of me, putting his fingertips to my cheeks and looking into one eye and then the other. I can feel his breath on my face and a blush roars up my neck. It's mortifying when he puts his palm on my forehead, I feel like a child trying to skive off school.

'I think you'll be okay. I'll pop the kettle on for you, then I'd best be off,' he says, standing up and stepping back into the middle of the room and swinging his arms around like a monkey to loosen up. 'I've got some things I need to follow up on, and I have a call with Sentient later. I need to check in to see if there's been any news at their end. I'm going to call a friend who can look into Sean's conviction for me too. I want to know more about what happened there, what the evidence was.'

'You don't think it's true, do you? That Lucas was involved?' My voice is an incredulous croak. I feel like my insides have dried out, my organs preserved like saltfish in a barrel. I probably swallowed enough seawater to do the job.

'I only believe things I've seen with my own eyes,' says Gareth with a funny sort of smile that makes me feel hot again. He bustles out the room leaving me sat on the sofa, and I hear him clattering about in the kitchen, collecting his things, talking to himself, but I can't make out the words.

'I'll give you a call later if I find out anything, Merry,' he calls from the doorway, popping his head round as an afterthought, giving a quick wave. 'Call me if you need anything, or if you start coughing or feeling off?' Then he's gone, banging the door and crunching away over the gravel, taking away in his van. Once he's gone, I notice how quiet my house is. It's oppressive. I feel cross about being so silly, so I tell the contraption to play Oasis, loudly, and I get up and get myself sorted out. I have things to do, and I don't need that man hanging around mithering at me all day.

I don't see why he gets to do all the investigating though. Lucas is my son, I should be the one to find him. I just need to gather the clues for myself, see how it all fits together. Heaving myself to standing is a lot more effort than it usually is. My muscles scream again in rowdy concert, and I make my way into the kitchen in a series of slow lunges and stretches. Where's a guru when you need one. Even my mug of tea is heavy as I carry it back through, my laptop equally burdensome under my other arm.

Crawling back into the cocoon of blankets I've left on the sofa makes me feel like a child. I'm feeling very foolish in general today, but the residual warmth in the soft fabric is comforting. I pull my legs into a cross and balance my laptop. I google Sean's trial. He's barely mentioned in the news reports, a minor player in a big game. They accused him of being a go-between, the man with the contacts in London and on the Isle of Wight. There's nothing about him giving up names. He did get a much, much shorter sentence though. The others all got more than fifteen years. His mugshot is in a row with the three other men's. The others look the same, dead shark eyes, smirks hovering on their lips. Sean just looks frightened, and confused, and young. I feel that tug of emotion again, a small murmur of memories of the boy I knew.

Then I stare at the screen. What is it I'm supposed to be looking for, anyway? I'm not an investigator. I make up puzzles for other people to solve. The gravel crunching, yet again, outside the window distracts me from my uselessness and I ease out of my burrow and sneak a look, wondering if Gareth has forgotten something. But it's just Gemma, Lucas's cleaner.

After a quick scuffle with my coat, sticking my feet into my slippers, I step outside the front door and walk over to where Gemma is sorting through all the various buckets of cleaning products in her car boot.

'Alright, Gem?' I ask her. 'Haven't seen you for a while.' Gemma usually comes in three times a week to clean the big house, which always makes me think that Alison must be really idle, but I suppose she could do things I'm unaware of.

'That's cos she let me go,' Gemma says, side eyeing me. Her usually cheerful round face is sullen, her mouth a thin line.

'What? When?'

'Last week. Said she doesn't need me anymore. I'm just here to do a last deep clean and then leave my keys before the photographers come in. And they sacked Jack before he even finished the grass.' She sniffs miserably and tugs on the end the plait that's always draped over her shoulder, but I am distracted.

'Photographers?'

'Yeah. Selling the place, aren't they?'

I open my mouth but no words come out. They can't sell the place and what – wait – how are they selling it if Lucas is still missing? I follow Gemma up to the big house and she lets herself in, giving me a funny look as I also barge in.

'Alison!' I shout, starting to feel a bit peculiar, stress building up inside me. 'Alison!' There's no answer, just my voice echoing off the high ceilings.

'Erm, Merry,' ventures Gemma, shuffling her feet. 'I don't think I can just let you in like this when she's not home.'

'Oh. No, of course not. I just wanted to speak to her. I'll leave you to it. Bye, Gem.'

'Bye,' she says, closing the door behind me.

I stand on the wide step for a minute, the cold wind biting at my exposed face and neck. This doesn't feel right at all. They aren't even allowed to sell the house. It was in the will. Julia told me it was in the will, the house stays in the family.

Back in my cottage I chuck my coat over the banister and go through to the kitchen, scanning for the card the selkie left for me. Her business card, where did I put it. I see Lucas's, and then glancing up, I spot the shining square of Macauley's, propped up against the books on the kitchen shelves. Finding where I left my stupid phone takes another age – it's in the shed, in my trouser pocket where I abandoned it yesterday – before I finally manage to call the woman.

I'm not sure I'm expecting an answer, but answer she does, after a few rings.

'Macauley.'

'Oh, ah, hi – this is Merry, from the er, Lucas Manning missing case?' I don't know why talking on the phone makes me splutter like an idiot.

'Hello, Merry,' she says in her smooth voice. 'What can I help you with?'

'Right. Well. I just found out that they're selling the house. The big house. Lucas and Alison. How can they sell it if Lucas is missing? It's his house.'

'Ah,' says Macauley. 'You've not heard then?'

'Heard what?'

'That Mr Manning isn't missing anymore.'

16

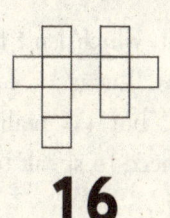

DOWN: 3. Not Father Christmas, the other type (6)

IT'S RARE THAT I'M SPEECHLESS, but I gasp like a fish out of water. Macauley takes pity on me, that or she wants rid of me.

'Lucas has been in touch with his wife and with us, Merry. You should talk to them, not me. We've closed the case. Sounds like everything got a bit much for him and he went away to let off some steam. It happens more often than you think. See you.'

She hangs up the phone before I can gather any more thoughts. I sit down heavily in the nearest chair, feeling like I'm about to have a heart attack, barely breathing with the huge sweeping relief that's rushing over me. Sobs burst out of nowhere, and I put my arms down on the table and hide my face in the crook of them and weep. He's okay. He's okay. I hadn't allowed myself to touch on my very real fear that he was dead, and that I'd never told him who I really was to him, that I'd never had the chance.

Eventually I pull myself together and find some kitchen roll to blow my nose on and scrub my puffy cheeks. Deep breaths, Merry. I pick up my phone and call Lucas, but his phone goes straight to the voicemail, which isn't full anymore – he must have deleted his messages. 'Lucas . . . hi, it's me, Merry. I don't know what's going on, but I'd really appreciate it if you could call me. Please. I need to speak to you about something. Please call me. Okay. Bye.'

The terrible message makes me blush, but I have hope now that maybe I'll see him again soon. How will I tell him though, about everything? This is a whole new terror, but I have to do it. I don't want his horrible brother getting to him before I can. They were like that when they were kids, constant one-upmanship, using what they knew as power over each other. Maybe it's a sibling thing; I wouldn't know, thankfully being an only child. My mother didn't even deserve one child let alone two. But I always thought they had a strange dynamic, loving one minute and dust-ball scrapping the next. Always grassing each other up for something, it drove Julia bonkers. She always told them they should protect each other. They did, to a point, but after the accident Sean was so angry. I could understand that, but children make mistakes. You shouldn't hold it against them.

Full of anxious energy, I fill the hours while I wait for Alison to come home pacing around the house. I put things away, find things I thought I'd lost or forgotten I'd ever bought. At three o'clock I find myself in the shed, almost about to grab my wetsuit, thinking of a swim, but something stops me. For a moment all I feel is that moment of otherness and suspension, when water closes over your head. The beat of the tide roars in my ears and I can taste brine. My arm isn't better. Maybe tomorrow.

By the time Alison pulls up in her dreadful car the house is tidier than it's been in years. I'm out and across the drive before she's had a chance to step down from the driver's seat. She doesn't realise I'm there, she's miles away, and when she sees me standing in front of her, she visibly jumps and clutches her chest.

'Fack!' she screeches. 'Merry, you scared the life out of me.'

I don't care. 'Where's Lucas?'

She stares at me for a long moment, looking fed up. 'You'd better come in,' she says in a distinctly resentful tone. I trot along behind her as she walks up to the big house. It's gleaming inside, a marked difference to the last time I saw it. Gemma is really very good at her job. There's a small bunch of keys with a yellow fob on the hallway console table next to a framed photo of a tanned and happy looking Lucas and Alison somewhere sunny, a beam of Mediterranean blue in the background. Alison picks them up and I follow her through to the kitchen. She opens the huge larder cupboard and pulls out a tin and puts the keys inside.

When she turns back to me her face is red and she has tears in her eyes and her bottom lip between her teeth. She wraps her arms around herself and makes a small, hiccupping sob, and my heart hurts for her. 'Oh, Alison. What's going on?'

'He's just left me,' she says, releasing an arm to rub at her face with her sleeve pulled over the heel of her hand. 'I feel like such an idiot. He called me yesterday, it was so weird, then sent me all these messages about how he wants a . . . a divorce. He wants to sell the house, but I don't want to move out. This is my home, Merry. I don't know what to do. I don't have anywhere else to go.'

'Where is he? Why didn't he tell you this in person? This isn't like him at all!' I feel a flush rise up on my face, angry at the thought that Lucas could behave so abhorrently to someone who loves him, someone I thought he loved.

'I don't know. I don't know what's been going on with him. He's been so quiet recently. Maybe he was just keeping secrets.' She moves to the kitchen table and sits down, and I follow suit.

As I sit down, Alison reaches into the pocket of her oversized cardigan and pulls out her mobile, tapping in the passcode and flickering her fingers over the screen. She pushes it towards me, it's open on her messages from Lucas. There are reams of them from her, *where are you, please call me, I love you, I love you*. For days. Then at the bottom, finally, a terse set of instructions.

I'm sorry, but we're done. Houghton & Co from Portsmouth will be round Tues re sale. I'll be in touch about the divorce. I'm sorry. L.

Stop calling me. I can't speak to you again, it's not good for you. You need to move on. You can stay in the house till it sells. Don't worry about money, half of everything is yours. L.

'Like I give a fuck about money! And now his phone is off again. One phone call after days of nothing, *nothing!*' Her voice rises in another screech and fury is written all over her face, the insipid blue of her eyes popping against her red cheeks. She grabs the phone back off me and looks at it for an instant and then screams in frustration and throws it across the room, where luckily it lands on the sofa and doesn't smash into a thousand shards.

As always in the face of emotions that I don't let myself feel, my skin crawls and I feel like my tongue is immobile in my mouth, a useless lump of flesh. I just look down at the table between us, and my ears burn with embarrassment. There's an agonising pause.

'Why would he do this to me, Merry? I don't understand what I've done wrong.'

I have to take a few breaths before I can answer, because I don't know what to say. This is so beyond any aspect of Lucas's character I've ever seen. But then what have I ever done except hide from my problems? Maybe it's a sour line in his genes, from me to him. Cowardice. 'I don't know. And you can't sell this place, can you?'

'Well, I don't want to, but what choice do I have? It's his house.'

'No, you can't sell it at all, either of you. It was in the will. The house can't be sold.'

Several expressions pass over her face in succession, too quickly for me to pin down.

'Sorry, what?'

It is a bit confusing, but Julia was adamant. 'Julia's will. The house passed to Lucas but on the condition it's never sold and stays in the family.'

'How can that be legal?'

'You'd have to ask the solicitors, I guess. I think they executed it. The will, I mean. You could probably contest that part of it, but it might take time.'

She pushes her chair out away from the table with a teeth-setting squeal on the tiled floor. I think for a minute rage is going to explode out from her again, but a shiver of effort keeps whatever it is she's feeling inside. 'Well, I guess he'll have to work that out, won't he. I'm sure he'll figure it out like he does everything else.' Her face is pale but set. 'Sorry, Merry, but I have stuff to organise it seems. Packing. Uprooting my whole life.' She looks ready to cry again, so I scurry away.

My legs feel distinctly Bambi-like after that assault on all my senses. People are too complicated, and they never act how I expect them to. Why would Lucas do this? What is happening in his life that would prompt his behaving like this? There must be more to it. I've seen them together; I've seen how much he adores his wife. This isn't right. I'm going to call Gareth.

Unlike Macauley, Gareth doesn't answer quickly. I have to redial several times before he picks up.

'Jones,' he says tersely. What is this thing of referring to yourself by your surname? How ridiculous. Though actually I am sort of guilty of that I suppose, so I can't really talk.

'Have you heard?' I demand.

'Merry?'

'Yes, obviously. Have you heard? About Lucas? He called Alison.'

'I did actually, I'm on my way to you now to speak to her again. I need to speak to him myself. He's still not answering my calls.'

'Me neither. Will you see me, after you speak to her? Or before. I asked her, I could just tell you everything she said, save you the bother of having her snivel over you.'

'Snivel?'

'Sorry, was that mean? It was mean. I didn't mean to say that. Sorry, I'm just – this is all a bit . . . I don't know. I'm all at two and eight.' My blathering is really getting bad; he must think salt water leaked into my brain yesterday.

'I don't know what that means either, Merry, but yes, I'll come see you. I wanted to see you anyway.'

He doesn't say goodbye or anything, which I don't mind. He's a direct sort of person, but I do feel guilty now for saying Alison was a sniveller. Of course she's upset. Lucas is behaving dreadfully. I wonder what Gareth wanted to see me about. Anticipation is only a small distraction from a new and unsettling thought that's worming around in my brain with a cold slither, evading my attempts to squash it. If Lucas could do something like this to his own wife, what else might he have done?

17

DOWN: 24. An impossible job, even for the Greeks (9)

'WHAT DO YOU MEAN, WILL I come to London with you?'

Gareth is doing his usual looming thing, so I flap at him with my hands until he sits down in the armchair, perching himself on the edge.

'We got a trace on Lucas's mobile. The one he used to call Alison is his work phone, and Sentient have a tracking system.'

'They track their employees? That's really creepy.'

'I think it's more they're techy types and they like that sort of thing. He consented to it. And it only works when the phone is switched on, and the app too. You'll have one on your phone you can let people have access to.'

'Will I?' I'm about to be affronted, but we're spinning off track. 'London though? He's there? And you want me to come?'

'Yes, and yes.'

'Why?'

'Because you know him. I don't know what sort of situation he's in, and frankly, if he's hiding or trying to disguise himself, I think you're more likely to spot him than I am.'

This seems very tenuous to me. I've never been to London. Julia told me it smells. She went once for a weekend and told me she hated it, though maybe that was just to make me feel better because she'd invited me, and I'd refused to go. I was too embarrassed to tell her that I've actually never left the Isle of Wight once in my whole life. How pathetically sad.

'Why would he use his phone if he was trying to hide?'

'Indeed. It's a real mystery, wouldn't you say?'

I don't say anything. I press my lips together instead. His face is almost smiling. He knows that I want to know all the answers. He knows I want to find my son, and I'm suspicious of why he wants me along, really. But I don't think I can resist, even if I do feel like I'm being manipulated. I guess I can leave here for once if it means finding him. I swallow my fear. It's what a real mother would do.

'Okay. Okay, fine, I'll come. When?'

Gareth glances at his watch, which is on his right wrist which is strange for a right-handed person. He was definitely right-handed when he was scribbling in his notebook, I remember. I wear mine on that wrist too; my mum, always said I was cack handed, amongst other nastier things. Maybe he is cack handed too.

'There's a boat at five-forty. Pack an overnight bag. Don't worry, I won't make you kip in the van. Sentient will spring for a room for you, I'll call them to arrange two. Can you be ready in twenty?'

I can. I throw stuff in a bag, tearing around the house plucking various things from where I left them. I'm not sure what to take, I've never even really packed to go anywhere, but I suppose all I need is my purse and my phone at the end of the day. If I need anything else I can just buy it.

'Okay, let's go.'

Gareth looks up from where he's sat waiting and smiles at me. 'Great, that was quick.' He stands up and winces with a smothered gasp.

'Are you okay?'

'Yeah,' he says, and he rubs his back ruefully. 'I've pulled something I think.' He eyes the armchair and I have to press my lips together to not laugh. Despite the dread I'm feeling at leaving the island and having the conversation I know I'll have to have with Lucas when we find him, I feel lighter than I have in years. Everything is going to be fine. He's alive.

I lock up the house and climb into the van where Gareth is fiddling with the heating. Warm air that smells like hot dust pours out of the vents and we back out of the driveway and onto the road. Fishbourne isn't far and we pull into a lane, directed by a waving high-viz-vest man. There are already cars coming off the docked ferry.

'That was good timing,' says Gareth. 'I hate waiting around.'

I feel like I've spent my whole life waiting around. It's never bothered me until now. 'I've never been on the car ferry,' I blab out without thinking.

'Oh no,' he says and laughs. 'You aren't one of those people, are you?'

'What people?'

'Natives who refuse to leave their patch.'

'No!' My face flames up with embarrassment. 'Well, maybe.'

'You aren't serious?' says Gareth raising his bushy eyebrows at me, the picture of astonishment.

'I've never had to,' I tell him. 'Everything I need is here, why should I?' How can I explain the fear I've always felt? My need to stay safe in my home, the only place I've ever been safe? I can see the world just fine from my telly. But he must think I'm a very sad case, and I don't like knowing that.

To my surprise he just smiles and doesn't tease me further as our lane begins to move and he drives us on to the boat. I find I hate the smell on the car deck, all metal and petrol, so unnatural. It spoils the smell of the sea beneath. An icy wind blows through the boat and Gareth hustles me up the stairs into the passenger lounge. We sit at the front and the huge windows show us a wide view of the sea and the lights of Portsmouth glinting beyond.

The sea is not too bumpy today, so at least hopefully I won't discover I have chronic seasickness, but the chairs are hard plastic and they hurt my bum. The ferry starts and the shaking sets all the car alarms blaring from below and the dogs on board start howling in protest. I have to focus to tune it out. Gareth buys a coffee and a sandwich for both of us. The drink is nice but the sandwich is like cardboard. I eat it anyway after picking out all the cress. Cress is a pointless embellishment.

'Where was the ping thing?' I ask him once the last stodgy cress-free bite has gone down.

He laughs. 'Near Lewisham.'

'How accurate is it? Is he in a hotel or something?'

'Mmm, it's pretty accurate.'

'What does "mmm pretty accurate" mean?'

'I'll show you.' He pulls his phone from his pocket and flicks through to his camera roll. 'This is just a screenshot, so it's a bit blurry but look, this is where the phone was switched on and used.' He spreads his fingertips over the screen to zoom into what looks like a satellite map and I lean over, my head very close to his. There's a fuzzy circle in a patch of green surrounded by a square of buildings.

'I don't understand – is the circle covering a house?'

'No. The phone was on and in use for about twenty minutes here, in this small park that sits in a square of houses.'

'You think he's in a park? Like rough sleeping or something?' The thought of Lucas, always so put together and smart, sleeping in a freezing cold park getting filthy and depressed is awful. And ridiculous, surely.

'I think he might be staying somewhere near the park, possibly in one of these houses.' Gareth traces the square. 'My plan is to start here and canvas with a photo and contact details. I've got flyers to put through all these doors and the nearest ones on the surrounding streets. It's a long shot I know, but I don't have anything else to go on currently.'

'But it could take days to knock on all the doors!' The task seems enormous. My brain is already feeling frazzled, and I think this was a mistake, why did I think I would be helpful? I can't think of anything worse than talking to a multitude of strange people, especially overners from London.

'I don't think it will take more than a day.' Gareth doesn't look at all fazed by the job at hand. 'I know it sounds like a schlep, but if even one person has seen him, and has any information at all, it's worth it.'

'How did you get into this?' I ask him, watching the shape his fingers make as they curl around his coffee cup. I'd never considered the mundane part of what he must do. Leaflets are not very glamorous.

'Investigating? I was in the military police, the RMP. I enjoyed the investigative side of it. I didn't want to join the civvie force when I came out, I wanted to work on my own and it was a good fit.'

I can understand that I wouldn't want to work with anyone else either. I want to ask him more questions but he's looking a bit morose, so I finish my coffee and watch him out the side of my eyes while he fiddles with his phone, answering emails and sending messages.

As he is being boring, my attention drifts instead to Lucas. What will I say to him when we find him? I'm not sure of the best way of approaching it. I could tell him what his brother is threatening me with, but then he'll think I'm only telling him because of that, when actually I just want to tell him. It's been long enough. Julia would want me to tell him. We spoke about it once: she wanted me to, but I wouldn't listen to her.

It was just after Lucas married Alison, just before she died. I think – I know – that she'd picked up on how sad I was feeling that I hadn't been at the wedding, even though I was trying my best to pretend I wasn't bothered, that I had no right to care. But you can't hide from someone who's known you for that long. Not from someone who already knows all your secrets.

I won't tell him, darling. But you should. I'll do it with you, if you want.

But I didn't. It never felt like the right time, and the guilt was always so heavy. Thinking of Julia makes my heart hurt afresh, it's a wound that never quite heals and cracks open whenever I think about her, about what she did at the end. How I found her there.

'Merry?' Gareth's voice is gentle, barely above a whisper. 'Are you okay?' His tone invites confidence, asks for secrets.

'I was thinking about Julia. She wanted me to tell Lucas that I was his birth mother.' A traitor tear slips over my lower eyelid and I brush it away on my shoulder crossly. He puts his arm around my back and presses me into him briefly before letting go. I remember with embarrassment belting him over the head when he tried to carry me on the beach. He's probably worried I'll do it again if he touches me.

'Alison told me what happened to Julia,' he says softly. 'It doesn't seem fair that one person should have to cope with so much trauma in their life.'

'No, it wasn't fair, she deserved so much more.'

'I was talking about you.'

I look up quickly into his face, his deep eyes, but look away just as quickly not wanting to get caught in them. My heart is fluttering like a trapped bird and I don't like it.

'My father died by suicide,' Gareth says out of the blue. 'We had no idea he was suffering. I've never forgiven myself. It was partly the reason I signed up. To run away. I think you're incredibly strong, Merry. Remarkable, really.' He's looking straight ahead now out of the window at the dark sky. This time I'm the one who leans against him, just for a moment, before pulling away.

18

ACROSS: 30. A long support (7)

THE VAN ROLLS OFF THE boat and into Portsmouth and my heart seems to pound in time with the banging of the steel gangway. Gareth's van is warm and the radio station is set at a soothing low volume which makes me feel sleepy. I don't know if it's some sort of self-preservation thing but I actually doze off and on all the way up to the outskirts of London, when we leave the motorway and the change in pace wakes me up.

'I'm glad you find me such scintillating company,' says Gareth with a glance and a smile across at me. 'At least you don't snore. Or dribble too much.'

'I don't dribble at all! I'm not a hound,' I tell him, but I don't feel offended as I'm pretty sure he's joking. I wipe my face surreptitiously all the same. The roads we're passing through now we're off the main roads have become residential, parades of scruffy-looking shops, bigger buildings sticking up like grey splinters in the distance. I mean, there are plenty of miserable places at home, but London just looks grimy and not green to me. Julia told me that when you blow your nose in London the tissue will be black. Give me sea air any day.

'How far away are we from the ping?' I ask Gareth.

'Not far. The hotel is just up this road, and we'll be able to walk in the morning. It's too late to be knocking on people's doors now. Here we are,' he says, spinning the wheel to turn into the car park of the hotel, which is low slung and not too mucky looking. I look at the floor before getting out. Fancy this being the first time my feet will have ever touched the mainland. I feel like a bit of a twerp about it now that I'm here and it's not that scary. I get out without collapse.

The receptionist looks bored when we walk in, but perks up as Gareth approaches, brushing her hair away from her face and smiling widely. He isn't that handsome. I feel my eyes wanting to roll but I control myself and hang back. They confer in low tones, and she looks confused and taps her keyboard, squinting at the screen. She must need glasses. After an interminable time, she slides over an envelope and Gareth comes back to me.

He looks very red. 'Ah, there's been a bit of an issue with the extra room,' he says looking distinctly sheepish.

'What sort of issue?'

'The "there is only one room" sort of issue. But it is a twin,' he waves the envelope at me, 'or I can sleep in the van. I think Sentient must have had a mix-up.'

I have to close my eyes briefly, breathe through my nose, and channel Julia, who was always calm and reasonable about everything. 'That's okay,' I tell him. 'Twin is fine. No funny business though.'

He looks relieved at not having to sleep in the car park. 'I wouldn't dream of it,' he says, and I feel slightly hurt, which is silly. All this is clearly playing havoc with my systems. He turns to the door at the end of the reception, and I follow him through it and down a dark corridor. Lights ping on as we pass, the fluorescent flickering making me feel slightly nauseous. I don't like long corridors; they feel like the beginning of nightmares.

'Here we are, one-zero-five,' says Gareth, fiddling with the envelope until a card slips out. He swipes it, a green light blinks and the door is pushed open. 'Oh, for fuck's sake.'

As I come through the door, I see the source of the swearing. While this is a twin room, it appears to be a conjoined one. The beds have been pushed together to form a large double with one duvet over the top. I'm starting to feel like I'm in some sort of idiotic romance film, except I'm not a twenty-something actress and I'm cross.

'Why have they done this?' I say, gritting my teeth until my jaw lumps. 'I'm not remaking them; you'll just have to go and get extra pillows.'

'What for?' he says, sounding similarly pissed off.

Would it be so awful to sleep next to me?

'To put down the middle,' I tell him. 'I won't maul you in the night, don't worry. And I can tell your back still hurts, so I'm not going to make you sleep on the floor or in your van and I'm definitely not sleeping on the floor or in your van.'

He looks slightly abashed and slings his heavy-looking bag on the bed with a thud and another 'oof', proving my point about his back.

'What the hell have you got in there, anyway? Bricks?'

'Take a look. I'm going to go find the barricade.' He leaves on a laugh, and I put my own considerably lighter bag next to his. Unable to resist being nosy, I do open the long zip. The bag is full of compartments. I love pockets. There are several phones and tablets, and little packets of things and gadgets. I have no idea what any of it is, but I am immediately entranced. I do so adore a contraption. I'm examining a little plastic disc trying to ascertain its use when Gareth returns with a bonafide bolster pillow under his arm.

'Where on earth did you find that?' I laugh. 'Is this a Victorian hotel?'

'Must be,' he says. 'Playing with the trackers then?' He nods to my hand.

'Ah, is that what it is? Do you stick it on cars?'

'Not that one,' he says as he walks over and positions the bolster down the middle of the bed, wriggling it down into the space between the twins beneath the sheets. 'That one is for slipping in pockets and handbags. I have an app that connects to each one so I can track people's movements.'

'How evil genius of you,' I tell him, turning the plastic disc in my hand, enjoying the smoothness of it. 'Perfect for stalkers.'

'Mmm, well,' he says. 'I don't really use those ones; they just came with the kit.'

He sits next to me on the other side of the bag and proceeds to tell me what all the different little things are; there are car trackers and listening devices and even some foam things you can put in your cheeks to make your face look entirely different, and a short blond wig. It's all very exciting and makes my life seem suddenly rather dull.

'It isn't as fun as all this makes it look,' says Gareth, somehow reading my mind. 'I hardly ever use any of this stuff. I got overexcited and bought it all, but most of my jobs just involve following oblivious people about to see if they're cheating on their significant others.'

I think of my cupboards, which are stuffed with projects I got overexcited about and then abandoned, and smile. 'Are they always cheating?'

'Hardly ever, actually,' he says. 'It's often extremely boring. They're usually engaging in some secret hobby. One man was sneaking off trainspotting, believe it or not.'

'No!'

'Yep. Followed him around for several weeks and all he was doing was sitting on railway bridges making notes in a little book. He was just too embarrassed to tell his wife he liked it. I think they both do it now.'

This image, spying on the unutterably boring, sets me off on a fit of giggles. I pick up my bag. 'I'm going to put my pyjamas on and brush my teeth. I'm knackered.' I potter in the bathroom for a little while but it's a bit cramped and not the easiest to manoeuvre around. I crack my elbow on the sink while trying to hop into my bottoms, which is unpleasant.

I'm halfway through brushing my teeth when my mobile starts ringing from the pocket of my trousers, which are puddled on the floor still. A glance at my wristband tells me it's a quarter to ten. Who would call so late? It better not be those accident arseholes again. Fishing it out, I can see it's a private number, which I don't usually answer but I do this time. An automated voice asks me if I'm willing to take a call from an inmate at Parkhurst and I have to lean on the sink. 'Yes,' slips out of my mouth before my brain properly engages and there's a series of beeps.

'Merry?' says that familiar whisper. 'I didn't think you'd accept my call after the other day. I wanted to apologise.'

'How did you get my number?'

He laughs. 'I asked around. Are you okay? I feel bad for throwing that at you, about Lucas. I was angry, but I felt awful after . . . It must have been a real shock.'

A shock? I nearly drowned myself after what you said is what I want to yell at him, but I don't. That wasn't his fault.

There's an intake of breath on the other end, almost a sob. 'It's just, I can't get anyone to believe me, Merry. About Lucas. It took me an age to realise that he must be behind it all, the conviction, his false evidence. We were together on the nights I said we were. We went fishing, we hadn't done it since we were kids. Mum wanted us to rebuild our relationship. She wanted me to forgive him.'

That much at least I know is true. Julia was always trying to fix them. But it makes no sense to me. 'I still don't see why he would do that to you, Sean. You must admit that it sounds far-fetched. That he would get you sent down but then give you names to get a shorter sentence. The others all got fifteen years!'

The line crackles softly for a moment before he speaks again. 'I don't know why he did it. I can only think maybe he wanted to get everything for himself. Don't you think it was strange what Mum did? What she supposedly did? He's certainly benefitted, hasn't he?'

'That's enough!' My voice is like the crack of a whip in the small room. 'Don't you dare insinuate that Lucas had something to do with that. Your mum killed herself. I know she did, I was the one who found her.'

'I'm sorry, I'm sorry – please, Merry, please will you speak to me again? I can call out between seven and ten, we have phones in our cells here and I have credit. I just want to talk to you.

I don't understand how I ended up here any more than you do. I only have a few minutes left, but can I call you tomorrow?'

The thought makes me feel faintly nauseous. 'I don't know. Maybe. Why now, though? You'll probably be out in a few days, why is it even important anymore? What's the point of any of this?'

'I've been trying to speak to you for the past two years, Merry. You never came to see me. You're important to me, you must know that. You were like another mum to me when Lucas was sick. I remember it all. I don't want you to hate me, I want you to know the truth about your son, about what he's done. He's not the person you think he is, and I wanted to warn you about him. It might be dangerous if you go looking for him, you need to be careful. He doesn't deserve your caring about him.'

I start to tell him that I'll ask Lucas myself, that I'm looking for him right now, but there's a long bleep and the call cuts out. Ten o'clock, lights out.

When I walk back into the room clutching my bag against my now unrestrained chest, suddenly wishing I'd made Gareth sleep in the van, he's cleared his stuff away and is dressed in some unthreatening nightwear.

'Everything alright?' he asks, and I nod. The bathroom door is heavy; I don't know how much of that he could hear, but he doesn't ask for any details. He disappears into the room himself, and I hear faint but vigorous teeth brushing as I chuck my bag on the floor and hurry into the bed. The covers are thick and cosy, and to my surprise I'm already half asleep – despite my swirling thoughts – when I feel him get into the other bed. He sighs softly and switches out the light.

19

DOWN: 28. A red-haired sea creature on screen (5)

I WAKE UP EARLY FROM the best sleep I've had in a long time. The room is delightfully dark, and I feel unusually relaxed and safe despite not being at home. It's been a very long time since I spent a night away from the cottage. It seems very strange to me to feel so secure, but then I realise I've been lulled by the sound of Gareth breathing next to me. It's like soft waves when the tide is on the turn, a hushing susurration very like the one that has been the soundtrack to my sanity for so many years, water slipping away over sand. I lie and listen for a long time before his alarm bleeps and he stirs into wakefulness, stretching from his arms down to his feet, and then relaxing again with a shudder.

'Sleep okay?' he murmurs, his voice drowsy and warm.

'Yes, thanks. I'm going to jump in the shower.' I find myself almost running into the bathroom and having a colder than normal shower. I'm a foolish woman and I'm much too old to be feeling silly feelings about unsuitable men. One was enough for me. The water needles my scalp and I deliberately turn my thoughts away from long limbs and brown eyes to the matter at hand. Finding Lucas, today. Finding my son.

Sean's words start playing on repeat again as I rinse out shampoo and then rub the free hotel conditioner through the ends of my hair. I don't want to believe a single word, but he sounded so desperate, and I miss who I thought he was before all that happened. A tearaway, yes, a jack the lad. But so sweet at heart. He always sent me flowers on my birthday, a card at Christmas. He would always visit me when he came home to see Julia. I cared about him, felt so betrayed when it all came out. I couldn't believe it then, so should I now? It's so easy for me to lose faith in people. I've never regained it, not once.

Brushing my worries aside I realise once I step out of the bath that I should have brought my clothes in with me. The towels provided, whilst reasonably fluffy, are not the biggest. The one I've wrapped around me barely covers my midsection. I peer around the door and Gareth is sitting up in bed, looking at a small laptop he must have produced from his bag of tricks. He's wearing clear plastic-framed glasses and seems to be intently focusing on the screen as I scurry across the room to snatch up my bag. I feel like I sense his eyes on me as I return and I look round quickly as I return to the tiny bathroom and he's not looking, but his cheeks have gone pink again. I'm not sure I've ever seen a man blush before, and it makes me want to laugh.

It's difficult to get properly dry in the steamy little room and my feet have that horrible slightly sweaty feeling in my socks when I emerge, drawing my comb through my hair. I probably shouldn't have washed it as it takes so long to dry, but I wasn't really thinking. He looks up properly this time.

'More Little Mermaid this morning,' he says with a laugh.

'What is it with you and the hair?' I grumble, admittedly feeling like I do have a very ridiculous amount of long hair.

'I like it,' he says. 'It's a lovely colour.'

'It wasn't when I was at school,' I tell him as I open the wardrobe to look for the hairdryer. 'I used to get bullied for it.'

'Kids are idiots. They'd all be jealous now of how striking you are.'

I ignore this and plug in the dryer, turning it on. It's very loud, so if he says anything else I miss it, but I do find myself watching his movements in the mirror as he takes his own clothes and washbag into the bathroom. No towel shows for me.

He doesn't take long, and I still haven't finished drying my hair by the time he comes out. It's too bloody thick. I watch again as he packs up his bags, neat economical movements, and then he strips the bed, folding the sheets and quilt with sharp corners. Army boy, I remember. And kind, to save the cleaner a job. My hair is still a little damp, so I pull it into a thick plait and band the end. I brought a hat with me at least, so hopefully I won't catch my death.

'Are you hungry?' he asks me.

'Not really.' I put the hairdryer back where I found it and quickly pace about the room putting my things back in my bag. I'm not as neat as him, favouring the stuffing it all in approach. Maybe I should get a bag with more pockets.

'How are you feeling?'

I glance over at him; he's sat in the chair at the little desk, watching me. I need a breath before I answer. When you're so used to ignoring your feelings, it takes a moment to catch one by its tail and examine it.

'I don't know. I'm nervous. I feel a bit sick.'

'That's understandable. We can just get a cup of tea first if you want. Chat it out?'

This sounds like a kind offer, but also slightly ridiculous. How can you chat out thirty-five years over a cup of tea?

'No, let's just get on with it. I don't even know if I want to tell Lucas yet. I just want to see him. This whole thing is so strange. It's not like him at all.'

'That's the impression I got from Sentient too,' says Gareth as he stands up and gets his coat from the back of the door, pushing his long arms into the sleeves, before picking mine up too. He holds it out by the collar, opening it like an embrace for me to step into, albeit backward. I don't think anyone has helped me into a coat since I was a child. He pats it down over my shoulders, and then to an almost spasm of delight, he takes my plait and tugs it from beneath the fabric to lay it down my back.

'Your hair's still wet,' he says, and I feel him run his hand down my hair. 'You're going to get cold – there's no rush, you can dry it properly?'

'I've got this: I'll be fine.' I turn around and pull my woolly bobble hat from my pocket and pull it down over my scalp and my ears. Julia knitted it for me, it's green like my scarf. To match my eyes, like that nosy selkie noticed. I bet she knows, I think suddenly, I bet she knows who I really am to Lucas. She's not silly. Green eyes.

Lost in thought I don't really notice that I'm still facing Gareth, that I'm looking up into his face and that he's looking down into mine.

'I like it,' he says, and he opens the door.

*

After we've checked out and put our bags in Gareth's van, he takes out his phone from his pocket and swipes the screen. It's a large one, almost tablet sized, but his hands are so big it doesn't seem outsized on him.

'Look,' he says, showing me the map he's pulled up. 'We're here, and the square we're looking for is just down here.'

'Has he used it again? The phone?'

'Not this one. But he likely has more than one phone he could be using for other stuff, a personal phone rather than his work one.'

'He definitely does. I've seen him with two before, when I've been round.'

'Right then, let's go.'

I follow him down the road, finding that despite his long legs and lope, I keep pace easily. I've always been a fast walker; I get lost in my thoughts and it seems to make my legs speed up. That and I'm fit from all the swimming, I guess.

'How's your arm?' he asks. 'I meant to ask if you needed me to have a look at it. I did some medical training when I was in the forces.'

'I took the bandage off, and the dressing. I don't think it really needed it to be honest, but thank you. It's healing up.' It's also really itchy underneath my long sleeves now he's mentioned it.

'Good.' We turn down a corner past the parade of shops we passed in the car last night. They look less grimy in the bright autumn sunshine, but the pavements are filthy and litterbugs have missed the bins with the wrappers from the fried chicken shop on the end. The smell of grease is pervasive, and my empty stomach twists nervously as we walk, down another short street and out onto the edge of a small park in the middle of a square. The houses that line it are large brown-bricked town houses with steps leading up to the front doors. Some are smart, with brassy knockers and shiny number plates, others are in distinct need of sanding down and repainting.

'Right, let's start here,' says Gareth, checking his phone again. He walks up the steps to the first house on our left and knocks on the door. No one answers for a minute, then I hear footsteps and I understand the expression heart in mouth. The door swings open to reveal a petite woman with a baby on her hip. She looks at us, and we look at her.

'Sorry to intrude,' says Gareth. 'But we're looking for this man, have you seen him?' He holds out a photograph: it's another one of Lucas with Alison. His arm is outstretched, he must have taken it himself. She looks at it briefly, and winces, but because the baby has entangled little fingers in her black hair and is pulling.

'No, sorry,' she says in a lightly accented voice. 'Della, stop that. I don't think I have seen him here, round the square. But I am not noticing a lot at the moment, this one keeps me busy.'

Gareth smiles, and she smiles back. 'Thank you. Could I give you my card in case you do see him?'

'Sure,' she says, and takes the proffered card with her free hand before moving back inside and closing the door.

Adrenaline I didn't really notice was surging makes itself known, and I feel sick again as we step away. 'This could take a while, couldn't it?' My voice sounds jerky.

'It isn't the most interesting bit, that's for sure.'

We make our way down the road. All the houses on this side seem smart, mainly single households.

'Is it worth looking for flats?' I ask him after the fourth door, and the third no answer. 'Is he likely to be in a proper house? They look more like flats over there, look at the strips of buzzers; flats have those.'

He looks over. 'Maybe, but it's always worth being methodical in case you miss something out.' He shuffles the leaflets he's had printed for the nobody homes – a picture of Lucas and Gareth's details – and pushes one through the letterbox with a clatter.

'What if Lucas finds one of those and runs again?'

He looks at me for a long moment, and his breath clouds in the space between us, mingling with mine. 'What do you think has happened here?' he asks. 'Truly, what do you think has made Lucas abscond like this, resign from his job, leave his wife?'

A wave of unquiet breaks over me, making me shiver. So many things. 'Sean might be getting out? Maybe he's worried about that.'

'Was that Sean on the phone last night? I could hear a few words, I wasn't eavesdropping,' he says, and tugs at his collar, lifting it up so it shields his neck from the cold breeze that's whistling around the square.

'Yes. He said he wanted to apologise for when I saw him. He's adamant he was set up, that Lucas lied in court. But I can't begin to understand why he would do that. And I definitely don't know why he would leave Alison. Maybe he was . . . maybe he was having an affair? But I don't think he's that sort of person . . .'

'People never cease to surprise me, Merry,' says Gareth and a dark look shades his features.

I remember he told me his wife found someone else because she didn't like him being away in the army. Had she cheated on him in the process? She's a fool if she did. Would Lucas cheat and lie to Alison? The thought makes me feel ill. I've done terrible things, but I'd never take someone for granted and hurt them like that. I couldn't. I have enough guilt already.

20

DOWN: 1. The lay of the upper classes, perhaps (8)

THE MIXTURE OF ANTICIPATION AND dread wanes with each door we knock on, with each person we speak to, with each leaflet we shove through a door. I am now frankly bored of it, antsy and feeling irritated that I'm having to do this, though I don't know if I should be blaming Lucas or the endlessly patient Gareth.

'Let's go and get a hot drink,' he says. 'It's brass monkeys out here.'

I agree with a shrug and wonder how I could work that expression into a clue. It's a bit rude considering the rest of the saying is about balls, but it might be quite tricksy to get it in there. Something to do with the cold, anyway, an icy jungle creature maybe. It's filed away to think about later. I could do a whole series on colloquialisms.

There's a café on the parade near the square, a real old school greasy spoon. The only customers are two older men sat separately, both with newspapers spread out in front of them and drinks at hand. A radio burbles in the back room, and it's delightfully warm.

'I've got all this on expenses, so what do you want? You should eat something; you look a bit peaky.'

I'm fairly sure peaky is my default colouring at the best of times, but I am hungry now after our morning schlepping about houses. We both order bacon sandwiches and mugs of tea and sit at a table by the window. The surface has been wiped but the plastic tablecloth still feels slightly sticky to touch. It's not long before a man in a blue-striped apron that's seen better days waltzes out and plonks what I can only describe as doorstop sandwiches in front of us. They smell delicious, and I've wolfed mine down before Gareth has eaten half of his.

'I think you needed that.' He laughs, and I have to agree. I've not been eating properly; I never do if I'm stressed. Looking after myself has never been particularly interesting to me, but I'll end up fainting if I'm not careful, and that would be embarrassing. The tea is hot and strong and almost as restorative as the bacon.

'Tell me about David Manning,' says Gareth before taking another bite of his sandwich.

'What?'

He looks at me like he's going to do his stupid don't-say-what-say-pardon spiel but must catch the expression I've made, quicker than I can get rid of it. 'Sorry, I should have eased in with that one. I'm still trying to get my head round any reason Lucas left. His adoptive father leaving like he did, it's an uncanny coincidence. Do you think there's a chance they've been in touch all this time? That he's pulling the strings?'

The pleasure of the meal disappears entirely. 'It's possible, I guess. But David was in his mid-thirties when he went. He'd be . . . seventy or so now.' The thought of an elderly David is strange, he was always so vital. Though seventies aren't necessarily doddery nowadays. He wasn't the sort to have let himself go either. Vain man.

'I was wondering, if he'd got back in touch, and he needed money, help, would that be enough to prompt this?'

'Lucas isn't a criminal. He wouldn't help a criminal.'

Gareth doesn't look convinced. 'Even his own family? And he was never actually caught or charged with anything. Legally, he's not a criminal.'

'That feels like semantics to me. Lucas told me once that he barely remembered David; he never even spoke about him much as far as I know. I think he was ashamed of him.'

'What was the dynamic like, in the family? Was David a good father?'

A small shiver runs through me before I can reply. 'I suppose, in some ways. He was away quite a lot in the years before he went missing, up to no good obviously, but when he was there he spent a lot of time with them. Things he thought were manly: camping, sailing, fishing. Lucas wasn't so keen on most of it apart from the sailing, and he wasn't sporty like Sean was. That was another thing David and Sean liked, both mad about football. He was a good player, Sean. Before at least. I know Sean really suffered after David went, he played up a lot, went off the rails I suppose you might say.'

Oh, that poor boy. He loved his dad, hero worshipped him. I should have done something; I should have supported him more. I can remember how he would come home from school all scuffed up and angry, having been fighting anyone who dared to tell him that his dad was a criminal, that he'd run away from justice. He just refused point blank to believe it could be true. It made it even more of a shock that he ended up where he is now, and his protestations of innocence niggle at me again. I have to take a sip of tea, feeling my mouth drying, not wanting to carry on down this path that leads to doubts.

Gareth opens his mouth to speak but his phone rings, making me jump as it vibrates on the table and lights up with an unknown number. He picks it up and slides his finger across the screen to answer.

'Hello, Gareth Jones speaking,' he says in a slow voice, an easy tone. 'Yes, that's right. I see. Can my colleague and I come back now? We're five minutes away. Number seventeen, right. A? Okay. Thank you very much.' He looks at me with a smile. 'Bingo.'

He deserts the rest of his sandwich, jumping to his feet and pulling his coat back on, waiting at the door for me to do the same. His eagerness is infectious, he almost quivers with it. 'Come on,' he says. 'They've seen him.'

My legs feel a bit wobbly as I walk beside him back up towards the square. I think part of me didn't think we'd find him, not really. Maybe I am just a negative sort of person, but now my heart is racing again. A clue, this person is a clue. Or Lucas could even be there! We stop to scan the numbers. Seventeen is one of the scruffier houses on the other side to where we started, the number of buzzers on the door suggesting the house has been divided into bedsits or very small apartments. Gareth raises a finger and presses the button next to the card labelled 17a.

The door opens almost immediately; the man must have been waiting for us on the other side. He's smaller than Gareth, not much taller than me, and pale. Almost like he's been through the wash a few too many times, with very light, almost white, blond hair and faintly blue eyes. Wearing a cream-coloured tracksuit has just added to his ghostly appearance.

'Y'awight,' he says. 'This yours then?' He holds up the leaflet that Gareth posted through the door half an hour ago.

'Yes,' and it's me that speaks, though I didn't mean to. 'Have you seen him? Lucas?'

'Yeah, I think I seen him,' says the man. 'I'm the landlord, Kris. Pretty sure he's been staying here.' Kris steps back and we walk into the house. The corridor is dingy, but clean enough, with piles of post on the long radiator that spans one side of it. 'Come down.'

Gareth stays behind me as we walk down the corridor into a galley kitchen. Each cupboard has a neat square of paper on it with a name or a room number. I don't see Lucas's name, but he must have a number.

'D'ya want a tea or anything?' Kris asks, with a shuffle that's telling me he's hoping we say no. The kitchen is as immaculate as the corridor, which surprises me. I always remember the bedsits me and mum lived in as being filthy and cold, but that was a long time ago in another life.

'No thanks,' says Gareth, still looming behind me. 'How long has Mr Manning been staying here? Have you seen him today?'

'Nah, not today, not the last couple of days maybe. He's been in and out. He dealt with my business partner, Michael; I haven't really met him properly. Don't say much, paid for a week up front but he owes us for two more that he booked. I'm starting to think he might've done a runner.' He laughs, but it isn't funny. 'He's not going by Manning though, your gent. He told Mick his name was David. David Stanton.'

Gareth's hand comes up and takes hold of my arm. I'm shaking without realising it. Maybe this all *has* got something to do with him, somehow. The idea sinks in slowly, that I might be wrong about everything, and then scurries under my skin, making me feel dirty. It sets off a nasty whisper in my head, *this is your fault. Everything is your fault.*

'Would it be possible to see his room?'

Kris looks discomfited by this. 'I can't really,' he says. 'I can't at all, actually. He signed a contract, even though it's short term he's got privacy guarantees and stuff. I wouldn't feel right.'

'What if we made up the missing rent? Have you seen him at all in the past week or so? He could be in trouble. It's very important we reach him,' says Gareth.

'I dunno,' says Kris, but I can see he's tempted, whether by the money or the morality I can't say. But people can surprise you.

'Look, I can open the door, and you can have a look see if he's there or whatever, or recently, but you can't go poking through his drawers or anything. Only I've not seen him for a while either, and you got me worried now. I don't want any money from you though. If he's buggered off, it's my fault for not pinning him down earlier. Come up.'

We trail back up the corridor and up two flights of stairs down to the back of the house. Kris knocks on the door, but it echoes into nothing. He takes a bunch of keys from his pocket, all colour coded, and shakes free one with a green casing. It sticks in the lock, and he has to wiggle it several times before it catches and turns and he can open the heavy door.

The room is empty.

It's small, just a basin and single bed, and a miniature wardrobe and a desk with a plastic and metal chair like you'd have at school. The wardrobe doors are open, and that's empty too. But the bed has been slept in, and the sink is marked with toothpaste. I can see all of this from the doorway, my eyes frantically scanning for any sign of life. It's the smell of the room that gives it away, that slightly damp and dusty smell that just says no one is here, no one has been here for a while.

Gareth walks into the room and over to the desk. Like the wardrobe, the drawer in the desk is open halfway and he reaches out and pulls at it.

'Er, mate,' says Kris. 'I did say no poking . . .' He trails away as he looks round too. There's clearly nothing in here, no bags, no clothes, nothing. So I'm surprised when Gareth reaches into the drawer and pulls out a slim rectangular case. He unzips the top and out slides a laptop into his other hand. He pushes it back in and goes into the drawer again, this time he pulls out a mobile phone. He looks over at me, but I can't read his expression.

Kris looks ruffled by this. 'That's not yours, is it, mate?' he says. 'If he's left stuff I'll stick it in the lockbox until I can get hold of him, if he's done one.' He holds out his hands, but Gareth shakes his head.

'This isn't Mr Manning's property,' he says, looking stern. 'His employers have hired me to track these items down. Look,' he puts the phone down on the desk and slides the laptop out of the case again. 'This is their stamp and logo. You can look them up and call them and check if you want, but I'll be taking these with me today.' His stance screams military and in charge. Kris raises his reaching hands palm up instead.

'I don't want any trouble. But I will want to speak to someone, I can't just let you waltz in and take someone's stuff. Even if they have buggered off.' He looks around the room with a frown. 'He was an odd one. Up to something if you ask me.'

I don't ask him. Lucas is not odd. I'm the odd one. I have to bite my lip to not shout it in his face. The kick of disappointment that he was here, that we missed him, is almost crippling. It's all I can do not to flump down on the bed and cry. Gareth doesn't look at me; he leaves the room following Kris to make a call to Sentient I assume. The room feels bigger without them here, but it's still tiny, smaller even than my bedroom. I stand and breathe for a while, slowly. There's no trace of him here, no familiar scent.

Seeing as Kris has gone downstairs and I have apparently been forgotten about, I decide to poke around a bit. Despite the cleanliness in the house, here there's a thin layer of dust on the windowsill and the surface of the desk. It's been clean, but it doesn't feel like anyone's been here for a while. The wardrobe is empty and there aren't any hangers. If Lucas was here, maybe he only used the bed and the desk. There's an indent on the pillow and I pick it up and hold it near my nose, but there's no trace of any scent save a faint memory of washing powder. I straighten the bed, looking down the side, but there's nothing there, not even a sock. He's gone.

21

ACROSS: 33. Who needs ethics if you can have money? (9)

KRIS SEEMS SATISFIED ENOUGH WITH his call to Sentient, who were ready with serial numbers and codes that were printed on the laptop and phone. Gareth tucks both away into his rucksack and slings it onto his back, his hands firmly on the straps.

'Thank you, Kris,' he says. 'We really appreciate your help.'

'No worries, mate,' says Kris with a grin. One of his front teeth has a small chip on the middle corner and it makes him look like a child. Gareth releases one hand to shake Kris's, a firm up-down that annoys me, but I don't know why. I just give him an awkward chin lift and half a smile before we turn away. 'I hope you find him,' he calls behind us and Gareth turns back to raise a hand.

'What happens now?' I ask him as we move away from the bedsits and circle back around the square, or square back around the square, however you do it. Clouds have rolled in while we were inside, and the colour matches my distress.

'I need to return this equipment,' says Gareth, adjusting his bag and looping the straps with his fingers again, gripping as if he's worried someone will come along and snatch it away.

'Where is their office?'

'About an hour back the way we came. Edge of south-west London.'

As he answers, I realise I know already. I spoke to Lucas once about his commute and if it was stressful. It wasn't long after Julia had gone and I'd barely seen him and didn't know how to, because without me realising, Julia had always created time and space for us to spend time together. I'd been for a swim and come past him on the bike as he was walking up the road, so I'd hopped off to push it the rest of the way. He'd looked tired.

We'd talked about his journey, how long it was. And it was long, an hour and a half each way including the boat. He was spending three or four nights a week in London then, in a cheap hotel near his office, but he didn't want to do it anymore; he didn't like leaving Alison on her own in the house. I should have offered to spend time with her, made more of an effort. Helped. I told him to ask them if he could work from home more, on Mondays and Fridays at least, if not more. They'd pushed back, but he was adamant, this or I leave. I was proud that he was someone who would stand up for himself.

How many conversations had we had like that? Just the two of us, where I'd helped him in some way. So few. Each one shines in my memory like a solitary silver fish darting in the deep, beautiful but not enough. I should have a whole shoal of them, enough light to banish the darkness entirely.

'Is that okay?' Gareth's question interrupts my reminiscing, and a pop of resentment makes my reply taste bitter.

'Is what okay?'

If he's confused by my snappish tone, he doesn't show it, just grips the straps tighter.

'Come with me to Sentient. To take this back.'

'Yes. Fine.' I assume I'll have to sit in the van while Mr Triumphant returns their precious bloody program. Then that will be it, won't it. Job done, and to hell with actually finding Lucas now they have what they want.

We're silent for the rest of the walk back to the van and though Gareth tries to make conversation as we're driving to the office, I find I can't summon the effort needed to reply. Pressing down the hurt and disappointment and anger I'm feeling is a full-time job.

I didn't know what I was expecting of the Sentient offices, but it wasn't this. It's one of those awful sixties buildings, all jutting concrete and Tory blue panels beneath the windows. How depressing.

Gareth pulls into a space and jumps out of the van, closing the door behind him. I watch as he walks towards the entrance, but then he stops and looks both ways like he's lost something before turning back to me, still sat in the van. He beckons me with his hand, and I see his lips form *come on,* so I do, reluctantly opening my door and climbing out.

'Come on,' he repeats. 'You helped me find this, you can help me bring it back. They might have something of Lucas's still in the office that you can take back for Alison.'

I didn't want to help him find the stupid laptop. I wanted to help him find my son. A slow burning fury is simmering in the pit of my stomach. Does he not care at all? I should have known that he was just using me.

The door buzzes open and the inside is much nicer than outside. It's almost like the building was in disguise. In here it's all shiny glass and steel and plants everywhere.

Gareth speaks to the smart young man on the reception, and they share a laugh. How could he laugh? How can anyone when the world is falling apart? I can't believe I thought he was attractive.

Someone comes down, another young man, this one in jeans and a scruffy t-shirt featuring a band who stopped touring at least a decade before he was even born. Idiot.

'G-man!' he crows. 'You got good news for us?'

I hate him.

'We have found the missing equipment, yes,' Gareth replies. 'This is my colleague Merry. She knows Lucas personally.'

The idiot looks at me and raises his bushy eyebrows. 'You know Luke?'

'He just said that, didn't he?' is my flat response.

If he thinks I'm rude he doesn't show it, just says, 'Come up!' and turns and leads us to the lifts.

The office is on the top floor and the windows look out towards London, but it's shrouded in clouds that are swallowing everything they touch.

We follow the idiot through to a large room where an extremely small woman is standing with her back to a wide desk with several monitors on it, speaking quietly into a mobile phone. As idiot knocks, she hangs up and turns to us. Her eyes go to Gareth, and she smiles beautifully, she's like a miniature version of an actress I like but can never remember the name of. She's very pretty, with a heart-shaped face and large hazel eyes beneath strong brows.

'Mr Jones,' she says in a voice that remembers the north. 'Thank you.' Then her gaze falls on me and her lovely eyes widen fractionally. 'Merry?' she asks, and my mouth opens wordlessly. How does she know me?

Gareth looks between us, confusion written on his face. 'How do you know Merry, Rhiannon?' He swings the bag off his shoulders and unzips it, pulling out the laptop and the phone and putting them on her desk.

Rhiannon takes no notice of the case but looks at me appraisingly with a small smile on her face, barely a curve on her generous mouth. 'I'll show you,' she says and gestures for us to follow her. Idiot is still lingering in the door, but she dismisses him with a jerk of her head, sending him scurrying the other way and into another office. We're taken to the room next door to hers. The door is locked.

'This is—was Lucas's office,' she says, taking a key out of her pocket and slipping it into the door. It opens with a muted click, and she flicks the light on because it's getting dark outside.

'Here,' she says picking something out of a cardboard box that's sitting on the desk. 'I asked him once, who you were.' She passes me a photo frame and it takes me a heartbeat before I can bring myself to look down on it. I don't remember this photo being taken; I've never seen it before. It's me and Julia, laughing. This was Lucas's thirtieth birthday party, a surprise one: Julia arranged it. We're sitting on the garden sofa, both of us creasing up about something one of us had said. What was it? I wish I could remember. Julia's head is thrown back showing her teeth in her biggest smile while I'm almost crying with laughter, leaning against her shoulder, weak with it. *When did I last laugh like that?*

I have to pinch my lips together between my teeth to stop the small sound of misery that wants to escape. I've been here with him this whole time and I never knew. Even if he didn't know the truth about me, he cared enough to have this picture here with him.

'I was so sorry about Julia,' Rhiannon says, and puts a small hand out to touch my arm. 'I don't think we met at the funeral.'

Shame barrels into me. She didn't meet me because I wasn't there. I was too much of a coward to face it. The feeling reignites the anger I'm feeling, and I thrust the frame back at her and move my arm away from her sympathy.

'Well, you've got what you want now, haven't you. I suppose we'll be off.'

I turn to look at Gareth, who is in the process of smoothing a frown off his face at my discourtesy, as if he's trying to pretend it wasn't there, but I'm not stupid. I'm even more furious – at him, at her, at Lucas. At myself.

Rhiannon is looking down at the picture. 'Do you want this?' she says. 'We weren't sure what to do with the things he left here. I hoped . . .' She trails off and swallows, rubbing her free hand over her face as if to gather herself. 'I'm hoping he'll come back. I really don't understand what's happened. This is so far removed from anything I thought he would ever do.'

It's obvious that she cares about him, probably more than she should. Is this the boss Alison described as a 'fucking prick'? She doesn't seem the sort, but appearances are always deceiving.

'What's so important about it anyway, this program he was working on, that you needed it back so desperately?' I ask her, not wanting to watch her mooning over someone else's husband.

'I'd rather have Lucas back than the program,' she parries. 'But this is a huge project for the company. If it works it could be massively beneficial for airport and security services, and it could save thousands of police man-hours.' She seems to perk up as she starts to explain, but I'm not actually interested in it. She's got what she wants.

'I'll take it,' I interject as she takes a breath. 'The box. I'll take it back to Lucas's *wife*, if it's not too much.'

I'm rewarded with a slightly pained look at the mention of Alison. I wonder if she was jealous. I knew she liked him too much. Maybe that was the stress, maybe she was harassing him, being inappropriate. She drops the frame into the box.

'No, it's not too much,' she says, running a palm over the rim as if it's a dog she's petting, before giving me a tight smile. 'I suppose that's it then. Please get him to call me when he can. Or let me know he's okay.'

I don't answer her. I just step forward and grab the box, hefting it towards me and holding it against my chest like a shield. It's not heavy but it is a bit unwieldy. We leave, and she pauses in the doorway looking back, and maybe I imagine a small sigh. She shouldn't have been so bloody hard on him, should she? This is probably all her fault, driving him to some sort of breakdown. He could be anywhere by now.

We walk back past her office, and she stops there. 'Please email me your invoice, Gareth,' she says quietly and this time it's his arm that gets her little paw on it. 'I'll get it paid as soon as I receive it. And thank you again.' She squeezes and I can see he's smiling down at her and a revolting flop of jealousy makes itself known in my guts. She's welcome to him. They're welcome to each other. I train my eyes on the lid of the box while they finish their small talk and then we're away, traipsing back down the corridor back to the lift and out.

Gareth lopes back to his van and I follow with the cumbersome box, my legs tired and heavy after a day spent on my feet. He opens the back doors and takes the box from me, sliding it in along the floor.

We climb into the front wordlessly. I'm aware of him flickering looks at me as if he's afraid to speak, and he doesn't, and our silence eats up the miles it takes to get back to Portsmouth and my boat home.

22

DOWN: 18. Is it really mutually assured? (11)

WHEN HE FINALLY OPENS HIS mouth, I'm so sunken into myself that it barely registers. It's only Lucas's name that I catch.

'What?'

'Pardon,' he says, not realising he's at risk of bodily harm at this point. 'What are the next steps with tracking down Lucas?'

I could almost laugh, but I think it would choke me. 'Why do you care?' I snipe instead. 'You've done your job, got what you wanted.'

'Merry . . .' he says, making my name into a heavy sigh that just screams every rejection I've ever felt, and it snaps something that's been winding tight inside me all day since we failed to find Lucas.

'Don't Merry me, you arsehole! You don't care about finding Lucas, you never did. You just wanted to find their bloody laptop, screw finding the actual real-life person, the one who's disappeared for no reason! You're just a bloody mercenary, aren't you.'

The high walls that ring fence the ferry terminal loom into sight as we drive around the park next to it, and they remind me of Parkhurst, of a prison. They remind me that I've made my life into a prison that I can't seem to escape from even now I want to. There won't be anyone to rescue me, and Gareth is going to leave like everyone else does.

'That's not fair,' he says. 'If you'd just let me finish, I can give you everything I have, and I thought . . .'

'Thought what? That I'd be grateful for your scraps after you've used me? You didn't have to drag me over here at all. What did you want from me? I'm just a sad little joke to you, aren't I. Arsehole. Let me out here.' I rarely lose my temper but when I do it's a flame that I can't put out. He's still driving, his own face thunderous, and not stopping until I scream at him, *'Let me out here!'*

He pulls the wheel round and screeches halfway up the pavement earning a beep from the car behind us. I can see he's about to talk but I've already got my seatbelt off and I throw open the door, almost falling out in my haste to escape him.

'Merry!' he shouts, hands scrabbling at his own belt, but I'm away to the back door, grabbing my bag and the stupid box. He's half out the door. 'Merry!'

'Just fuck off!' I yell back over my shoulder, running out and across the road without even looking. Unfortunately, there's nothing coming and I make it over without injury. I don't look back, I just keep running into the port, down past the rows of waiting cars and into the office. He doesn't follow me.

I don't have a ticket, so I have to buy myself one at the desk, still in that shaky post-anger feeling, barely able to articulate to the girl what it is I want. She slides the ticket over the desk, and I manage to grab it and stuff it into my pocket. At least the boat is here. I walk up the side of the gangway, shifting the weight of the box, trying to balance it on one hip and under my arm, but I don't have enough hip to manage it and it starts to slide and I drop it with a *thunk*, letting out a small wail of frustration. Someone helps me pick it up and I snarl at them ungratefully and feel even worse.

The boat is really busy, and I have to share a sofa with a woman and her two dark-haired sons, who are fighting in an increasingly less playful way as we wait for the cars to finish loading. Their voices are drilling right through my head. I squeeze my eyes closed and just want to be home, safe, away from everything. They remind me of Sean and Lucas and I don't want to think about that anymore, about anything at all, it's too much.

Just to add insult to injury, the sea is really lumpy on the voyage back, the ferry pitching from side to side as we leave the harbour. All the car alarms are shrieking in protest again, which in turn makes all the dogs on board howl in misery again, and this time I feel like I could join them. I am so stupid. Never get close to anyone, Merry. It's not worth it.

Rain is lashing by the time the boat pulls into Fishbourne and I have to call a taxi because I've missed the bus with the boat being slower, which annoys me further. I'd usually just walk it but I'll drown out there tonight. I should have got Gareth to give me an extra tenner on his sodding 'expenses'. The prat.

Thankfully my driver, who I vaguely recognise but don't know to talk to, is the silent type. It's only ten minutes in the car and he drops me right at my door before circling up and around the long drive and away. There's only a dim light showing at the big house, Alison must be sat in the kitchen. My heart wrenches for her again, feeling like I've failed her as well as myself and our Lucas, and I turn to my house. The door is ajar.

From wrenching to hammering in an instant, my chest feels fit to burst. I locked my door. I remember locking it. Gareth was there, watching me as I did. I jiggled the handle to check, then he smiled at me when I turned round. Someone has been in my house.

Mouth dry, I reach out and push the door open. The hallway beyond is dark and silent, all I hear is my pulse thundering in my ears.

'Hello?'

I don't know why I am saying hello to the burglar or rapist or murderer who has broken into *my house*. Fury takes over and I slam the door open, it clatters against the radiator, and I yell out, 'Who's here?' The box drops to the floor, and I kick it aside, clearing the hallway.

There's no answer except the faintest ricochet of my own voice. I flick on the light and there's no movement except my thumbs rubbing over the clenched fists of my hands. I can't sense anything untoward but as I edge along the hall, glancing up the stairs, to push the door to the lounge feeling like I could genuinely wet myself for the first time in forty-five years or so, I realise that nothing in my home is right.

In the front room all my books have been pulled off the shelf, and my armchair tipped over. All the cushions and blankets have been ripped off the sofa and scattered like fat confetti over the coffee table. All those drawers are open too and emptied.

My tide table has been torn in half. Hot tears spring to my eyes and my nose blocks, my breath huffing now. I stagger back and through into the kitchen, where the destruction continues.

Everything that can be overturned is. The tables, chairs. My cookery books are off the shelves and scattered all over the floor. They've upturned my coffee and sugar jars, pulled tins from the cupboards. My cheeks are fully wet now with useless tears. It's hard to pull myself away and upstairs, where the destruction is just as bad as downstairs, nothing where it should be, everything upside down. I need to wash my face. In the bathroom I fumble for the cord, and when I catch it and pull it the flight flickers on to reveal my white face in the mirror, fractured by red lines. They make up words, but it feels like a long time before I can process them. *Keep your big nose out.*

I don't have a big nose.

23

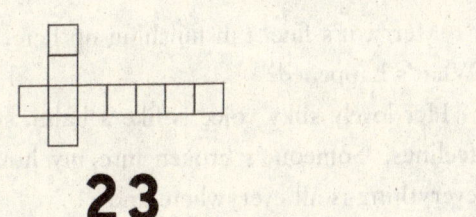

ACROSS: 29. Everything's all upside down said Tim (5,5)

KEEP MY BIG NOSE OUT. Of what? Finding Lucas? I don't understand what is happening. Did he send someone to do this? Did he do this? No. No, he would never. I turn back away from the horrible mirror and scurry down the stairs, gripping the banister to stop myself tumbling on weak legs. At the bottom I sit and reach to grab the bag that I abandoned and pull it towards me, tugging my mobile phone out.

The selkie was one of the last numbers I dialled, after Gareth's and Lucas's. I press the number and hold the phone to my ears, my eyes squeezed shut to stop any more stupid crying.

She answers after three rings: 'Macauley.'

I can't speak for an age, my throat won't work.

'Hello?'

'I'm . . . sorry . . .'

'Merry? What's wrong?'

'My house . . . I know I should have called the 111 but your number was just on my phone and if you're busy I'll call them – I'll . . .'

'Merry, it's fine. I'm finishing up here, I can come see you. What's happened?'

Her lovely silky voice is like a balm, smoothing my jagged feelings. 'Someone's broken into my house. They trashed it, everything is all everywhere and . . .'

'Okay, Merry, stop there. I'm going to see if I can get our fingerprint guy out with me. I won't be long. Don't touch anything.'

She hangs up and I sit, still in my coat on my bottom step, staring into nothing while I wait. I couldn't say how long they take, but there's a car noise, and footsteps, and then Macauley is there in her smart coat with another man who has a case in his hand. I hadn't even shut the door and the cold is blowing through the house, and the rain is coming in.

'Merry,' she says and walks to me, crouching down and putting her green gloved hand on my shoulder. 'Are you okay? Did you disturb anyone when you got home?'

I shake my head. 'No, they had already gone. I was in London, today, last night. I don't know when this happened.' Shivers start somewhere inside me, radiating out to my limbs. I feel violated. This is my home, someone has done this to my home. Macauley pats me and then moves away, whispering something to the other man, who follows her through to the kitchen. I hear him right the table and put his bag on it, the latches make snicking noises. All my senses feel heightened, it's almost painful.

Macauley walks back out to me and crouches down in front of me. 'Derek is going to try and dust for some fingerprints. Can you tell me what's missing?'

The question feels fudgy in my head. I don't have anything worth stealing, except maybe my laptop. I pull myself up on the newel post and the detective stands too. 'I'm not sure, I didn't really look it's just . . .'

'Don't worry, let's go and have a look together, okay?'

This must be so far below her paygrade, and I feel embarrassed that I'm bothering her with this, but I'm so grateful that I almost start snivelling again. We go through to the front room where I try and remember where I left my laptop. It was on the side table, I think. I put it down when I went out to speak to Gemma and I don't think I picked it up again. As I walk around the coffee table to the other side of the sofa, I can see that the table's also been pulled down. My laptop is on the floor, half under the chair. Picking it up, I open it. The screen's fine.

'Was that in plain sight?' asks Macauley and I nod. A frown flickers across her face.

'I'm not sure this was a burglary,' I tell her, and the flickering settles into a blank face.

'What do you mean?'

'I'll show you.'

I trudge out of the room and up the stairs again, feeling almost more exhausted than I did after my near drowning. I just want to sleep. 'There.'

Macauley moves into the doorway of the bathroom and looks at the mirror for a long time. When she turns back to me, any feeling I had that she might be feeling sympathetic is gone.

'What do you think this means, Merry?'

'I'm not sure. I mean, I was in London with that Gareth Jones, from Sentient Systems, the investigator. We were looking for Lucas.'

'Did you speak to his wife?'

'I did, but Alison didn't know where he was. He called her but wouldn't tell her. And his company just wanted his stupid laptop back. That's all Gareth cared about,' I say, and the last words sound bitter, and I flush.

Macauley leans her head to one side, just slightly, and narrows her eyes. 'You don't sound very happy about that.'

'I want to know where he is. I'm still worried something's going on. We didn't actually find him, just the things that Sentient needed back. Isn't that a bit odd to you? Why wouldn't he be there too?'

'Mr Manning is an adult, Merry, and it sounds like a run-of-the-mill marriage break up to me. Lots of people will run away from their problems rather than face them. I'm not sure what something like this could have to do with that.' She gestures vaguely with her hand at the writing.

I don't understand what she means.

'Why are you so keen to find your neighbour personally, Merry?'

Suddenly I don't like her accent anymore. I don't like the way she keeps saying my name. It's patronising. We stare at each other.

'Do you want to check if anything else might be missing, or are you sure there isn't?'

Gritting my teeth to keep myself together, I go into my bedroom. I don't have a jewellery box, but there were a few bits in the top drawer that Julia gave me over the years. All my clothes are scattered everywhere as if by a whirling dervish, but the little velvet pouch is still in the drawer. Everything is still there. 'It wasn't a burglary,' I tell her, easier with my back turned. 'This must be something else. There must be something else to do with Lucas going missing. Why would anyone want to warn me off finding him?'

When I turn round Macauley has her appraising look on, and it makes my armpits prickle. I don't like the way this is going.

'Mr Manning has made his wishes quite clear to his wife, Merry. Sentient Systems have their property back. Indeed, why would anyone be warning you of anything?'

She doesn't use them, but I can hear the bunny ears in her voice, putting the word warning in invisible finger quote marks. She doesn't believe this has anything to do with Lucas, but what else would it be? I literally have nothing else in my life. A burglary, sure, that can happen to anyone, but nothing's gone. The house is ransacked, defiled. It's a warning. I know it.

'I don't know. But someone did this.' I hate the pleading note in my voice.

'Let's go back down.' She turns away and I follow like a kicked puppy. She glances through the bathroom doorway again at the mirror and the lipstick smeared all over it.

'I've got loads of prints, Mac,' says Derek. 'Some palm prints, but they're all pretty small, so they're probably yours. I've found a few much bigger ones though.' He directs this at me, dark eyes sharp under beetling brows. 'Made a proper mess, din't they.'

'They did,' says Macauley. 'Are you finished?'

'I could do some more surfaces; I've not done the front door yet . . .'

'I think we probably have enough to be going on with.'

If he's confused, he hides it well and slips his little plastic squares back in his bag, picking up his brushes and powder.

It's smeared everywhere, like thick dust. He's put the chairs back up for me, the table now a little oasis of normality in all the destruction.

'Do you need mine?' I ask him, and he looks up in surprise. 'Sorry?'

'My fingerprints. So you can rule me out, see if anyone else has been here, if there are anyone else's prints?'

'We usually run them all to see if we get any hits off the database. Yours will just be the most common I've picked up. If there are any others, I'll check those.'

'Oh, okay. That makes sense. I've never had mine taken for anything; I won't be on the database.'

He makes a sort of laughing noise at this and finishes zipping everything up. His bag reminds me of Gareth's bag of tricks and I'm furious again that the only person who seems at all worried about my son is me. I wish Julia was here. This never would have happened if Julia were here, I'm sure of it.

'What will you do now? About Lucas?' I ask Macauley. 'Don't you think this is weird? That someone has ransacked my house to warn me off looking for him?'

She gives me a long look. 'There isn't precisely enough here to say that's what this is though. Is it a warning because you're looking for Lucas, or has someone taken umbrage to something else? It could even be mistaken identity. Unless I have evidence of a crime, there's nothing I can do. We're understaffed here as it is, without mysteries like this.' An eyebrow quirks dismissively, and then I know for sure. She doesn't think this is a warning, or a mistake. She thinks I've done this. She thinks I've done this to my own house to try and get attention, for Lucas, because I'm so obsessed about him, about where he is.

'You know, don't you?' Querulous, unable to stop my voice pitching. 'You know he's my son? You guessed; I know you did.'

'I did think it might be the case, yes,' says Macauley, all honeyed sympathy again. 'I realise that it must be very difficult for you, but there's nothing we can do. You'll just need to try and contact him yourself. I'm sure he's fine.'

'But what about all this? I didn't do all this! Someone has threatened me!' I'm almost shrieking now, horrified and furious in equal measure.

'Call the station if you need anything else, Merry. We'll be in touch if anything comes up with the prints.' With that, they both turn away and walk down the hall, letting themselves out. As the door opens, I can see that Alison's car is pulled up behind the police car those two useless gits arrived in. Her face is a pale blur behind the wheel, and she opens the window to speak to Macauley as they walk past. Whatever they say is brief and beyond my hearing, which is no longer sharp with adrenalin, but dull with a heavy shame, even though I've done nothing wrong. The door closes.

I'm just sitting and staring at the mucky prints all over the table when the door knocker is softly lifted and tapped, almost nervously. I don't want to answer it, but I know it must be Alison, so I force myself to stand and to go open it. I'm so tired.

'Merry, what's happened?' says Alison and she sounds so kind that I burst into tears. 'Oh, Merry!' I'm pulled into a hug and Alison rubs my back while I cry on her shoulder, just so fed up and exhausted and, frankly, frightened. Why did Macauley think I could do this to my own home?

24

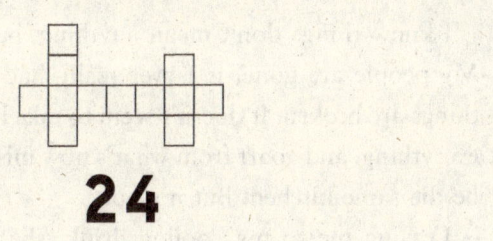

ACROSS: 22. Smaug's handiwork (10)

ALISON HOLDS ME FOR A long time in the cold hallway and when I finally pull away, I can see that she's been crying too.

'What has he landed us in?' she says. 'I don't know what's up or down anymore.' She looks down the hall through to the kitchen, and then leads me there and sits me down. 'What a mess.'

I can't even look at it anymore, I just rub at the ashy marks on the table with a fingertip, blurring the fingerprints left in them into nothing. Alison begins to move around the kitchen, rinsing the kettle out and putting it on to boil. She picks up all my cookbooks and puts them back on the shelf. They'll all be in the wrong order now. Everything will be. Tea that isn't in my favourite mug appears, and she asks me where the broom is. So many of my silly little things that don't mean anything to anyone except me are smashed on the floor. Tat from the 2p machines in Peter Pan's that Sean won for me when I was looking after him. A little glass full of coloured sand that I made on a school trip to Alum Bay, one of the only things I have from my childhood, shattered.

I know things don't mean anything, but I only had things. My people are gone, if I ever really had them, and now my things are broken. It doesn't seem to take her very long to right everything, and apart from what's now missing, it could almost be the same kitchen. But it's not.

Leaving me to my cooling drink, she goes into the living room and starts the same process. I should be helping but I feel like I'm made of stone, heavy and lifeless. If I move too much I might shatter into as many pieces as have just been swept away. I slowly put my head down on my arms instead, and somehow must fall asleep, because Alison wakes me. There's scum on the tea, and she looks exhausted. I've been remiss, she's been looking worse and worse since Lucas left, and what have I done? Nothing.

'I think I've sorted most of it out for you, lovely,' she says, before rubbing her face with her palms. 'I don't understand why anyone would do this to you. What the hell was that message on the mirror about? I got most of it off, but it's still a bit pink round the edges. Newspaper is good for cleaning mirrors, you'll probably get the rest off with that. Are you okay? Do you want to come and stay with me tonight?'

She drags the other chair around the table and sits beside me and takes my hand in both of hers. I don't deserve her compassion or her hospitality. My son has upended her life and hasn't even got the decency to tell her where he is or why he's left her. Maybe he was born that way, secretly full of cowardice, cruelty. I always thought he was more of Julia, kindness, thoughtfulness, her nurture vanquishing my nature. I should stop caring. I should stop looking. What if Sean was right? What if he wasn't lying? His parole is at the end of this week. Has Lucas run because he's afraid of what he did? Is he the criminal? I don't think I have the energy to care anymore.

'Thank you, Alison, but I want to stay here. If I leave now, I might never want to come back, but this is my home. I don't want to let anyone take it away from me.'

She squeezes my hand. 'No one can take it away from you. And I'll arrange a locksmith to come out and change the locks for you, okay? And we could probably do something about these windows, get some locks on those too. Lucas can pay!' A laugh shrills out of her from some painful place, and I make a sorry effort to join in.

'It's the least he could do,' I half-heartedly parry back, and in a moment of weakness can't help but ask her, 'Alison, what did Lucas tell you about his brother?'

She blinks slowly and then looks away through the window where the lights of the big house twinkle in the darkness beyond. 'It was a while before he ever mentioned him. It was Julia who talked about him to me when I came to meet her for the first time; I asked about the picture she had of the two of them. You know the one that used to be in the front room?'

I nod because I do know the one. I think it was one of the summers Lucas was home from uni, one of their better patches. I can't remember what the event was but they had their arms slung round each other's shoulders and looked happy in each other's company for once.

'It was a bit embarrassing asking like that and her saying it was his brother. I had no idea. We had a bit of a row after. I looked him up, read about the trial. Lucas didn't want to talk to me about it. He always seemed ashamed about it. A bit like he wouldn't talk about his dad. They're a bit of a fucked-up family when you think about it, maybe I should have expected something like this!' She makes the squeaky laugh again and I'm too exhausted to ask her anymore.

'Thank you for helping me tonight. Really. I don't know if I could have done any of this by myself. You go get yourself to bed, you look done in.'

She leans forward and hugs me again and gives me a soft kiss on the cheek. 'I'll pop in and check on you in the morning.'

I can't even muster the energy to see her to the door. She lets herself out and her car pulls away and up the drive. The house is silent, but where I usually find it calming and insulating, it feels oppressive again, and lacking. My whole life lived in silence and shame, thinking it was for the best, and where has it gotten me?

'Come on, Merry, you sadsack,' I whisper, talking to myself to break the spell. 'Let's get to bed. After all, tomorrow is another day.' Scarlett O'Hara wouldn't let herself be worn out and kicked down. I stand up with a burst of energy that makes my knees crack like pistons. I chuck the cold tea down the sink, rinse and put the mug on the drainer.

The walk to the front door seems to take longer than usual, and I take my keys out of my pocket and shakily find the double lock one, slot it and turn it, and for the first time in years I slide the bolt at the top. In the front room, which Alison has done an amazing job of tidying up. I check the window latches are tight and I straighten a couple of things. As I turn away to go, my eye is caught by the frame laid flat on the coffee table. It's the picture of me and Julia and Lucas, and the glass is smashed. Not just cracked, it looks like a heel was deliberately brought down on it.

I bring it carefully back to the kitchen and get last week's *County Press* out of the recycling, pulling out the middle few pages, then tap out the glass as carefully as I can before looking. There's a deep scratch in the corner of the photo that bleeds into the side of my face, but it's mainly unharmed, and if I had any tears left, they'd come now, but my eyes are dry, because if anything is going to come now, it's anger.

This is my *home*. This is my *life*. How dare someone come in here, and do this to me? For what? Looking for my own child? Admittedly they can't know that, but still. Fuck them. I'm not going to stop because of this. I don't care if the police now think I'm mad. I'm going to find Lucas if it's the last thing I do, with or without help.

The back door doesn't lock as securely as the front, and I end up putting a chair against it up against the handle. Does that ever actually work? How is it supposed to work? I don't know. My brain is fizzing. I'm too wired to sleep so I find my un-stolen laptop back where I originally left it, on the shelf of the sofa side table, and I plug it in. I'll write a puzzle. It will calm me down.

The software opens up and I start with *missing*. One down. For the clue: *a short girl laments for the lost*. Is lament the right word? Maybe croons. I like the word croons. It's a bit easy, but it's a start, it will do for a placeholder or an easy cryptic. A girl is a miss, a short miss is a mis, and to croon is to sing. Mis-sing. Like Lucas. Everything makes sense in this world, there are rules. It fills up quickly, missing, mystery, stupefied. Son, wife. I pour everything in my head into the first puzzle, start another and another. It makes no sense but my head feels slightly clearer.

I'm leaning my head back against the sofa and staring at a grubby mystery mark on the ceiling when my phone starts buzzing in my pocket. Feeling like it's probably Gareth, I'm already half furious by the time I've yanked it out but the number on the screen is the unknown one again. Sean.

'Yes,' I tell the automated questioner again and wait for the pips.

'Merry?' says Sean, sounding slightly breathless. 'Are you there?'

'I'm here,' I tell him, my voice still not right from all the emotion of the day and night. It's late again, not long to talk.

'What's wrong? You sound upset.'

He sounds genuinely concerned and it makes me feel all twisted up. 'Someone turned my house over. A warning I think. I've been looking for Lucas.'

There's a hissing sort of sound as he takes a sharp breath and holds it. I'm wondering if he's even there anymore, it takes him so long to respond.

'You need to be careful,' he says eventually, slowly. 'Merry, you really need to be careful. I think Lucas is mixed up with some really bad people. I've had threats even in here . . . I don't know where I'll go when I come out but I can't come back to the island. It's not safe, not for me or him.'

'Why wouldn't he warn me of any of this?' I spit, fed up. 'Why wouldn't he warn his own wife?'

'Maybe he's trying to protect you both from what he's done. Like Dad did.' There's another long pause that I don't fill before his voice comes again, stronger now.

'I've changed my mind – don't look into any of the stuff I told you, it's too dangerous. I wasn't thinking. I don't want you to get hurt, you should stop. I don't have any time left, Merry. I'm so sorry you got dragged into this. I wish—'

But I don't know what he wishes because the line bleeps and then he's gone.

Discarding my phone on the sofa, I get myself a glass of water and venture up the stairs, my skin prickling, my head swimming again. My room is mostly righted, clothes away, pillows and blankets back on the bed, and I put the drink down beside my lamp and switch it on so the soft golden glow pools over the bed. It takes me a few minutes to find my pyjamas: Alison had put them in the bottom drawer when I keep them with my underwear, and I pull out my oldest and most comfortable, quickly changing as if someone could be looking at me. In the bathroom the mirror is as warned, tinged red, with small ridges of colour pushed to the edges.

I reach out and almost touch the garish smears, but stop short, and drop my hand. My toothbrush is still downstairs in my overnight bag, but I don't have the energy to go down and get it. Mouthwash will have to suffice, decay be damned. I unplait my hair. How was it only this morning that I laced it together, that Gareth touched it? What a fool I am to even think I could trust another man, any man, when I can't tell their lies from the truth. My hair crinkles limply around my shoulders, grey and red, blood and ashes.

25

DOWN: 26. A pirate's pastime (9)

IT'S A PERFECT EARLY NOVEMBER morning, cold but still, almost bright enough to hurt my eyes. The beach is scattered with the pebbles that wash in every winter to be dredged away every spring and gnarled dried black seaweed crunches underfoot. My feet are freezing.

I left my bike up on the prom, my towel in the café, and ran down like I always do, breathing in the thick tang of the air, footing gradually getting firmer, and now I'm here, on the hard sand, the water lapping my toes, invitingly, the clarity of the sea just feet away.

But I can't go in.

I ran, I ran here to dive, to swim, to be alive, but I can't go in. I haven't been since the storm. I haven't really thought to, or had time, with everything going on, but this morning when I woke up in my not-right house, my ears still ringing with Sean's voice, it was all I could think about. I knew it would make me feel better, but now I'm here all I feel is yet more fear. The sea is calm, but waves are roaring in my head, and it's dark, thick green, and I can't breathe. My suit is too tight.

My legs fold beneath me like paper, my bottom thumping down on the ground sending a shockwave up my spine and my fingers scrabble at the back of my neck for my zip cord, pulling it down to loosen the bonds of the wetsuit that seem to be constricting my ribs. It's right there, the sea, my sanctuary for my whole adult life, the place that kept my mind quiet, where I could leave my secrets, but I can't reach it. I'm afraid.

Pulses of panic begin to ebb away as I suck in huge gasps of air, as slowly as I can. It's been so many years since I had a panic attack, but the memories are razor-sharp. Swimming was how I conquered them in the first place, will they come back if I can't do it anymore? I can't not swim. I can't swim. Forcing myself up, I stumble forward into the waves, as high as my knees, but as soon as I feel the suck of the tide my chest constricts again and ripples of terror rush through my whole body, and I have to get out and away, running up the beach again, almost blind with it, all the way to the café.

'Merry! Are you okay? Did you step on a weaver? Wait, no, not this time of year . . .' Nicky is babbling as she runs around the counter and out to me. 'Sit down!'

'Just . . . just . . . towel, home, I'm fine, I'm fine!'

'No you're not. Sit!' She manhandles me down. 'Put your head down. Slow. Down.' She starts rubbing my back, up and down in smooth motions that help me match my breathing to them. Up, breathe in, down, breathe out. When it's calmer she stands up and grabs my warm towel from the radiator, wrapping it around my shoulders.

'Not seen you in here for a while, love. Everything been okay?' I can't look at her face because I know it will match the concern in her voice and I can't cope with that right now. She doesn't push it.

'I'm going to make you your drink, okay? You just sit here.'

The familiar noises, clinking and hissing, of the glasses and the machine, help me push away the remnants of the panic attack that followed me up the beach and I sit up and look out of the window. The sea is calling to me, still, but where anticipation used to lie is an oleaginous layer of dread, like river silt, slimy and cold. I can feel the weight of all that water pressing me again into the seabed, forcing its way up my nose, into my lungs, beneath my eyelids, burning salt.

This is the last thing lost. Everything I ever loved is ruined or gone.

Nicky puts the hot chocolate down in front of me. She's put squirty cream on the top, and sprinkles. A masterpiece of confection from a kind woman.

I manage a smile. 'Thank you, Nicky. Sorry about that.' The first scorching sip is divinity and warmth, but it doesn't make me feel any better where I need to feel better. My head is still whirling. I want my life as it was, quiet and simple, knowing what was going to happen every day. I can't cope with not knowing where Lucas is or why he left. I have to find out what's happened. I *have to*.

'I realised the other day,' says Nicky, who is still hovering and looking worried, 'that my Manning was related to your neighbour. Do you remember I said?'

I nod vaguely, not really in the mood for island gossip.

'He never said to me, but Lucas is his brother. I went to look him up and I found all that stuff about him being in prison. I didn't see it at the time, in the news or anything, I'd just had

George and my head was up my arse for about six months, little sod didn't sleep for more than ten minutes at a time. I couldn't believe it.'

'When did you know him?' I should have realised they were about the same age.

'Long time ago. My family had only just moved here from the mainland, I didn't know anyone and he was sweet. I felt a bit sorry for him to tell the truth, what with the limp and everything.'

I wince at the thought of what caused that limp; it rolls over like a bloated corpse rising to the surface of my mind, sickening. 'That was a long time ago,' I whisper, lifting the drink again. It tastes cloying now, spoilt.

'Yeah we were only about fifteen. He was lovely though, I was so shocked when I saw about all the drug stuff. I would never have thought someone like him would get caught up in all that.'

'Neither did I,' I tell her. And I didn't. I never believed it. My stomach roils again so I drain my drink, thank Nicky, who is still looking worried, make my excuses and leave. All the energy I didn't burn off swimming goes into pedalling so hard the chain rattles fit to ping off and I make it home in half the time I usually would. Ripping off my wetsuit and throwing it in the shed leaves me standing on my lawn in just my costume. It's freezing, but I'm so used to the cold now, the true cold of sea water, that it barely even registers. I must look like a madwoman. I certainly feel like I could become one, with no other outlet for the maelstrom.

Back in the kitchen, I look at my phone, thinking about how Sean sounded last night. Worried about me. Warning me.

The screen shines to life and there is a missed call notification from Gareth. I don't return it; I'm still angry that he used me to find what he really wanted, that stupid laptop and not my actual son. I don't want to hear from him so I delete the notification and the accompanying voicemail. Instead, I scroll to Lucas's personal mobile number and I call it. It rings out, again and again. He must have it switched on. After a shower and an ineffectual scrub at the pink mirror, I return to the calling. Again and again, just ringing and ringing. The voicemail is full again, but I can keep calling, so I do. By lunchtime it won't ring anymore, it must have been turned off or run out of battery.

There's a pile of notebooks at the end of my cookery books in the kitchen, which I have a bad habit of buying and not using, and I grab the first one. I need to make a timeline and write everything out. Ten days. How has it only been ten days? It's the fourth of November already. The date nags, and then I remember, Sean's parole hearing is in two days. Did Lucas really set him up? If he can desert Alison, land his job in trouble, and ignore me like this when I'm so clearly worried about him then maybe I don't know him at all.

I write down the name Macauley and try and remember everything that she told me. Lucas is unaccounted for from about 4.30 a.m. on October 25th, until the ping in London two days ago. She didn't think he'd left the island, there was nothing on CCTV that day. There wouldn't be anything stopping him leaving in the following days if he was staying somewhere, there's any number of little hotels and B&Bs he could have holed up in first. And he obviously wasn't trying to sell the software or anything nefarious, because I think he left them there in London on purpose to be found. Maybe he just hadn't considered Sentient would send someone to find him, or he'd planned on sending it back at some point but then just left it there before he moved on instead. That might mean all of this was spur of the moment, unplanned, unpredicted. That there was a threat, and he just ran.

It feels impossible. He could literally be anywhere. Frustration burns me up and I rip all the pages that I've written on out of the poor notebook and screw them up, throwing them in the direction of the bin in a rage. I feel like I could trash my house all over again myself, which is laughable, considering Macauley thinks I did it in the first place for attention. There must be something else I can do, someone I can speak to. I try and remember what Gareth asked me, about friends of Lucas's. I don't recall any of the names apart from Lucy's. I wasn't precisely honest with him about that. I don't have her number but I know exactly where Lucy lives. I could talk to her. I'll need to be quick to make the bus though, the number 8 goes from outside the library at half past eleven.

I manage to rush out the door and down the road and across the town in time to make it to the bus stop, where the bus is ten minutes late anyway, so I'm sweaty for no reason. As always when it trundles up and I get on, it smells vaguely of cabbage and has gotten outrageously more expensive. The everlasting loop around Nettlestone makes me feel carsick like it does every time, but I'm happier when we come down Eddington Road and the view down over the Duver and the beach opens up past the holiday camp at Nodes Point where I used to clean chalets in the summer as a teenager. It's one of my favourite outlooks.

I get off the bus outside The Vine and walk along the green. The enormous pile of wood at the Brading end looms in my vision before I turn up round the back of the houses and it reminds me that it's nearly bonfire night. I hate fireworks, hate them. Don't think of that. Lucy's dinky house isn't far, I hope she's at home. I hope she still actually lives here. I didn't really plan this very well and I'm already berating myself as I walk up the path to rap the knocker.

I hear a dog barking and a voice shouting and I know it's Lucy and her silly little dog Smokey, who is one of the longest sausage dogs I've ever seen. He has a very particular yip-yap. The door swings in, and Lucy is there.

'Merry!' she says. 'Hello, how are you? I haven't seen you for ages. Erm, what's up?'

She looks a bit confused, pulling her cardigan around her body guardedly, and I'm not surprised: it has been a long time since she moved out of the big house to here. Julia and I had helped her move, it's how I knew the address. 'Sorry to just drop by like this,' I force out. 'I was wondering if you'd seen Lucas recently.'

Her smile drops for a moment and her forehead quirks, but then she pulls it back. 'Come in,' she says. 'Sorry about the mess.'

Unlike when I say it, her house is a bit of a mess. There is a pushchair in the hallway and in the little front room there are toys all over the floor. So she did have a baby. Julia said she thought she'd had a baby not long after she left Lucas.

Lucy sits on the sofa and, as it's the only chair, I sit at the other end and watch as she hoists Smokey, who has got rather porky in his old age and is now the fattest as well as the longest sausage dog I have ever seen, onto the cushion between us where he immediately curls up and goes to sleep.

'I did see him not long ago,' she says, pushing shiny strands of almost black hair behind her ear. 'But why are you asking? The police did want to speak to me about him going missing or something but when I called them back, they said he'd turned up again.'

I can't help but sigh before I explain what's been happening, his strange abscondment, his desertion. Lucy's eyes get wide and, as I always have, I note their unusual prettiness. They're blue, but as far from Alison's watery version as is possible to get: a limpid twilight navy.

'Oh dear,' she says uncertainly.

'Indeed,' I reply, and an errant thought passes through my mind of Sean telling me I didn't really know Lucas. But surely Lucy did. 'Did you go to Sean's trial?' I ask her.

'Um, for one day I did, when Luke was giving evidence.' She always called him Luke, so I refrain from correcting her. 'Why?'

'I went to see him. Sean, I mean. He told me that it was Lucas who tried to set up the smuggling deal. That he gave him names to tell the police after he was arrested, so he'd get a lesser sentence, even though he wasn't involved. Apparently.'

Lucy doesn't scoff like I expect her to; she looks pensive instead. She reaches out and strokes Smokey's silky ears. 'It was a weird year,' she says slowly, and I remember that they broke up not long after the trial finished.

'What happened with you two?' I blurt out, knowing that it's rude to ask but also wanting to know. I liked Lucy. I liked how their names fitted together, how they looked together and laughed so easily together.

'I'm not sure, now,' says Lucy, looking away and out of the front window. 'We were fine, really happy. Trying for a baby, even. The trial was stressful, but in hindsight even a bit before that something was up with Luke. He was distant, and secretive. We argued one night, something stupid that blew up, and I stormed out. When I came back, he was just . . . gone. I didn't see him for days; he didn't call or text or anything. I was so angry at him for doing that to me that I did something really stupid, though it worked out okay in the end.' She smiles vaguely at this, casting her gaze down over the floor and the toys.

'And by the time he showed his face again I'd had enough. I left him. Did Julia never tell you about it? She was so cross with him.'

My stomach sinks as she talks – he's disappeared like this before? I had no idea. Julia never told me. 'You don't think he could have been involved, do you? In the smuggling?'

'To be honest, I really don't know. Something was going on. He was acting weirdly. But I don't know that he would have done that to Sean, even if he was involved, it seems very out there. They were quite tight when Sean moved back, before he got in trouble. And they were close as kids, weren't they?'

'Mmm. They had their issues. But you said you saw him recently. How recently?'

Her eyes move from side to side as if she's scanning an imaginary calendar. 'Not long at all; it was completely out of the blue actually. He turned up here, like you just did. It was the end of September; I remember because it was just before term started again.'

Lucy is a tutor for the online university, but I don't need the potted history. 'What did he want?'

'To apologise,' she says. 'For how things ended with us. He said that he'd made mistakes, choices he regretted. It was odd, after so long. And he wanted to meet Ainsley. When I realised I was pregnant I hoped she might be Lucas's. I told him, and he went absolutely mad at me. Told me it was impossible and said the most awful things. He wanted to apologise for that too, because he'd never told me he thought he was infertile when we were trying. I thought maybe that was why he'd been acting so strangely at the time, because it wasn't happening for us, and he really wanted a baby.'

'Did he have tests?' I ask her, thinking of what the doctors had told Julia when he was having chemotherapy as a child.

'I don't know,' she says. 'Maybe. He didn't tell me. But it wasn't a problem on my end.'

Lucy glances at a picture on the mantlepiece with a goofy sort of look. 'She's at nursery today while I'm working.' Her little girl is gorgeous, but very clearly not Lucas's. I think Julia had harboured a small thought or hope that she might be, but she isn't.

'How did you meet her dad?' I ask, unable to not be as nosy as ever.

'He was the "something really stupid".' She laughs. 'I think I knew Lucas and I were done, especially after the disappearing act. It was a one-night thing with a colleague while he was gone. Gabriel was on secondment from a university in Brazil. He's back there now, but he visits as much as he can. I have no regrets.'

'Unlike Lucas.'

'Unlike Lucas,' she agrees. 'I'm sorry I can't help you more.' The dog grumbles and shifts. 'I need to take this one for a W-A-L-K,' she spells out. 'I can give you a lift back through to Ryde if you like. I was going to pop in and see a friend down Arthur Street and go with her to the beach and the café for lunch.'

'Oh, thank you, if you're going anyway. Yes, please. I hate that bus.'

We make small talk in the car. Lucy is interested in gossiping about Alison.

'Julia worried she might have been a bit of a rebound from you,' I tell her while trying to keep a hold of the stupid dog, whose seat I am sitting in. His fat bottom keeps sliding off my lap.

'How did he meet her?' she asks.

'They used to get the same train in London from Clapham, got chatting, kept bumping into each other near where Lucas worked, as far as I know. Lots in common, blah blah.'

'You make things sound so romantic, Merry! I always wondered about that boss of his, you know. She's very pretty.'

'Yes, I suppose. But Lucas is very professional. I'm sure he wouldn't want to mix things up like that.'

Lucy makes a noise of agreement that could be a laugh in disguise, but it's true.

'Did he say where he went? When he left, after your big row?'

She shakes her head. 'I never asked. I was furious that he could do something like that to be honest. But like I said, something was up with him that last year. He wouldn't talk to me about it, but we'd been together since school. I knew him. I knew something was wrong. Maybe it was all the stuff with Sean, maybe it was about his fertility, who knows. It's too late now.'

*

Her words about it being too late echo with me for a long time after she drops me off. I've been adamant that Lucas would never have set Sean up, and I still believe that, but could Sean genuinely think he had some involvement? They were closer as adults than they had been as children, I can't pretend that was all rosy. Not after what happened to Sean, though I always thought it was a tragic accident caused by a little boy who had no way of knowing what could happen. Maybe I was wrong about that. Maybe I'm wrong about everything.

26

DOWN: 23. The opposite of belief (5)

GARETH HAS LEFT ANOTHER MESSAGE on my phone by two o'clock, but I delete that too. I'm getting somewhere myself now, I definitely don't need or want him. At all. I have managed to make myself even more confused though. Lucas has gone missing before when things were difficult. Obviously Lucy didn't report it to the police like Alison did, but it could be the same thing. But is it the same reason? Everything always swirling back to that vile business of David's.

I'm looking at every news report I can find online about Sean's case. There was quite a bit locally, and a little bit nationally, but not enough really. I need to speak to people who were there, people who might know for sure who was involved and how. The court transcripts are available online but reading them doesn't really help because most of the witness names are redacted. It's obvious which parts are Lucas's though. His answers are terse but damning.

Were you with the defendant on the evening of March third 2013?

No.

Were you with the defendant on the afternoon of March fifth 2013?

No.

Can anyone else attest to where you were on the aforementioned dates?

I don't know. I was at home but my girlfriend was away that week. Maybe my neighbours saw me. But I wasn't with my brother.

Were you aware of the alleged activities the defendant had become involved in?

No.

It goes on in a similar vein. Most of it seems quite spurious, and, like I told Sean, I can't find anything to suggest Lucas could have been involved. It doesn't really make sense and considering how much cocaine was involved, Sean was frankly lucky to only get a few years.

Would Lucas have wanted to help him though, by supplying names of bigger fish that Sean could use as bargaining chips? It's not like they'd be hard for someone as clever as him to track down. I still can't bring myself to believe that Lucas would set him up, but I'm halfway persuaded to think there could have been some sort of other mistake, that maybe Sean wasn't involved after all. But Lucas might have felt bad because of the horrible accident he caused when they were younger, how it derailed Sean's life, and just wanted to help anyway he could. That would make sense. I'm looking at the rest of the transcripts when I spot an unredacted name that I do recognise with a small lurch of revulsion. Peter StJohn. He's the harbourmaster now, but forty years ago he was the ringleader of all the awful kids who made my life hell.

His transcript is interesting, because while it confirms suspected movements of some of the suspects, he never actually identified Sean. It's a frustratingly brief testimony. And he must have known Sean – and David, and Lucas, now I think about it – from their sailing, because he worked at the yacht club before he got the harbour job. I saw him there once when Julia had dragged me along to an awards night. He tried to talk to me, but I blanked him. I wonder what he thought about everything that happened.

I look at my wristband, and it's only half three, somehow. He could well be at the harbour. I feel completely ridiculous scurrying about all over the place like some demented ferret down a coney hole, but something is driving me. I don't like sitting in my house; the wrongness is still poking at me. My chest feels tight as I set off on my bike and my shoulder hurts for some reason, but I'm still moving. I don't know how to stop.

At the harbour the hut is empty, and frustration makes me feel a little sick and lightheaded. I need to eat. I'm contemplating going up to Tony's on my way home when I spot someone clambering off a boat down on one of the floating pontoons. It's Peter, looking ridiculous in one of those big puffy jackets. It's an effort to make my lip stop curling as he strides along and climbs the ladder up the wall. He does a stupid double take when he sees me standing in front of his office.

'Hello,' he says. 'Long time no see.'

'I wanted to ask you about something.'

'Alright,' he says with a confused frown. 'Bit chattier than last time I saw you then?'

He remembers the yacht club then. 'Yes, I suppose. Do you remember who I was there with, last time you saw me? It was a long time ago.'

'How could I forget?' He smiles, showing slightly yellow, slightly too long teeth. 'You were with David Manning's missus and their kids. You didn't look anything like you used to at school!' He laughs, and I want to push him into the harbour, but I'm still sat astride my bike and I don't think I could get enough momentum. Instead, I smile back, as if he's funny.

'It's them I wanted to ask you about. The kids. You testified at Sean's trial. It was incriminating, but you didn't identify him. But you knew him, didn't you? Why couldn't you identify him?'

An uneasy look passes over his face and he rubs his hands together briskly before taking a pair of gloves out of his pocket and pulling them on, delaying his answer. It's infuriating.

Eventually he clears his throat. 'I couldn't be certain which one it was,' he says, pulling at the fingers of the gloves, straightening the seams.

'What do you mean? The other men involved?'

'No.' He shakes his head. 'I knew who they were. It was their boat they kept here. I meant I didn't know which one it was seeing their boat off that morning. Which brother.'

The lightheadedness comes back with a vengeance. 'You mean it could have been Lucas you saw?'

The shrug is only just discernible beneath the thick shoulders of his coat. 'Maybe. Only I saw both of them quite a few times just before the bust, and they look the same from a distance. I actually spoke to Lucas the day previous. He was asking me stuff about the boats, what records we kept, said he was thinking about buying a new one. We ended up talking about his dad, other people I thought were involved with all that, who'd got away with it. Probably not something to be blabbing about but it's quite a lonely job down here. I was just gossiping really, you know what it's like. But the police were interested in Sean, not Lucas, and they had stuff on him, didn't they? But I wouldn't identify him, because I couldn't tell for sure who it was by the boat when I saw the others go out to fetch the stuff that had been tied round that buoy. And I was gone home off my shift before the police intercepted the boat on the way back in. I always miss all the fun.'

'Fun. Right. So they didn't arrest Sean on the boat with the others?'

'Nope. Whoever it was on the pontoon left when the other three went out, then I went home meself. I clocked the other buggers clear as day on their way down to their boat but I only caught a glimpse of the fourth man, could've been anyone really: it was right down the end there. Might not even have been either of them as far as I could see. The police tried to push me into saying it was Sean, but I wouldn't. I just couldn't tell from here.'

He points to the furthest pontoon, which probably is too far away to make out a face, and then turns back and smiles at me again uncertainly, like he's expecting something more from me, but I don't have anything left to give. If they were both here, who was involved in what? I would always put my house on Lucas being innocent, but Sean's words are insidious, and now this. Lucas might have known names to give Sean, was possibly snooping around the boats where the other men were planning to go pick up the drugs. I mean they both love boats, it's not strange that either of them would have been down here chatting to Peter in the general scheme of things, but it's disrupting my equilibrium, my certainty.

'I'm sorry.'

'What?'

Peter is looking at me again, and his eyes look a bit hazy. 'I'm sorry,' he says. 'For picking on you at school. I've always felt terrible about it, especially when I realised, when I was older, what it might have been like for you at home. My cousin knew your mum.'

I grit my teeth so hard they could break. I can do without this. 'Well, I'm sorry you felt terrible, Peter. I'm glad you got that off your chest.'

He flushes but doesn't say anything else as I push away on my bike. I half expect a conker to come bouncing off my head, his weapon of choice when we were ten, but of course all I feel is a cold breeze and guilt for not accepting his apology like a gracious adult would. My legs are wobbling like mad all the way back up the hill and I regret not waiting to go down there until tomorrow. I've done too much today and everything I've heard has knocked me off centre.

All the new information I've discovered is swirling like a dervish round and round and round inside my head and I can't seem to pin any of it down. I feel very strange and it's difficult to pull my thoughts straight when I'm thinking about so many things I've tried so hard to forget. It's all battling together and not making any sense.

Whatever the answer is, I feel like I've had enough. Lucas has disappeared and come back before, maybe he'll do it again. It's time to stop believing in this gilt-edged version of him I've got in my heart and accept he's flawed like everyone else. I just wish I know how flawed that might be. It's a bitter pill to swallow and I go to bed feeling more miserable and alone than ever, with an ache in my chest that won't go away.

Gareth calls again in the morning. It makes me so furious that he's still pestering me that I'm genuinely eyeing things I could throw across the room when my phone pings with a message *again*. This time when I look at it, angrily ready to swipe and delete, my heart flips. It's from Lucas. It's his name there on the screen in a little bubble. All my feelings amalgamate together into an odd kind of nausea that makes my ears ring. My hands shake almost too badly to pick up the phone and open the text, eyes barely capable of moving.

It hits me like a punch to the solar plexus, I'm winded. I can see the words, but they don't make any sense. This isn't from him. This isn't from my son. Someone else has written this, someone who doesn't know me. It begins with my name. Lucas would never, ever use my given name to address me; he knows I hate it. He's never called me anything but Merry his whole life. I scan the rest again, but it is meaningless. *I'm fine, just needed to get away, in touch soon*. It's bullshit. This isn't him.

I can't breathe. It feels like an avalanche has been set off in my brain. If it's not him using this phone, was it even him in London? Does someone have all his things so they can pretend to be him? Why is someone pretending to be him, someone who doesn't know him, or me? A stranger with Lucas's phone. He must have my first name in his contacts for some reason, he probably thought it was funny, but the person with his phone obviously wouldn't know that. They've just had about a hundred missed calls from me and want me to stop.

I don't know what to do. I have to tell Alison. Something must have happened to him. All my worst fears come flooding back as I scrabble to get my shoes on and my coat. It takes another age to unlock the door, confused as to why I can't open it, forgetting the bolt from last night, finally flinging it back on its hinges with a smack just in time to see the tail end of Alison's car run past the house and out onto the road. 'Fuck!'

My phone with the hateful lie on it is still on the table and I grab it and call her, leaving a garbled message asking her to call me immediately. I must sound like I'm raving. I am raving. It's not until I put it down that a lightning bolt ploughs through my scrambled mind, and then there's nothing else but the vicious white light of it.

Alison told the police that Lucas had called her.

She had messages from him, on her phone, she even showed them to me when we were sitting together in her kitchen. But it's *not him*. Surely she would have known it wasn't him. A wife would know her husband's voice. A deep dread sweeps through me. I open the kitchen drawers, rifle through them, pull everything out. There. Keys to the big house. My door is still open and I run out of it and up the drive, almost winding myself as fat drops of rain begin to fall from the blackening sky. Willing the keys to still work, I push the first one into the Yale lock, and it slides in and turns in one silky movement, and the door gives. It's not even double locked, and it swings open, the house yawning in front of me.

I don't even know what I'm looking for. I know it wasn't Alison who sent me that message. I don't know if she even knows I'm not called Merry. Lucas probably put my real name into his phone thinking it was funny, but he would never use it, especially not for that sort of message. The phone isn't here, it's probably with the same person who took the laptop to London, along with the work phone, to set a trap. To make me believe he left.

What if he never left?

When I helped Alison look before – was that all a lie? Was she just trying to trick me, to befriend me so I wouldn't suspect her? I obviously didn't look in their room. Would there be something there? I don't know what I'm doing now; propelled by a throbbing panic that I can't control, I pound up the stairs. They still use Lucas's old room, at the end, next to the master at the back of the house. He said it had the best view of the sea; I can almost hear his voice telling me how he loved it.

The room is a terrible mess, with clothes taken off and left on the floor, empty cups on the side, even a pizza box! It looks more like a student's hovel than anything and it makes me feel worse. Lucas is a neat person. I open the drawers, still full of Alison's clothes, all jumbled in. One after the other. Where are Lucas's things? The wardrobe is worse, a large three-door one, the first two full of women's clothes, the last is his. The smell of them assaults me, so uniquely him. Something you only notice when confronted with a garment that belongs to someone you know, a scent that you didn't realise you knew. I feel sick, I'm going to be sick. I have to run into the en suite, throwing myself onto my knees. I heave and heave but nothing comes up. I've barely eaten again. All I've had today is a bit of toast, maybe nothing at all yesterday apart from Nicky's hot chocolate.

A horrible sweaty-but-cold feeling washes over me. I must be as pale as the toilet I'm hanging over. A minute passes before I sit back against the narrow bath, splaying my legs out and hanging my head so my chin rests on my chest. When I look up for tissue, I see the box tucked down beside the loo.

The stick just slides straight out of the open end of the box when I grab it and clatters to the floor. I don't need to pick it up to see it for what it is. How did I not realise before? The greasy hair, the pale face. I thought it was grief. It wasn't grief. Alison is pregnant. And it's not Lucas's baby, because he can't have children: he told Lucy, didn't he, that he was infertile. It must have been the leukaemia treatment, the poison they had to use . . . this time I am sick, just a string of acid bile, coughing it up until I can't breathe.

I have to get away. Pushing myself to my feet, I almost tip over backwards into the bath. Back in the bedroom, I'm drawn to the window, to the view Lucas loved. *When did he last look at it properly? What's happened to him?* I lean forward again, still spinning, and rest my forehead against the cool glass, my yellow face reflecting back at me. Out past it, through the glass is the stretch of lawn and that fucking building, and that mess of turf.

I don't know if it's a flashback of another time, or if Lucas is speaking to me somehow, but I can't tear my eyes away from the grass, where those beautiful flowerbeds used to be. The new turf viewed from above clearly hasn't taken. It wasn't put down properly.

Who didn't put it down properly?

I think I hear someone screaming as I run down the stairs and into the kitchen. The back-door keys are still in the door, but I don't know who turns them, who opens the door, who runs into the garden. Is it me now, or is it me before? Two nights seem to be blended into one horror, one peak of frantic terror as my feet carry me over the grass. I still hear that faint echo of screaming as I fall again to my knees at the edge of the dying turf, and my eyes pick out a small square of plastic. It's an acrylic fingernail.

As I begin to rip and to claw, pulling up the grass strip with my own hands, with my own nails, plunging them down and down into the black earth again and again, all I can hear is a woman screaming, a man's voice shouting, until there's an enormous pulsing pain in my chest, in my arm, and then nothing.

27

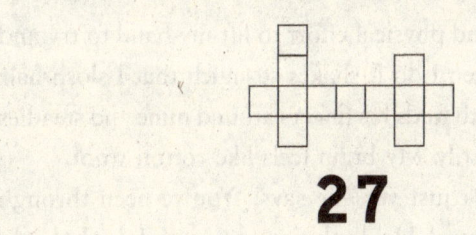

ACROSS: 19. It wasn't me (8,8)

SOMETHING ROUGH IS SCUFFING THE back of my hand. Something is holding it. It's hard to open my eyes, they hurt. I'm so tired. Then everything rushes back with a howl, and I do open them, and I gasp.

The rough feeling is Gareth, running his mouth and stubbled face back and forth over my knuckles, my hand clasped in his. He jerks away as I wake up. My mouth is so dry; I try to speak but I can't. I want to sit up; I want my hand back.

'I thought you were dead, again,' he says. 'Hold on, mind your arm.'

I look blankly at my other arm. There's a tube in it, leading to a bag, on a pole. A drip. Wires attached to a bleeping machine thread out from beneath the horrible gown I'm wearing. *What?* He's fiddling about at the side of the bed, emerging with a remote-control thing. He presses it and the back of my bed lifts me until I'm sitting, then he puts it down and pours me a glass of water from the plastic jug next to me on a little table.

It takes a mental and physical effort to lift my hand to try and take the cup, and when I do it shakes so much that I slosh half of it on the bed. Gareth folds his fingers around mine and steadies it so I can drink thirstily. My brain feels like cotton wool.

'Don't try and talk just yet,' he says. 'You've been through it these past few days.' He looks at me, and I look back. Everything I don't want to think about is trying to crowd into my head, but I don't listen. *Why am I in the hospital?* He must be psychic because he answers my thought.

'You had a false heart attack. The doctor said it was something they call a Takotsubo cardiomyopathy episode, brought on by severe stress, and your extremely low blood sugar probably didn't help. When did you last eat? I hope it wasn't that bacon sandwich.'

It was, pretty much. We went to London, to find Lucas. But he wasn't there. He was never there. My fingers hurt, and I lift my hands. Two of my nails are split. Digging. Black earth. My boy. Pain folds me up inside, but I don't even have the strength to actually curl up as I cry. Gareth tugs his chair even closer, and gently pulls me to him. I never cried before all this, never. There must have been a whole ocean of tears inside me just waiting because it feels like I've done nothing but cry since Lucas went, and that I might do nothing but cry from now on. I wish it had been a real heart attack.

'He's dead,' I croak into Gareth's shoulder. 'Alison buried him in the garden.'

He pushes me away and wipes my cheek with his thumb. He looks confused for a second. His face is very close to mine, his hand still cupping it. 'Merry,' he says, quietly but firmly. 'Lucas isn't in that garden, I promise you.'

I pull back, break the spell between us, push his hand away awkwardly. 'What? But I found one of her nails, in the dirt. She must have lost it when she was . . .' I can't get the words out.

'I don't know why that was there, but I promise you, it wasn't Lucas under there. It wasn't him. Merry, do you know?'

I can't tear my eyes away from his. It wasn't Lucas, but it was someone. I can't say. I can't. I promised. Oh, God, what have I done. My lips are pressed in a tight line, and I shake my head. I can't say.

'I came to see you because you were ignoring my calls. Some additional information came up, but I'll tell you about that later. Look, I heard you screaming, up and away behind the other house. I've never heard anything like it. I rang the police as I ran over. You were raving, screaming that he was down there, pulling up the soil with your bare hands, and then you collapsed. I thought you were having a heart attack, so I rang an ambulance as well. I told the police you were saying that there was a body, and then I came with you here, and I've been here since. You've been asleep for a long time.'

He takes my hand again. 'I tried to call the Scottish detective. She wasn't on duty at the time, but her colleague didn't like the sound of what had been happening. They brought a dog in, a cadaver dog, and it signalled not far from where you'd been digging. They have found a body, Merry, but it wasn't Lucas. You know who it is, don't you?'

Of course I know who it is. I buried him there. It's David.

I can't hear Gareth anymore, if he's still talking. I just lie back and close my eyes. All the things I kept in that little box, that I don't think about, that I spent every day since trying to forget, crawl out gleefully.

It was all the blood, there was so much blood. Julia moaning that it was her fault, but how could it have been her fault? He'd been attacking her. It was self-defence. There was so much blood. I had to help her. We dragged him out into the garden and we planted him under the flowerbed and we left him there to rot. The whole night is a broken series of moments of horror, punctuated by blanks. Washing my hands again and again. Scrubbing at the floor, again and again. The smell and the taste in the air. Julia crying. David's dead eyes, staring.

He was a terrible man; he deserved a terrible death. I just wish Julia could have believed that too. I'm sure that's why she killed herself. She couldn't cope with the guilt anymore, the secret. It was supposed to stay secret. The house doesn't sell, the garden is untouched. It's why I was so furious when they were digging about and building. They could have found him, but they didn't. It's me that's done that.

'The police are going to want to talk to you, Merry, as soon as you're well enough.'

'I am well. I want to go home – I . . .' My voice disappears as the door to the room I'm in opens.

'You're awake! Oh, thank God, I've been so worried.'

It's Alison. I'm so shocked I just stare at her blankly.

'Is she okay? Did she just wake up?' she says to Gareth, who must nod because he doesn't say anything. She puts down a little pile of magazines and a crossword book on the other table behind my IV, and then perches herself on the edge of my bed.

'What did you do to Lucas?' I hiss at her. 'Where is he? Where did you put him?'

Her face creases with confusion and she slides her eyes to Gareth again. 'What? I don't understand. I didn't do anything with him . . . he left me, Merry. I told you. I showed you.' One hand reaches up and pulls at her collar. 'Should I get the doctor?'

'No. Those messages weren't from Lucas, were they? Only I got one too. It was from his phone, but it wasn't from him. I could tell. You said he called you; you said you spoke to him.'

'I did speak to him . . . I . . . I think it was him?' She still looks confused, and hurt too, colour is rising in her face. 'It was a bad line, I could only just hear him, it was only a minute . . .' She bursts into tears, making me jump. 'Oh God! If it wasn't him then who was it? Where is he? What's happening?'

My head hurts and my eyes are stinging. 'But you're pregnant! Lucas can't have kids, so you must have been cheating on him! Did he find out? Did you hurt him?'

Her hands fly to her stomach. 'How? Yes, I am. But the baby *is* Lucas's. We had tests. He wasn't completely infertile, Merry, but it was badly reduced from the chemo. We were looking into getting IVF, but then a miracle happened.' Even though she's still crying, her face lights up. 'He doesn't know yet; I've been calling and calling . . .' She dims again. 'I only just found out. How did you know?'

Shame sweeps over me. All those clues I thought I'd put together and I blamed her. 'I'm so sorry. I went in your house. I saw the test. The garden, the lawn . . . your nail, your false nail was in the grass. I thought . . .'

Alison looks at her nails, which are fixed again. 'I broke them. I was pissed off at the rolls of grass. Lucas told me he was going to sort them out, and then he disappeared. I just rolled them out myself. I was angry, pulling it. My nails were too long and two snapped off.' Her pale blue eyes pin me in place. 'I can't believe you thought I was a murderer.' An angry bloom of colour suffuses her cheeks as her breathing quickens and whistles through her nose and she shakes her head. 'I don't know what's happened to my husband, Merry, but I love him. I'd never hurt him, ever.' She puts a hand over her mouth and a small whimper escapes through her fingers.

'I want to go home,' I whisper. 'I'm so sorry, Alison, I just want to go home.'

'I'll go and get the doctor,' says Gareth. I'd almost forgotten he was there, but he's been holding my other hand this entire time, it's the only part of my body that feels warm.

Alison watches him until the door closes behind him, and then she leans forward and says in an urgent voice, 'Merry, it's okay, I understand everything now. I know about you. When I was looking through the house after you were rabbiting on about clues I found some of Julia's old things and there was, this, well, a letter for Lucas. I don't know if she ever wanted to give it to him, really, or if she just wanted to get it out, but it explained everything. I know you're Lucas's birth mum.' She takes my hand, and she presses it against her stomach. 'And that means you're this baby's grandma, or nana, or whatever you want her or him to call you. Okay? And we'll find Lucas. We have to.'

28

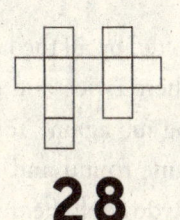

ACROSS: 11. Tentative approach (8)

IT TAKES FOREVER FOR ME to persuade the doctor to let me leave. In the end I insist on checking myself out; there's nothing wrong with me, it wasn't even a real heart attack. I made Gareth google it for me: they call it broken heart syndrome too, because it can happen because of stress and grief. But my several ECGs with their nasty sticky tabs were all clear, and actually very healthy. I have the cardiovascular system of a thirty-year-old apparently.

'It was still basically a heart attack, just without any of the blockages or damage.' Gareth's lecturing me in the van on the way home from St Mary's. I ignore him, looking out instead at the dirty lights of the prison as we pass. The parole hearing is tomorrow, but Sean might not even be there. It was a big case, so they've probably taken him to London, though I don't really know how it all works. The words he spoke to me in there still linger in my head, that Lucas ran because he was the guilty one. What if he really was telling the truth?

'Why were you calling me?'

'Sorry?' he says, distracted by all the lanes at Coppins Bridge. I failed my driving test here twice and gave up.

'When you were saving me again. You were calling me, and I ignored you, so you came round and heard me.'

'I think the whole of Ryde could hear you, Merry. I still think you should be in hospital. You weren't right at all.'

'Gareth! I'm fine. Why were you calling me?'

'Sentient had a look at the laptop. I don't think I told you when that email from Lucas arrived resigning—'

'That email supposedly from Lucas,' I interrupt.

'Yes, that one, when that came through, they immediately disabled his access to the systems and shut down the laptop remotely.'

'Why did you call me about that?'

'If you let me finish, I'll tell you.'

'Sorry,'

'Right, anyway, they looked at the laptop, and don't ask me how they know, but there's evidence of hacking attempts.'

'Hacking? Someone was trying to get into it? For the program?'

'Potentially, yes.'

'So it can't have been Lucas then! Someone must have taken it, or him, or both. I knew he wouldn't steal it.'

'Well, not necessarily. Lucas could have been the one trying to hack in after it was shut down. He had the skills.'

'But you don't think so, do you?'

Gareth keeps his eyes on the road, but his face is solemn, and he sighs. 'No, I don't think so. I don't like any of this.'

'But why did you come back? Why are you on the island again? You could have told me that on the phone or not told me at all. It makes no difference to me. Lucas is still gone. He's probably dead.'

There have been many words in my life that I wish I could take back, to suck back into my stupid mouth and swallow down to burn away, but none more so than those last three. They just came out from the pit of despair that's inside me. But saying it out loud, it scars.

Gareth takes one hand off the wheel and reaches out, taking my own that's made into a fist on my knee, covering it, squeezing until I release it and then he doesn't let go. He threads his long fingers through mine. He doesn't let go until the next traffic lights when he has to change gear. Why doesn't he drive an automatic? My skin tingles and it helps me not think about what I just said.

'I was going to come back anyway. I wanted to help you find him. I'm not actually a mercenary.'

My cheeks blush as I remember shouting at him in this same space on the way back from London. 'I can't afford you,' I tell him, and he huffs.

'I don't want your money, Merry. I want to help you. I . . . well, I want to help, okay?'

'Okay,' I whisper. 'I'm sorry I called you a mercenary.'

'Amongst other things.'

'Amongst other things.'

A quick smile cracks over his face and I feel even more embarrassed. 'And, actually, Sentient have offered to cover my expenses while I help. Lucas is extremely well regarded, you know, Merry. They're all really worried about him.'

'Now they have their stupid Terminator software back.'

'I'm not even going to ask what that means. I'm going to stop up here at the shop and get us some food. You have to eat before we do anything else, okay? Are you allergic to anything?' We pull into the little car park, and he unclips his belt and cracks the door, one foot already swinging out before I can answer.

'No. But I don't like fish.'

'You don't eat your brethren then?' He laughs and shuts the door before I can answer. He really is the most infuriating person I've ever met. I find myself running the fingers of my other hand over the one that he held.

I still feel so tired, and I have started nodding by the time he comes out, carrying far more bags than he needs for one dinner. He slings them in the back of the van and comes back round.

'You okay in there?'

'Mmm. I'm tired. I feel bad. I don't know. I'm just so confused about everything.'

'You need some food, and more sleep.'

I nod and close my eyes until the sound of the gravel on the drive alerts me again. Gareth gets the bags out of the back and puts them down by the door, fishing in his pocket and producing my keys.

'How did you get those?' I ask him as I get out, slowly. I feel beaten up.

'The door was open, before. When I called round. They were in the back of the door, so I grabbed them to close it, and then I heard you screaming. Still in my pocket.'

We go in straight down to the kitchen, where he stops in the doorway, and I almost walk into his back.

'What happened in here?' he asks. 'Where are all your little bits? It looks different.'

He's so observant it's uncanny. And I'd forgotten, I didn't tell him. 'Someone broke in. While we were in London. They smashed everything up, pulled it all down. Alison tidied up, so everything is in the wrong place.'

He looks at me aghast. 'What? You got burgled? Oh Merry, I'm so sorry.' He drops the bags and pulls me into a brief hug. 'Did they take anything important?'

'They didn't take anything at all. I called Macauley in a panic and she came round but I think she thought I did it.'

'What?'

'There was nothing missing, valuables still here. Just messed up. And a message on the mirror in lipstick. "Keep your big nose out."'

'You haven't got a big nose,' he says. 'So she didn't do anything?' He looks really cross.

'They took prints. She still thinks Lucas just left. I think she thought I was a mad old woman trying to get attention. She guessed too, about Lucas being mine. And Alison knows.'

'You aren't old either. But I can see her thinking that, wrongly. But this means someone here is warning you off. I feel like the laptop and phone turning up in London is a red herring. The answers are here, I'm sure of it. Go and shut your eyes, I'll shout when this is done.' He gestures vaguely at the bags, and I obey. I sink onto the sofa and close my eyes for what seems like a second before he's there again, his hand on my shoulder.

In the kitchen he's laid out plates and glasses and my mismatched cutlery. There's a pan in the middle and he takes the lid off and my stomach growls loudly. He's made some sort of mustardy, creamy chicken with vegetables and there's a stick of bread warmed in the oven to mop the sauce up with. It's delicious and comforting at the same time, and I have two helpings.

'Thank you for this,' I tell him. 'I can't remember the last time someone else cooked.'

He smiles and raises his arms in a stretch before standing and gathering the pots to put in the sink.

'Leave those, I'll do them in the morning. The chef doesn't wash up.'

'If you insist.' He fills up the pan to soak regardless and sets it aside, and wipes over the sides, which he's actually already tidied. The meal has reignited something for me: the kitchen feels safe again. A new memory made to lay over the recent bad one, a good one.

'I'll sleep in the van tonight,' he says. 'I've not booked anywhere yet and I don't like to go too far after what you told me earlier.'

'It's November! You'll freeze.'

'I won't, it's insulated, and I have thermal everything, don't you worry. And it's been very mild for this time of year.' He laughs in his easy way.

'I'm not worried,' I tell him, swimming with exhaustion again, with emotion, and it loosens something in me. 'I just don't want you to go. I want you to stay here. With me.'

He looks at me for a long moment. 'Okay,' he says, and he holds out his hand for mine.

29

ACROSS: 9. Solving step by step (12)

THERE'S A CUP OF COFFEE that I didn't make on my bedside table gently steaming. I can hear Gareth moving around downstairs, he's doing that bloody washing up. Sitting up is a small issue because everything aches. My fingers will hardly flex enough to pick up the handle of the cup. I can only curl them round the whole to take a sip of the rich sweet liquid that seems to seep straight into me. There's a dent in the other pillow of my bed where Gareth slept after helping me get changed and into bed. I hope I didn't snore.

It's an easy distraction from thinking about Lucas, about what's happened to him. I know he must be dead, that he got caught up in something awful somehow, but until I know for sure, how can I ever accept it? How can you grieve for someone who was never yours? He was born right here, in this room, but I didn't even hold him. I never even told him I loved him. It's so hard to filter through everything that I'm feeling before putting it aside. I try putting it in the place where I don't think about it, but it's not working. I created my very own Pandora's box full of bad things and now it's open I can't get anything back in and not even hope is left.

After the coffee, a shower. I wash and dry my hair properly, try and find a nice top to put on. Nothing romantic happened last night, just being held until I fell asleep, which is sort of romantic, maybe, I don't know, but I feel nervous. I could do without it, to be honest. This is all getting too much, and when it's all over, when we find out and he leaves, what will happen to me then?

'Sort it out, you silly bint,' I hiss at myself in the mirror. 'He's just being nice to you because he feels sorry for you.'

Recriminations done, I creep down the stairs. Gareth is doing a crossword at the kitchen table, and there's something in the oven. When he looks up at me and smiles, my heart cracks. I don't know how I'm going to cope when he goes.

'Morning. Fancy a sausage sandwich? Kettle's just gone.'

'Please,' I say, not looking at him, but going to make tea. 'Do you want a drink?'

'I've just had one. I don't know how you do these, I really don't.' He's back at the puzzle. Glancing over his shoulder, I see it is one of mine, and it's in my favourite newspaper to work for. He hasn't got very far and one of his guesses is wrong, which makes me laugh.

'Nearly, there.' I tap on the word.

'I didn't think that one was right. Mmm.'

I sit down and watch him as he scratches his head. He pencils in a few more, then gives up and moves across to the everyman puzzle instead, which he rips through in a matter of minutes.

'I know there are rules to the cryptic ones,' he says as he stands up and goes to open the oven, the smell of sausages increasing exponentially in the room and makng my mouth water. 'But I can never get all of them aside from the obvious anagram ones. You'll have to teach me.'

I don't offer to; he might not be here long enough for that. I could get painfully used to the food though, even the simple sandwich I'm presented with tastes like a gourmet meal to me. I've starved myself of everything my whole life, because of what? One person hurt me, once? Could I have had this with someone, this domesticity? It feels so easy.

When we're done, he tidies up again, and I still feel too beaten up to even protest, just gratefully accepting another tea and watching the way he moves and fills up all that space I never knew was there. Afterwards, he brings through his laptop and bag, and takes mine down from the shelf, before sitting next to me, his arm pressed against mine.

'What do we know about what exactly was happening with Lucas in the months before he went missing? None of this feels random. This had to be planned.'

'Do you think it was about his work?'

'It could be, but I still think that was a red herring to make us think he was there when he wasn't. And the program wasn't affected, and couldn't be copied from where it was stored, from what they can tell. There were security layers that hadn't been accessed for a few days – the weekend likely – before Lucas went. The hacking attempts were later in the week when he was already missing.'

'So the person who took Lucas didn't know what it was worth and tried to get it afterwards?'

'Yes. Like a bonus, maybe, as well as to mislead.'

'But what other reason could they have to take him? Lucas

was just a normal person, if they didn't know what he had was worth millions, why would they take him?'

'I think we need to look closer to home.'

'If Lucas did find names for Sean to do a plea deal with, they could have found out and this is revenge.'

He huffs and frowns. 'Or Alison could be involved. You always need to consider the spouse.'

I shake my head. 'I've seen how upset she's been. I don't think she could fake that.' And the baby, I think. She's having Lucas's baby, and she wants me to be part of its life. I'm going to be a grandma. The warmth of the thought is a golden speck in the rest of this awfulness.

He agrees. 'You're right, I'm not sure it could be Alison. I know Lucas is a big man, she's tiny – I don't think she could physically do anything to him and cover it up, not on her own and leaving no trace.'

He's still talking but I can't hear him, because suddenly I'm back in the kitchen of the big house again, blood everywhere, on the floor, on my hands, my knees, Julia there white-faced and staring. She couldn't have done it on her own either, but *I helped*. Maybe this is my punishment for what we did, losing Lucas like this.

'Merry?'

His fingertips turn my face away from my blank screen to look at him, but I can't. I close my eyes instead, feeling my breathing coming too quickly. His hands smooth back my hair away from my face and he makes small hushing noises like I'm a child, but I can't even feel cross because everything is red. I'm rubbing at my wrists again but I can't get it all off, it's everywhere, how will it ever come off?

Faintly, somewhere a chair grinds on a floor, and I'm leaned forward, my head against something, warmth around me, but my chest hurts and my eyes hurt, and an iron band is squeezing and crushing me and I can't breathe, I can't see, it's all red and pain and loss and the box won't shut.

When I open my eyes again, it's to the cotton of Gareth's t-shirt and his arms are wrapped around me, and mine around him, and he's kneeling on the floor and still making that shushing sound, rocking me gently. I can breathe again, but I'm shivering fit to fall off the chair.

I whisper into the soft material in front of me. 'I helped her bury him in the garden.'

He pushes me gently upright again but stays where he is. There's no judgement on his face, but he thinks for what feels like forever before speaking.

'What happened?'

I shake my head, trying to release the memory, but I've never been able to remember, not properly.

'I don't know. I can't remember the whole night, not really. It's like looking in a broken mirror, it's all fractured, in pieces. I've been trying to forget about it for so long, and then it's me that ended up messing it all up. Everyone will know now that she did it. I don't want her memory to be that. She was such a good person. He was attacking her, he'd broken her arm before, her ribs. She was terrified. There was so much blood . . . that's the only thing I can truly remember, all the blood on the floor . . . we buried him in a flowerbed, and then I cleaned all the blood up. The boys were out at a friend's house for the night, thank goodness, so they never came in or saw anything. It took me hours.' My hands squirm against each other again, always trying to get the blood off.

Gareth runs his fingers over his hair, scruffing it back and forth. 'He was a bad man, and Julia is dead now. It happened a very long time ago and I don't think there's any point in you disclosing your part in it to the police. They are going to want to speak to you at some point though. I told Macauley you weren't well enough yet. What will you tell her?'

'What do you mean?'

'You'll have to talk to Macauley. What will you say?'

'I don't know. Julia gave me a letter in case this happened, but I don't know. Maybe I should just confess to what I did. Maybe all this with Lucas is a punishment for what happened.'

'That's not how life works, Merry. And what do you mean, a letter?'

'I didn't want it, but I've got a letter. In case the garden ever got dug up, or he was found somehow. She gave it to me, as an in the event of my death thing. She didn't want anything to happen to me. It's still sealed, but I don't want to give it to the police if I don't have to. I don't want that to be her legacy.'

'Where is it?' he says.

'There's a shoebox on top of my wardrobe, it's in there.'

As the thumps of his footsteps recede up the stairs I remember when Julia gave me the letter. We hadn't spoken about it for so long, it was almost an unsaid pact between us that bonded us almost as much as Lucas. But she'd come round with it, made me sit down right here. Told me that if he was ever found, I was to be safe. That I had helped save her life that night. I just put it away where I couldn't see it. Just another thing to not exist if I didn't think about it. All my secrets are being unburied, and I'm not sure I can cope with it.

Gareth comes back with the letter. The envelope feels old now and crinkly. Julia's elegant handwriting looks up at me; *to be opened only in the event of David's return* it says. I thought that was a strange way of putting it at the time, but I didn't want to talk about it anymore, I'd stuck it in the box, and we went back to pretending he had just left. Gareth is smiling.

'Clever,' he says, but I don't understand. He reaches out and touches the writing. 'If she'd written anything else, like discovery, it would look like you knew what had happened, or could have guessed at least from what was written. She wanted you to be in the clear.'

'But I don't deserve to be in the clear,' I tell him, feeling that wave of panic building again and hearing it in my voice. He kneels next to me again and pulls me against him and I rest my head on his shoulder while he strokes my hair and my back.

'Look, don't think about it for now. I'm going to put this up on the shelf and I can get to this research by myself if it's too much. It's too traumatic, I wasn't thinking.'

I push away again, pull at him so he gets off the floor. 'No, I want to help. I need to. I have to know. I can't spend the rest of my life not knowing, I'll go insane. I might as well go to prison.'

'You aren't going anywhere,' he says, and he puts the letter up on the shelf above the cookbooks out of the way before sitting down again and picking up his pen. 'Remind me what Sean told you when you went to see him.'

I tell him what I can remember. That he blamed Lucas for his sentence, much beyond the refusal to corroborate his alibis.

That it was Lucas who set the whole thing up with Sean as his patsy, so he would go to prison and Julia would disown him, that he'd lose everything. That he believed Lucas had run either because he was getting out, or because he was mixed up with dangerous people.

'That doesn't make a lot of sense, but there is a motive in there, from his point of view,' says Gareth, making notes. 'Do you think there's any truth in it?'

'Well, Julia did leave the house entirely to Lucas, but I don't know if there was additional provision made for Sean. I never saw the will. And Alison told me that the person she thought was Lucas on the phone told her he wanted her to sell the house.'

'So that's the money angle. It wouldn't be easy to do without Lucas in person, though there are ways if someone looks enough like him to sign documents and whatnot. Identity documents can be forged easy enough.'

'And someone has his phone, and they definitely aren't Alison or Sean.'

'How do you know?'

'It's what . . . set me off. I had a message from Lucas's number, I just kept ringing and ringing and then it came through, but I knew it couldn't be him. It used my first name, and I never use it. No one calls me anything but Merry. Lucas would never address me by anything else. I just knew. And if he doesn't have his phone anymore, who does?'

His eyebrows seem to knit together as he thinks. 'It's hard to piece together a proper timeline, of when he was operating and when these unknowns come into the picture. We know he was in London last week, the landlord saw enough of him to identify him from my flyer. When did Alison get that call? Do you think there was a chance that call was actually real, and that someone took his phone and the laptop afterwards and then left them there to be found? Or that he left them and was taken after?'

All I can do is shrug and watch in fascination as his brain starts ticking.

'I did think it was strange she wouldn't realise it wasn't him, so maybe it actually was. Maybe he's in trouble and needs the money from the house sale. I've seen their accounts – they're well off, but none of it is easily accessible ready money, most of it is tied up in long-term investments. He could have turned to trying to sell the house quickly when he realised he wasn't going to be able to sell the software, or thought better of it. It sounds like he needs a lot more money than he has readily available, anyway. There could be more people involved in this than we know. They could be holding his phone and just sent you that message to get you to stop ringing. He could even have been allowed to message you and used your first name so you'd realise something was wrong.'

I never thought about that. 'Like a coded message?' I put my elbow on the table and rest my forehead against the heel of my hand. 'But none of this makes sense, Gareth. Why does he need so much money? What has he done? I don't know how we're ever going to find out what's happened or who he's gotten involved with, or why. How do we even start?'

'Methodically,' he says, squeezing my shoulder. 'Like your crosswords. Let's start with what Sean said.'

My head is pounding as Gareth pulls together pages of notes he's already got and starts on more. I wish now that I had gone to the trial. Sean had begged me to be a character witness, but I was so angry at him for getting mixed up in all that. Julia was there. She was there every day. Reading the transcripts didn't help me at all, but Gareth is now reading them anyway, jotting things down.

'I already spoke to someone from those,' I tell him, and he jerks his face back towards me.

'Really? Who?' He looks impressed and I feel a small glow of pride.

'The harbourmaster. He saw the boat go out. The other three men were in the boat and it went out to pick up the drugs, but Sean wasn't on it. And Peter – that's the harbourmaster – said he was too far away to identify, though it could have been him. But he also said . . .'

Gareth puts his hand over mine again and squeezes it, helping me find my voice again. 'He said that it could have been Sean or Lucas, that he'd seen both of them down there quite a bit. He said that he and Lucas had been talking about David's circle, about who was still operating. It might mean there's something in what Sean said, about him finding out the names of bigger fish. He might not be lying.'

'Or not entirely,' says Gareth. 'Sometimes it's a mix, isn't it, of the truth and untruths. And what Sean believes is the truth isn't necessarily what happened. But there could well be unknown people at work here.' He looks back to his notebook and begins tapping again at his keyboard, so I look at my own screen.

Though I haven't in a long time, I click onto Facebook. Lucas made me set up an account even though I don't have any friends and he isn't on it anymore. He made both of us make one, said there were groups and forums we would like. I only have one friend on my account, Julia. Her page is still there. She loved it, reconnected with old friends from school, joined Isle of Wight heritage chats and lots of crafty pages. The profile picture is from a few months before she died. How did I not realise how much she had been suffering? Why didn't she just tell me? I had to find her, instead.

I scroll idly down the page at the various posts and witterings she used to put up. I'm tagged in lots of them, and there's a picture of us swimming. I think Lucas must have taken that one. It's not as painful as I thought it would be, looking at this. Julia managed to have a lovely, full life, even after what happened. It just makes it so much harder to comprehend what she did.

'Does Sean have a profile?'

Gareth's voice makes me jump. I hadn't noticed him transferring his attention to what I was doing. 'I don't know, maybe. I don't think it would have been his bag really.'

'Ugh, you'd be surprised. Let's have a look.' He angles my laptop towards him and puts his name in the search bar. Several Sean Mannings pop up, and halfway down there's one with no profile picture, just a motorbike.

'That one,' I tell him, pointing. 'That's his bike, I'm sure of it. He got in trouble about how he borrowed the money to buy it off someone and never paid them back. I think Julia did in the end.'

He clicks on the name, but it's private. 'That's annoying.' He clicks back through to Julia's page and looks at the list of her friends. There are hundreds, and there in the middle is his. He clicks again, but it's still closed entirely apart from some random music albums and film likes.

'Can you remember Julia's email address?' he says.

'What? Why?'

'This page isn't a memorial one, it's still open. We could log in if we know the email and can guess the password, and we could look at Sean's page. If we can access his friends list, it might be something. This could have been done by someone he knows.'

'I know Julia's password,' I tell him, as it dawns on me that she always used the same one for everything. 'She told me: we were talking about her memory getting a bit hazy because of, er, her age.' I'm too embarrassed to say the word menopause, which is ridiculous, and I resolve to put it in my next puzzle to make up for it. 'She said she just used the same thing for everything. It's SeanLucas48.'

'And her email?'

'I don't know, we didn't really need to email much . . . I can't remember!'

'Don't worry, let's look.'

The email isn't listed on Julia's page, but Gareth switches away and opens my email account instead. He clicks 'sort' and scrolls past 'J' and through to 'M' but there's nothing there.

'I clear them, I'm so sorry . . .'

'No worries.' He dives into the sent folders and the deleted ones but there's nothing again, and my heart sinks. Why can't I remember? She definitely emailed me the odd thing or forwarded stupid poems which I hated but didn't have the heart to tell her. I always just deleted everything. I'm on the verge of tears again when he clicks on the compose button and types a J in the address bar and there it is, still in the memory, in the autofill.

'Bingo.'

He switches back across to Facebook and logs me out and types in the details, and Julia's page opens. There are hundreds of notifications and messages, but Gareth ignores them and goes straight to Sean's page. There's nothing since he's been inside, obviously, but there are various posts and the odd picture he's tagged in. Gareth starts by scanning his friends list – there aren't very many, less than fifty – and he writes down each one on his notepad. Having had my laptop hijacked, I go to make another cup of tea.

A flash of movement catches my eye through the window about the sink up at the big house. It's Alison on her mobile, walking back and forth. I hope she's not letting herself get cold. She stops and puts her phone in her pocket, then puts her face in her hands. I feel a swoop of concern and I'm wondering if I should get my shoes and run up there, but then the door of the house opens and it's that poxy detective. She must be grilling her about the garden, I dread to think what sort of a mess they've made dredging up the past. They talk a moment then Alison goes in and Macauley runs down the steps and strides around the house to the back, flicking a glance my way as she does.

'Merry,' says Gareth and the low urgency in his tone has me spinning back to him. 'Do you recognise this person?' He turns the screen towards me.

It's Sean, with a girl in a pub by the looks of it. His arm is around her and her face is buried in his chest; she looks like she's laughing, but her long pale hair is obscuring anything recognisable. 'I don't think so, but I can't see much of her,' I say.

'Not the girl, the man in the background.'

There is someone there in the shadows, also laughing, and in profile. He also has pale hair, most of it in a long fringe swept over his forehead. I do recognise him, even from the side. I do. 'It's the landlord. From London. It's that Kris!' I look up and Gareth nods.

'I'm such an idiot!' I cry, smacking my hand down on the table. 'Why did we believe him when he told us he saw Lucas? He might not even have ever been there! He must be involved somehow, doing Sean a favour or something worse. Has this been Sean all along? How?'

Gareth puts his hand over mine again. 'I was thinking about him after what you told me about the message. That someone could have been pretending to be Lucas to mislead you and Alison. This man is a likely suspect for that. He's not tagged in the photo, and none of the profile pictures of the people Sean is friends with look like him; his hair is very distinctive, and I'm pretty sure it's him.' He tugs his own phone out of his pocket and taps a few times before putting it to his ear. Nothing happens. 'Huh. The number he gave us is switched off. No voicemail.'

'Where is this picture? I don't recognise the pub. Is it on the island? Can we find out?'

'There's another picture in the album, here, look: they aren't in it but there's a window and there's a bus stop outside, a London one. Did Sean spend a lot of time in London?'

'Yes, he lived there for most of his twenties. He'd only been back six months when he got arrested. The police thought he'd been trying to revive David's old network. That's why he tried to use Lucas as an alibi, because they'd been spending time together, getting along better.'

I remember when he was back, how well they'd all been getting on. Julia had been delighted. She took me out for dinner with them both one night, Lucas and Sean, at the Buddle Inn. We'd laughed the whole night, she'd had a wonderful time. It made it so much worse, after, that it was all a betrayal.

'So it was this guy? He did something to Lucas and stole his laptop, and is pretending to be him? Is he doing it on Sean's orders? *How?* How is he getting anything like that out of prison without it being monitored? We should tell the police; that Macauley is over in the garden of the big house now, she needs to know.' I flick my eyes again to the window, to the big house.

'I spoke to her this morning while you were asleep. She knows we found the laptop. I gave her a piece of my mind about not believing you that someone had broken in here to warn you off. We can speak to her later, I want to find out more first.'

'Was that him too? Kris? Is he here somewhere now, do you think?' I stand up and go to the window, looking out and scanning the grounds of the big house, as if Kris is going to be creeping out of the woods at any minute. I have to wrench my eyes away, feeling like this is a spiral into a paranoid place I don't want to be in.

Gareth looks perturbed. 'I don't know. We drove straight back after Sentient and we weren't there very long. I don't think he could have beaten you here and done that before you got home. It would have been extremely tight and risky timing. There might be someone else involved, or he paid someone, has connections here.'

'What about Alison?' Anxiety starts to rear its ugly head again. 'If Sean is behind this and he wants the house, the money, she's in the way. If he's done something, or organised it, he can't get anything because Alison is Lucas's wife. It would all be hers. And she's pregnant! She's in danger.'

'Do you want me to go and warn her?'

'I don't want to stress her out even more, it's not good for her. And we don't know anything for sure, do we? There are still police swarming all over her garden, so I think she'll be safe as long as she's at home.'

He beckons me to sit back down beside him and I comply, feeling the warmth emanating from his body as I do.

His voice is equally as warm and reassuring as his presence. 'There's no way her being harmed will help Sean get anything, so for now I don't think that's a worry, but if you are concerned about her if she's away from the house, we could slip one of these in her coat pocket.' He reaches down and unzips his bag of tricks, pulling out one of the slim plastic discs. 'I can set it up on your phone so you can keep an eye on her.'

The disc seems to glow at me from his palm. I'm torn between grossly invading her privacy while keeping her safe at the same time. It wouldn't hurt, just to be on the safe side. I expect people have these things all the time now, don't they, to keep their loved ones safe. Somehow it ends up in my hand, and Gareth is running a program on his screen again, tapping in numbers from the disc, taking my phone and fiddling about with that too.

'Here we go.' There's a new icon now on my phone, a little radar symbol. He taps on it and it opens and there's another little icon with a capital A. When he presses that a map pops up, which I recognise immediately as here: there's the road and the path down through the woods, there's a block where the big house is and a little flashing light where my cottage is. I close my fingers around the disc and squeeze tightly.

'Will you be okay to put it in her pocket, or would you like me to come with you and I'll do it while you distract her?'

'I'll do it. Her coat is always on the end of the banister. I'll walk right past it if we go through to the kitchen, it should be easy enough. I'll go now.'

'I'll keep looking for this Kris guy, see if I can track him through any of these other friends.' He turns his face back to the screen, fully focused, and I watch him for a minute before pulling myself away and getting my own coat. My hand, clenched around the disc, feels like a hole is being burnt through it. I can't balance feeling guilty and wanting to keep Alison safe.

30

DOWN: 15. Working undercover (9)

THE WALK UP THE DRIVE seems twice as long as it's ever been before and my arm aches as I raise it to rap the knocker. It takes her a while to come to the door and when she opens it, she looks sick and exhausted, but still lights up with a smile for me, and gives me a hug. 'I was hoping you'd come round.'

As I thought, she turns around and goes through to the kitchen, and I slip off my coat and before hanging it over hers I reach my hand into her pocket and I drop the token, pushing it right down with my fingers, before yanking my hand back and flicking my coat so it layers over hers.

I'm not really thinking as I walk through after her, but of course I can see the whole garden from the huge windows and glass doors. There's a white tent where the flowerbed used to be, and two people are lurking by it talking. I can't see Macauley, which is a relief. I don't want to speak to her. Not yet; I need to pull myself together first. With a shiver of horror, I realise I'm standing right where he was lying, that night, and I shift away, sitting at the table before I fall. The room has been renovated twice since then: the first time Julia and I did the floor ourselves, pulling up the tiles and chipping away at some residual rusty stains beneath, erasing every trace of David.

I've ignored it for so long, but all I can see again now are those smears and puddles and gouts that came out of him. I close my eyes, only opening them when Alison clunks a mug in front me. I've already had far too much caffeine today, but I take it anyway.

'How are you feeling?' she says, pushing her hair away from her face and putting her chin on her hand, elbow on the table.

'Fine, a bit tired. This is all . . .' I gesture at the window, and she frowns.

'I know, it's awful. All this time there's been a body in the garden.'

'Have they identified it yet?'

She looks at me quizzically for a minute but then replies. 'Not officially, but they're pretty sure it's David. I had the third degree all morning from that Scottish woman, but I don't know anything. And Lucas certainly didn't. We wouldn't have dug up half the garden if we knew, would we?'

Her eyes pin mine with this last statement and I feel a hot blush start to rise up from my chest, but she doesn't say anything else. She clearly knows that I knew something – why else would I have been so over the top about their renovation?

'I know this might be difficult for you,' she ventures softly, and I brace myself to lie about what Julia and I did, but she blindsides me. 'Who was Lucas's birth father? I found his birth certificate and it has Julia and David's name on it. How did they manage that?'

'David's parents did it. I don't know how. Lucas's dad was . . . a silly fling. I was young, I thought I was in love.'

She looks relieved. 'I'm glad he didn't hurt you, well, physically,' she gabbles. 'I always thought you were a bit prickly, and I wondered when I found out about Lucas if there might have been a lot of, well, trauma, that had affected you.'

'Prickly is just me,' I tell her, but she's probably right. I don't know who I would have been if it weren't for all this, every road that led me here. But Lucas's conception, that hadn't been traumatic, at the time it had felt like every dream I ever had finally coming true. But it wasn't. It was just a break in the nightmare.

'Tell me about it,' she says. 'Please. I want this baby to know their history.' She puts her hand against her flat stomach and manages a wobbly smile. 'If it isn't upsetting for you. I need a distraction.' Her hand moves back to her face to heel away a threatening tear.

I don't know where to start. If Pandora's box is open in my head then I may as well open my mouth, but some secrets are deeply rooted, too deep to pull out in one sitting. But I can try, I can give her this if she needs it. 'I met him on the beach, the summer I was sixteen. You must remember how you were at that age. I was a late developer, and just starting to get interest from the boys at school who used to bully me. It was weird.'

Alison reaches out and touches my arm. 'I bet you were beautiful. You are beautiful, Merry. I hope the baby looks like you.'

I feel a flush at the compliment. I hate them, but I'm deeply pleased too that she would want the baby to look like me.

'Was it someone from school then?' She lifts her mug and blows on the surface of her tea, her eyes still trained on mine.

'No, he was older than me. Older than I realised I think, you can't really tell at that age, can you, and I was so naïve. He told me his name was Frank, that he was a lifeguard at Appley. I never really went down there because that's where all the popular kids went and I hated them. He was surprised he'd never noticed me. Especially with all this: I suppose it stood out then.' I tug on my hair and she ghosts me a smile. 'He taught me to swim, actually. He said I couldn't be an island girl and not know how to swim. We spent a few weeks together, swimming every day. One night he challenged me to swim out to the little spit, and he'd already been there to set up a picnic and a bonfire, and one thing led to another I suppose.'

'That actually sounds so romantic,' says Alison, hugging herself.

'I never saw Frank again, after that.' Her face falls and I feel bad. 'He just disappeared, and I realised I was pregnant a few months later. Textbook idiot. But I was happy, for those few weeks. And I thought I loved him, so there's that at least.'

'Oh,' she says, looking embarrassed now. 'Maybe not so romantic then. I'm sorry.'

'Alison, what do you think has happened to Lucas?' Thinking about how he came to be just reminds me that he's gone and the words come out of nowhere, and I wish they hadn't because she immediately tears up, biting at her bottom lip.

'I don't know, I don't want to think about it. When I thought he'd just left me, I was angry. So angry. But now I don't know what to feel. He must be gone!' She puts her head down onto the backs of her arms and sobs loudly.

I reach out and grip her elbow, rubbing with my thumb. I feel empty now, there's nothing left in me, no hope, no curiosity, nothing. He is gone. We might never know the whole story; and what evidence do we really have? A ten-year-old picture and our word that the person in it was the landlord of the house where we found Lucas's laptop. It could even be a coincidence, everything could be.

Eventually she pulls herself together again, scrubbing at her eyes with her hands. 'Sorry,' she says. 'I can't seem to hold it in at the moment. Must be the hormones.'

'When are they going to be finished out there?'

'She said tonight. They've had the dogs out again all over and in the woods, but nothing else is out there. I can't even think about it. It's so horrible, a body there all that time, and no one knew.' Her eyes are swollen and sore looking now, but she has that same appraising look again. I look at the drink she made me, still full, but I can't make myself swallow any of it.

'What do you think has happened to Lucas, Merry? Is it something to do with David? Do you think he got mixed up in it too?' Her pale wide eyes are beseeching. But what can I tell her?

'I really don't know. I went to see his brother last week. Sean said it was Lucas who was involved in it, that he set him up.' A bitter laugh squirms out of me. 'I don't know what to believe anymore.'

'He would never tell me about Sean. Why do they hate each other so much? What happened?'

I feel tears burning my own eyes now, but they don't spill. I think I've cried myself out today. 'There was an accident, when they were younger. Lucas was about eight, or nine. Sean was twelve. They were chasing each other through the woods and

Sean put his foot down a hole and snapped his ankle clean through and ripped all the ligaments. He'd been selected for football trials at Portsmouth, but he never regained enough mobility in his foot to ever make it again. He was so angry.'

'That doesn't sound like it was Lucas's fault though?' She's staring into her own drink and slowly rotating the mug between her hands. 'If they were playing?'

'Lucas had made the hole. He deliberately ran Sean near it. I think he was just trying to play a trick on him, make him fall on his face. You know how silly boys are. He confessed straight away; he was so upset. Sean blamed him for everything. But he made his own choices after that. He didn't have to end up where he did.'

'Must have been hard for him though, Lucas being the golden child after what he did, getting everything from Julia. I can understand that. But I don't see how he could arrange anything like this from prison.' She sounds convinced. 'It must be something else, maybe someone really was after that program. Or maybe there'll be a ransom soon, if they can't get money that way, or from tricking me into selling the house, like that would have worked! He must have been kidnapped for money, it's the only explanation.'

Her voice has a slightly manic quality to it, and the pitch is making my head hurt again.

'I'm so sorry but I can't stay, Alison. I have to get back to Gareth.'

'Is he still here?'

'Yes, he brought me home yesterday.'

'When is he going? He found their stuff, didn't he, Sentient's. Why is he still hanging about?'

'Loose ends I guess,' I tell her, too embarrassed to say I asked him to stay and that he's still investigating at my behest, embroiling himself in a pointless endeavour. 'I expect he'll be off soon.'

I don't let her stand up to see me out. I leave my cup in the sink without looking into the garden again, and when I grab my coat I feel a sickening stab of guilt about the tracker, but I leave it where it is. I have to keep them safe.

31

ACROSS: 13. 1994 Madonna single (6)

WALKING INTO MY HOME WITH someone else already there is a strange feeling. I can sense the other presence even though Gareth's not making any noise. In the kitchen he's still sat at the table, his face lit by the glow of the laptop in front of him.

'Do you like pizza?' he asks without looking up.

'Doesn't everyone?'

He laughs. 'I got one yesterday. I'll pop it in the oven. I'm waiting on a call from a contact of mine in the OCP.'

I sit down. 'The what?'

'Organised Crime Partnership. They had someone at Sean's parole hearing, and they're waiting for the verdict now.'

'What? How – it only just started, didn't it? How is it done already? Are they always that quick?'

He looks at me properly. 'Merry, what's the date today?'

'It's the sixth.'

'It's the seventh. You were in hospital for two days, not one. The hearing was yesterday, and deliberations are this morning. They're expecting a verdict any minute.'

Ignoring the fact that I've somehow managed to forget an entire day of my life I push on, anxiety ramped up again. 'Would he be released straight away if it went in his favour? Is that going to happen?'

I can tell from his face that it is. 'Prisons are overcrowded and he's been a model prisoner by all accounts. It's possible.'

'But he did it, didn't he?'

'That doesn't matter. If they think he's served enough time and is unlikely to offend again, and I do think it was a first offence despite the gravity of it, then he could get parole.'

He begins to bustle around again like he owns the place, but I'm not annoyed, I'm too worried. I can't get my head around the *why*. There are supposed to be rules, reasons. And Gareth was right, I can't see how Kris could have got here before me to turn over my house so thoroughly without risking me catching him in the act. Someone here must be involved – were they the one who hurt Lucas? If they did, where is his body? How did they take him? There's nothing, no trace of him. It just doesn't make any sense.

Half a pizza is put in front of me, but I can't really eat much of it. I'm not hungry, but Gareth eyeballs me until I eat two slices. I can feel it lodged in my stomach, doughy and undigested. He puts the rest of it in the fridge to threaten me with later.

'I can't find any other trace of Kris anywhere near Sean,' he says. 'I think we should consider the small possibility that him being in the background of that photo is either a pure coincidence, or that it's not actually him.'

'Have you found him at all?'

'No, not precisely. Not without a surname. I'm waiting to

hear back from someone who makes Land Registry searches for me, I need to find the owner of that building, see if I can track him down that way. They'll be back in the office tomorrow.'

'If he's not involved then we're back to square one!' I can feel that my face is settling into a rictus of panic, wild eyed, but Gareth reaches out and touches my cheek, sliding a thumb over my cheekbone, and it's disturbing but calming at the same time.

'Don't worry just yet, we've plenty of things to be looking into.'

He spends the rest of the afternoon tapping away and writing things down, making phone calls. Usually I would find this focus fascinating, but the numb feeling I've had all day has just grown. This feels pointless, impossible. I go out into my garden for some air, hoping the chill will revitalise me, but it doesn't. I watch over the hedge for a while instead as a van drives past and the men around the back of the big house begin to bring round their equipment and load it away.

When I go back inside the door, another person in the room makes me startle. It's Macauley.

'Good afternoon, Merry,' she says. 'How are you feeling?'

'Fine.' The last time she was here she didn't believe me, and I feel a spark of something, at least, even if it is just a sullen resentment.

'That's good because I'm going to ask you to accompany me to the station. We'd like to speak to you about David Manning and the events of seventeenth August, 1985.'

Gareth interrupts. 'I don't think that's a good idea just yet, detective. She's not fully recovered yet, the doctor told her she had to rest and she—'

'I can speak for myself!' I don't mean it to come out so sharply, but he doesn't look wounded, just concerned. But I have been expecting this moment for more years than I care to count, and there's no point putting it off. 'I'll come.' I notice him flick his eyes up to where the letter is sitting and back to me but I frown and shake my head. If I can protect Julia I will. I have to try.

The young lad, the Harding, is in the driver's seat of the unmarked car the selkie must have arrived in, though he has his uniform on. Macauley opens the door for me and as I get in, I look up the drive. Alison is out on her phone again, and she sees everything that's happening. Shame pulses past the numb feeling, and nausea.

It's only a short drive down the hill to the station, where I'm checked in at the desk by another seemingly teenage policewoman, and then taken down a dim corridor. I can hear someone shouting somewhere in the building, but the sound doesn't penetrate to the room I'm led into. It's overly warm and I can feel sweat tickling under my hair and starting on my back. The chair is hard, but then what part of this is supposed to be comfortable?

Macauley clicks the black recorder on the table, speaking into it in a low clear voice and a strange spurt of hysteria makes me feel like I'm an extra on that old television show, *The Bill*. Like none of this is real, like the past twelve days have just been an extremely long, bad dream, but then I nip on the side of my cheek, hard, and the metal tang of blood reminds me that it very much isn't.

'Can you please state your full name for the recording?'

I do and she has the good grace not to even suggest an expression about it. But then this isn't a laughing matter.

'Ms Merriweather, can you please tell us everything you remember about seventeenth August, 1985.'

I clear my throat to give me a second to compose myself. 'I don't remember anything, really. It was just a normal day.' I'm trying to remember every crime novel I've ever read, every liar who ever sat in an interrogation room, not wanting to give anything away. I need to be trying to find what's happened to Lucas not getting myself arrested.

'When did you hear that David Manning had gone missing?' Macauley is tapping the tip of her green biro gently on the surface of the table but she's watching me keenly, waiting for me to slip up.

'Sean, his oldest son, asked me if I'd seen him, but I don't know if that was the next day or the day after. It's really a very long time ago, I don't really recall. I could have just told you this at my house without all . . . this.' I gesture at the room and try and look exasperated. My heart is thumping. I can feel it at the base of my throat, hear it in my shaking voice.

Macauley keeps her expression deadpan. 'Did Julia Manning tell you anything about her husband's disappearance? What did she say?'

'I went to see her after I saw Sean, to see what was going on. She said he'd disappeared, that the police had been round looking for him, that he was suspected of some nasty things. She was devastated. I always assumed he had done a runner. It was a real shock when I heard he'd been discovered in the grounds after so long.'

'About that,' she says as she leans forward slightly, and the room seems to close in around us. 'Why were you digging with your hands in that garden, hysterical that someone was buried there? Because you were right, weren't you? You were the reason we brought the dogs. Mrs Manning was rather hysterical when she called us saying you thought there was a body in the garden. Mr Jones was quite concerned too.'

There's another blurt of shame at the stress I must have caused Alison, sneaking into her house, and then having a breakdown in her garden, and causing all this. I didn't know she'd seen me that day. But I can't think about that, I must try and protect Julia's memory, whatever I do. 'I thought Lucas was there. I saw all the turf had been laid down funny and just panicked. I didn't know about David – why would I have done that if I'd known David was down there? And I was mistaken to boot. I think the stress of the past few weeks got on top of me and I had a funny five minutes. You not doing your job properly didn't help.'

'I'm sorry?' She looks offended. Good.

'Lucas is still missing. It wasn't him on his phone to Alison, it was a trick. He's still missing and all you care about is some long-dead scumbag who would have been better off staying where he was. You didn't believe me when my house was broken into, I know you thought I'd done it, but I didn't. There's something much bigger going on, and you're not doing your job properly.'

'We're not here to talk about the Lucas Manning case—'

I cut her off, it's my turn to lean in now and I hiss, 'You said he spoke to you. When you told me he'd contacted Alison. You said he spoke to you too. How did you know it was him? Did you confirm who you were speaking to? Did you get proof? Did you do your job?'

Her eyes narrow briefly, and I don't know if it's because she's angry or I've hit a nerve about her missing something. I don't think she did check who was claiming to be my son. They dropped the ball.

'We're not here to talk about the Lucas Manning case,' she repeats. 'Did Julia ever give you any reason to suspect that David was not missing, but dead?'

'No, never. She thought he had run away too.'

'What do you think happened to him, Merry?' She's trying to change her tune now, wheedling at me with her lovely voice. Not a chance.

'I think his associates caught up with him and stuck him in the flowerbed. Are we done? I'd like to go home now please; I've told you everything I know.'

There's a moment where I remember with a shiver all the bad legends about creatures from the sea, her face is still but terrifying, then she leans forward again. 'Interview terminated at seventeen-fifteen on seventh November.' She clicks off the button again. 'I don't believe a word you say,' she says as I stand up and readjust my coat, sweat now cold and slick on my spine.

'That's your problem, not mine. I don't know anything, and neither did Julia. When are you going to find Lucas?'

'I'm not convinced by your conmen on the phone tales, Merry. I think you're leading poor Mrs Manning down the garden path with all this.'

I open my mouth to furiously tell her about my own message, the one that couldn't have been from Lucas, but then think there's no point. She's made up her mind not to believe me. And when I do lie so much, why would I be surprised by that? The detective isn't stupid. She knows a liar when she sees one.

We walk back to the reception in a stiff silence, and she signs me out before lifting the receiver of the phone behind the desk.

'Jon, can you come down and run Ms Merriweather back please?' There's a painful pause while we wait, where she just assesses me with those silent pool eyes of hers, but then Jon blunders down the stairs and we go. The fresh air is mercifully cool on my face, but I can still feel her watching me.

We don't make small talk on the way back. He hums to himself, some tune I don't recognise but find deeply irritating nonetheless. I so desperately want to go for a swim, but even the thought of it sets the waves thundering in my head again, that feeling of being crushed down against the seabed with air being slowly pressed from my lungs is still all too real.

He drops me off and I have to knock on my own door because I forgot to take my keys. Gareth answers and it's all I can do not to fall on him. He nods at the policeman in that way that men do, and then steps aside, but he catches at my arm as he closes the door.

'My contact called,' he tells me, and I feel like I'm sinking. 'Sean was released four hours ago on parole.'

32

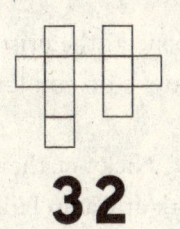

ACROSS: 27. One who looks out against the darkness (5,8)

WE GO THROUGH INTO THE lounge instead of the kitchen and he sits down next to me of the sofa. It's not large, and I feel quite pressed up. I don't really like it. I feel too hot, panicked.

'He could be here then. He could be here already.'

'I don't know, but it's possible, yes. Or he could have gone to London. I have a few people on retainer and I've got someone watching the bedsit. There's been no sign of Kris.'

'We need to watch Alison; if it is Sean and he's out he might try and hurt her, or take her too. We can't see the back of the house from here – he could even still have keys, Gareth. Should we warn her?'

He leans back and stretches out his long legs, the muscles in his thighs moving beneath the thin material of his trousers drawing my eye. 'I don't think he would make a move yet. This feels like it could be a plan that's been in the making for a while. Lucas disappears before he's released, there's not really a better alibi for him than that. We need to find evidence that he and this other guy, or someone, have been collaborating.

I need to speak to someone at the prison, see if I can find out anything about his visitors – do you know anyone who works up there?'

'No, not at Parkhurst. Nicky at the café, she told me once her husband used to work at Camp Hill, but that closed about five years ago. But he might know people who still work in the service.'

'Have you got her number?'

'No, I only know her because she works in the café. She'll probably be there tomorrow; she does most of the winter shifts. It opens at nine.' I'm embarrassed again, because I probably should have her number. She's been kind to me for years, making the odd overture that suggested she wanted to be friends, to pop round for a drink one night, that sort of thing. But I kept her at arm's length like I do everyone. Not anymore though, I'm not going to do that anymore. I want people in my life. I'll take the baby, in the summer. We'll visit the café and go paddling, and build sandcastles, and I'll have friends. I will.

'Merry?' Gareth has been talking and I wasn't listening. 'Are you okay?'

'Yes, sorry, just thinking.'

'What about?'

I laugh, but it's not a funny sound, it's sour. 'About how I've wasted my whole life, avoiding people, not letting anyone in. Always afraid of being left. It's ironic really. I think I have made myself what I didn't really want to be. Alone.'

He puts his hand on mine, the feel of the callouses on his palm sets the hairs on my arms tingling, and he does the finger threading thing again. I like how it looks.

'Merry, you don't have to be alone if you don't want to be. You've been through more trauma than nearly anyone I've met, and you're still standing here. I think you're an amazing person. A bit spiky maybe, but amazing.'

I'm cringing so hard I think I might have another heart attack, but the warmth of his words drifts somewhere deep inside me, where I can hold on to them and think on them occasionally, because I still can't quite believe he won't leave me too. But I don't want to be ruled by fear anymore. I've lost too much without ever being able to appreciate it already, so I look at his lovely face, and his funny brown eyes and I reach out and touch his cheek with my other hand. 'Thank you.'

It feels very natural as he leans towards me. He pauses for a second, as if asking for permission, but when I don't move except to hold my breath, he continues, and puts his mouth on mine, so softly. I can't help but gasp, just a little, and the kiss becomes firmer, asking questions of me that I answer with my own. I run my free hand over his short hair and then down over his shoulders, the firmness beneath his clothes so alien to my touch. He releases my hand and plunges both of his into my hair, making a low sound of appreciation, his thumbs stroking against my scalp, cupping my head.

I don't want it to ever stop, but he pulls away with a small laugh and a smile. He tucks my hair behind my ears, smoothing it away from my face. 'So beautiful,' he says. 'But I don't want to take advantage of you. I want you to be sure you want me too.'

I do, I think, *I do*, but I don't know how to say it. And a flurry of other things crowds in, where we are, why we are, what we're trying to do. 'What are we going to do about Alison?'

He sits back, away from me, and I feel a bit bereft. 'I set up my hide, while you were out.'

'Your what? A hide like a birdwatching hut?'

'If you can call Alison a bird. In the woods, and it's more a small tent, but I can watch both entrances to the house from there. No one will go in or out without me seeing them.'

'Tonight?'

'Yep. Won't be the first time. I've got my thermals, flasks for coffee. You call her and check on her and I'll head out there.'

'What about me? I want to do something.'

'It's not big enough for two, and you're too much of a distraction. You need to get some sleep, you can watch tomorrow in the daytime.'

I don't like the idea of him out there in the cold all night, but I suppose he probably did worse in the army. He heads back into the kitchen and starts rattling about while I sit for a minute, fingertips to my lips. You'd think you'd forget how to do it after so long. I'd definitely forgotten how wonderful it felt, to be kissed like that. When I feel like I've regained a modicum of equilibrium I follow him.

He's making sandwiches and has two large flasks lined up on the side next to the kettle, which is coming to a boil. There's a square black case on the table, the sort of case that protects something techy. 'What's this?' I ask, tapping it. 'More gadgets?'

'Have a look,' he laughs, now tipping an obscene amount of coffee granules into each flask and topping them up with hot water.

The case has some sort of headgear in it, with lenses. 'Are these night-vision goggles?' I'm delighted by the idea in some sort of childish way.

'They are. And heat sensors. If anyone comes near the house, I'll see them.'

'And you'll call the police? You won't try and do anything yourself, will you?'

'I will call them, yes. I'm not a kamikaze type, but I do have experience in combat, Merry. You don't have to worry about me. I know how to look after myself.'

Well, that's a stupid thing to say. Of course I'm worried. If someone can make Lucas disappear without a trace, then they can do the same to Gareth. Or Alison. I'm glad he's going to watch though. 'I'll call Alison.'

I ring the landline and she picks up with a curt hello.

'It's Merry,' I tell her, not sure suddenly of what I'm going to say.

'Oh, hi. You okay?'

'Yes. I'm fine. I just wanted to check you were locking up properly.'

She laughs a bit. 'Sorry, what? Locking up?'

'Yes, the house. With the bolts on the inside. Do you put the alarm on?'

'I don't even know the code, Merry; we never use it. Lucas leaves all the windows open half the time. He only used to set the alarm when we went on holiday.'

'It's seven-five-seven-five,' I tell her. 'He told me in case it went off when he was away, so unless he's changed it that should work. You should try it.'

'Why are you so concerned about my house security? What's going on?'

I can hear the suspicion in her voice tinged with concern, and I feel guilty, but I don't want to worry her more than I clearly just have. 'I just thought, you might get some weirdos sneaking round the garden looking for bones or something.'

'Weirdos after bones, right. Well, thank you for thinking of me. I'll be sure to lock up, don't worry. Bye, Merry. Get some sleep, yeah?' I think I hear a smothered giggle as she hangs up.

Feeling distinctly stupid, I put the phone down. Gareth is putting milk in his coffee, but I can see his back is shaking with laughing at me.

'Weirdos in the garden,' he says, also giggling like a girl.

I don't think it's funny, so I ignore him. There could be a lot worse skulking around for all we know, and I go and draw all the curtains, feeling watched. My skin feels like it's creeping over my flesh, and I rub my arms vigorously to try and dispel it.

I put the radio on in the front room and try to get some work done while Gareth finishes whatever it is he's up to. I'm so behind and have had several emails from various editors, but I'm finding it extremely difficult to concentrate on anything, so I fudge up several very old puzzles to make not-really-new ones and send them off with an apology. It's not good enough, but it's all I'm capable of for now.

'I'm off,' says Gareth from the doorway. He's dressed in some sort of black utility suit which appears to have a great many pockets and he has a big black rucksack slung over both shoulders. As I watch he pulls out a large black hat from one of the pockets and tugs it on. It looks lumpy.

'Balaclava,' he says, being a mind reader again. 'Warmer and helps hide the reflection of a white face in dark woods.'

'Will you be okay out there?'

'I'll be fine. You warm the rest of that pizza and then get to bed, okay? You still need to rest, you look exhausted. I'll lock the door behind me.' He steps back into the room and leans down and kisses me, one hand to my cheek. I can feel the ghost of it resting there as he leaves.

33

DOWN: 6. A sleeping child, taken (6)

I TRY TO REST, BUT all the small noises that make up a normal night suddenly seem sinister. The wind blowing against the windows at the back of the house becomes someone testing their security. The owl that lives in the copse calls, and the sound shocks me awake. When I do sleep, I grind my teeth until the pain in my jaw wakes me up again. Silver is showing in the curtain gaps by the time I drift away properly.

The sound of water wakes me. It's my shower, and though every particle of me tells me it's Gareth, my heart still thumps as I creep down the corridor towards the bathroom. The door is ajar, and I peep around it to look in. Definitely Gareth, his black clothes are folded neatly on the unit. I don't mean to, but as I withdraw, I catch his reflection in the mirror; he has his back to it, washing his face in the stream of water from the showerhead. His naked broad shoulders and other parts make me blush and I jerk back and run down the stairs to make breakfast.

It must take him a while to warm up because I've done the sausages by the time he gets down and am buttering the bread.

He rips through his hungrily and I let him finish before starting on the third degree. 'Did you see anything?'

He sits back and rolls his head on his shoulders, making a deep click go off in his neck. 'Not much. A few foxes sniffing around, Alison on her mobile about ten o'clock, but nothing else.'

'I don't think she gets any reception in the house, it must be the walls or something. I see her out there all the time in the evenings.'

'Did you get some sleep? You still look tired.'

'Flattery will not get you anywhere with me, Jones. But there's another sausage if you want it.' I reach over and swipe the plate off the worktop and wave it at him.

'Merry.' He's not sidetracked. I like his directness.

'No, not really. Some, but I felt too, I don't know. A bit scared I guess. Worried for Alison.'

He does take the sausage and eats it in three bites. 'I should have said, I was watching here too. You don't have to worry when I'm here, Merry. I can look after you.'

'I've looked after myself for a long time. I don't need babysitting.'

'I know,' he says. 'But I'd want to, just so you know. Look after you a bit I mean, you're probably past the babysitting age.'

The washing up seems pressingly urgent all of a sudden, so I stand up and gather the plates and stick them in the sink with the pan, turning my back on him. My ears are burning.

'I'm going to go and see if I can speak to your friend at the café. If I can get a lead on anyone who works at the prison who might be inclined to talk to us or who knows anything about Sean's visitors while he was in there, it could be useful. They might recognise Kris, or whatever his name really is, if he visited. This wasn't something that they could write about in letters, or talk about on monitored calls; there had to be someone physically visiting, probably often. Do you want to come with me?'

I do, but I don't want to go near the beach. I don't want to feel that fear of the sea again. Without looking around at him I tell him no. 'I want to keep an eye on Alison. As much as I can, anyway. I'll stay here.'

'Okay. I'll call you in a bit or see you back here soon.'

The room feels colder when he leaves, and I curse myself under my breath. Would it be so hard to tell him that I want to look after him too? It just won't come out. It's trapped beneath all of this, all of everything. How could I start something when I don't know where I am, or what's happened? Where is Lucas? All I should be focused on is my son and finding out what's happened to him. And it wouldn't be fair to Gareth, to lumber him with a broken person like me. I would just make him as miserable as I've made myself.

I finish the pots and stack them on the drainer, not liking the greasy feeling left on my hands from the water. I'm washing them and watching the big house, but there's no sign of life. She wouldn't mind if I called her, would she? Talk about what she told me in the hospital, about the baby. I wonder if she'd want me to come with her to her appointments, to the scans and things. Like a proper Grandma, like Julia would have been. She would have been so excited.

Feeling like everyone has now arrived at Merry's pity party for one, I shake it off by having a cold shower and getting dressed. I don't wash my hair, just plait it and roll it into a tight bun and pin it out of the way. It's a more reasonable hour by the time I finish faffing, so I unplug my phone and I ring the landline of the big house. There's no answer.

I try her mobile, but that doesn't ring at all, so she is probably there. Maybe she's showering herself. I wait twenty minutes, and then I call again. Still no answer. I'll just pop over and check she's okay. She might have morning sickness. I'll take her some of the ginger biscuits Gareth bought. I can't stand them, I only like ginger in cakes, and I'm sure he won't mind. My boots and coat are by the door, and I stick my phone in my pocket.

It's cool again today and it must have rained in the night because the grass is soggy and squishing beneath my feet. My breath doesn't leave any trace of silver in the air. I knock at the front door, but there's no answer. Alison's car is on the space at the side of the house and I walk around and peer in it, though I'm not sure what I'm expecting to see. I walk round to the back of the house and immediately notice that the back door is wide open and I miss a step, almost slipping as I hurry over. Maybe she's airing the kitchen, burnt toast or something. I'm always burning toast.

In the doorway I stop again, hanging on to the frame to stop myself falling. It takes a strange time slip before my brain catches up with my eyes. There is a smashed bowl on the floor, milk and flecks of cornflakes in a white puddle around the shards. A chair is on its back. The biscuits I'm clutching drop from my suddenly nerveless fingers and roll away. 'No, no, no . . .' A low moan comes out of my throat. 'Please no, please no.' I was supposed to be watching her, I was supposed to be keeping her safe! A scene plays out in front of me, of Alison being dragged from her breakfast. But where? I didn't hear a car, unless it was when I was in the shower, and how long ago was that? Thirty, forty minutes?

Feeling panic blasting though me and with tears starting in my eyes, I yank my phone from my pocket and open the little radar app and tap on her name, hoping beyond reason that wherever she is she has her coat on and that it isn't still in the house. It's not in the house. The circle is still in the same patch of map, but it's not here. It's in the woods.

With my phone in front of me, I dash out of the big house and across the lawn to the treeline and the path that twists down to the beach. The dot on the screen is moving down towards the beach. I try and run, but I've lost some condition, being sick and not swimming or eating properly; my legs and lungs start to burn almost straight away, though I try my hardest to push past it. The woods are wet and dank, and the path is treacherous, but I move as quickly as I can. My feet slip on leaves and mud as I go, and I almost fall when I try to look at the screen again. The circle is still moving away from me. I'm not fast enough and my breath feels like it's tearing something in my throat.

I can see glimpses of the sea through the barren trees where the path twists round to the shore and I risk another glance down at my screen. She's down on the beach now. My phone slips out of my sweaty hands as I hit another patch of slimy ground and jerk to steady myself and I have to stop to pick it up and flick back to the right screen because it's switched itself back to the homepage somehow. It doesn't make any sense. The little green dot is over the sea. Is it broken? Why is Alison in the sea? Are they going to drown her and make it look like an accident?

I put the phone back in my pocket and I sprint, as fast as I can, ignoring my protesting body, fuelled by panic. Crashing out onto the pebbled shoreline, I almost fall again. There's no one here, no one in the water. But I can hear something, the small *put-put* of an outboard engine, and when I look out, I see it. The little dinghy that's been tied to the jetty for the past few weeks is making its way across the narrow stretch of water to the spit. There's a low morning mist ghosting on the water, but I can make out enough to see that there are two people in that boat and then I know. It isn't heading out into the Solent; it's veering away to the left. The sandbank island, where they used to bury the drugs. They hid Lucas's body on the island and now they're taking Alison there too. No one would ever even think to look out there.

Shaking almost too much to function, I grab my mobile again, and I call Gareth. He answers as I'm running up the small jetty, already shrugging out of my coat. I don't let him speak. 'Gareth, call the police, they'll need a boat. Someone's taken Alison, they're in a boat — there's a small spit, a little island, across from their bit of beach, I think that's where they put Lucas, they're going to put her there too! You have to get help, quickly!'

'Where are you?'

'I'm on the jetty. I'm going to swim—'

'What? No! Wait there! Call the police too, I'm on my way back, I'm almost there. Merry, don't do anything. Don't you dare!'

'It might be too late! I have to go, I'm sorry, I have to! They can't take her too.'

If he answers I don't hear him. I throw the phone down on my coat, kick out of my boots and I run and dive from the end of the jetty. The shock of the cold water is immediate, but

I am used to it, even without my wetsuit. It's not so easy to swim in my clothes, but they fit close enough and my body remembers. This is home. The tide is in my favour and it helps push me towards the tiny island. My arms slice through the water and my legs propel me as well as they have ever done. Any fear I had of the water is gone, drowned by my terror over what I am heading towards now.

I kick and pull through the water, the cold air burning in my chest, but in a good way, the best way, how it always has. I've swum this gap before, so long ago, and it was at the end of my limits then, but I was new to swimming, just a girl. This distance is nothing compared to what I'm capable of now.

I drag myself out of the sea next to the motorboat, which has been pulled up and tied to a tree stump on the grubby shore. There are big boot prints in the sandy earth, and lots of smaller footprints, and I follow them along a path lined with stubby bushes. And now I hear voices, or one voice, one male voice. Sean. He's in a clearing, standing in front of a thick metal door that's opened upwards from a mound of sand. That's not a hole, it's an entire bunker! Lucas must have lied to Julia about having it filled in, and now Sean is going to put Alison in there. One of his arms is tightly around her shoulders, and the other is holding a small black gun. He laughs, and suddenly I am all rage.

'Let her go.'

He whirls around and points the gun at me, but I don't care. 'Let her go, Sean.'

'Oh, the whole family is here! This couldn't be better.' He laughs an awful hyena laugh again. 'Just in time,' he says. I don't understand, but he steps to one side, pulling Alison with him and there beyond him in the bunker is Lucas. Thin, filthy, but *alive*. He looks at me, barely strong enough to keep his head up. There are food packets and empty water bottles scattered about him, and he's chained by one arm to a thick metal hoop on the wall.

'I was just telling Lucas a story about a cuckoo,' says Sean. 'About a cuckoo who laid her egg in someone else's nest and hatched a filthy bastard child who stole everything from me. And here's the cuckoo herself, ready to watch her chick get exactly what he deserves.'

He lets go of Alison and he raises the gun again. 'Stop, please!' I run towards him, but then veer past him, into the stinking bunker, and I throw myself down in front of Lucas, shielding him with my own body. Some part of my brain registers the awful smell, the damp, salt and shit and sickness, but I twist around to face the threat and ignore it.

'I'll happily shoot you before I kill him,' says Sean. 'No one will find you here.'

'You can't kill him, he's your brother!'

He spits, and sneers. 'He's not my brother, he's just your little bastard.'

'He is your brother. David was his father too. You must be able to see that.'

The gun wavers in his hand, and then drops to his side. 'You're lying. He wouldn't cheat on my mum, especially not with someone like you. His dad was some cunt called Frank. I know you're lying!'

A swell crashes over me, and I reach back with my hand, find Lucas's arm and squeeze, desperate to ground myself before I'm swept away. *How does he know about Frank?* 'Like he would never have beat the shit out of her? Broken her arm? Her cheek? Come on, Sean. You were older than Lucas, you must have noticed what he was doing to her. He cheated all the time. He was a criminal.'

'You killed him, didn't you?' he says, the gun swinging back up, the whole universe shrinking into the tiny black hole of its barrel. 'That was you!'

'No.' I shake my head. 'You know it wasn't.'

'I know who it was,' he says. 'But you helped her, didn't you? How could you do it, fuck her husband and be her best friend and then help her kill him? The stupid bitch even raised your kid!' His face is puce with fury, spit flying with every word.

My own face is so cold that I feel the warm track of the tear that falls over my cheek. 'I didn't know he was married. I met him on the beach, he brought me right here. He groomed me. He told me his name was Frank, and then he disappeared after he got what he wanted. I agreed to let Julia adopt Lucas before I realised that David was Frank. He was away when Lucas was born, when your grandparents arranged the adoption. I had no idea; I was barely more than a child myself.' My last secret hits Sean like a slap, but I can see that he knows it's true. Alison also looks shocked, but I can hardly think of her with Lucas right here.

He coughs behind me, a thick wet racking sound that terrifies me almost as much as the gun. There's more heat pulsing through my palm where I'm gripping him tightly. He's burning up. I have to try and reason with Sean, surely he's not so far gone that he would kill us in cold blood now he knows the truth. 'You can't think you'll get away with this, Sean? Killing all three of us and leaving us here? You'll be caught, you'll be back in prison for good. You can just go now, we won't tell anyone.'

He pauses, cocking his head slightly, and a terrible grin spreads slowly over his face. 'All three of you? Who said anything about killing Alison?'

She steps forward and he puts his arm round her again, pulling her roughly towards him, kissing her hard on the mouth. 'My girl!' he says gleefully, madly. I look at her and glance down at her stomach and back and she shakes her head, a tiny movement of *no*, and my heart breaks as her expression takes on a wicked smugness. It was her all along. She's the girl in the Facebook picture, the one with Kris in the background. I didn't see it before, her hair's much darker now, but her eyes, they aren't the same shape as her brother's, but they're that same washed-out colour.

'He's your brother, isn't he? That man in London. Kris, or whatever his name really is. He was helping you. And it was you, who broke into my house. I should have known.' The message on the mirror. I don't even own any lipstick; she must have had it on her. A finishing touch. I feel cold now, colder than I've ever been, my clothes feel frozen against my skin. I paw down Lucas's arm until I find his too-hot hand. He can't even squeeze back, both of us are shaking violently, one with ice, one with fever.

'You trapped him here so Sean could kill him, didn't you? Your whole marriage, you faked being in love with Lucas that whole time? Everything? How could you?' The only heat I can muster now is in my words. She told him about the adoption, about Frank. I trusted her, and she used me.

She shrugs a shoulder. 'A long con,' she says. 'Always worth it in the end. Though it has been especially painful having to put up with you and your endless fucking interference.' A cold smile of her own appears, showing teeth that suddenly seem sharp and ready to bite. 'I've waited a long time for Lucas to get what he deserves. He took everything from Sean, wouldn't even give his own brother an alibi, then stole his inheritance to boot. Well. Now we're going to take everything from him. And you.'

The pain of her betrayal makes me gasp and behind me Lucas moans, and coughs again. 'You'll be caught too, there's no way you'll get away with it. I called the police already, they'll be here any minute!' I'm shouting as loudly as I can, but there's no one coming. There's no time left.

'I'll be long gone,' says Sean, that sick look still on his face. 'I've got friends waiting for me out there, and this mist will help nicely.' He swings wildly out in the direction of the Solent. 'You'll both be dead in a minute and poor Alison might have a flesh wound, but she'll tell them what happened. A mad man, wasn't it, babe? Wanting a ransom for your poor husband. Merry, you really shouldn't have come on your own after us.'

'Silly Merry,' she says with a hard barking laugh. 'Do it now, Sean, you have to be quick, the pigs won't be long. I love you!' She kisses him hard and then steps away and closes her eyes, and to my absolute horror Sean points the gun at her and shoots her through the top of her shoulder, and her scream rends the air as she collapses to the floor. 'Fuck that really hurts!' Tears are pouring down her face and a red patch is seeping through the beige material of her coat, spreading rapidly. She makes panting noises of pain and writhes on the floor.

'Sorry, love,' he says. 'Needs must.' He turns back towards me and Lucas and points the gun again. I shuffle as far in front of my boy as I can, desperate, and I close my eyes and wait for the bullet. At least I'm with him at the end, like I was at the beginning. But the bullet doesn't come. Instead of a bang there's a strangled sort of grunting noise, then a thud. I open them to Sean convulsing on the floor, silver threads leading away from him to a figure in the undergrowth holding a small black box with his finger on a trigger. It's Gareth.

He runs over to Sean and picks up the dropped gun, flicking a button on it before switching it round in his hand so he's holding the muzzle. He brings the handle down hard on Sean's temple before running to us. Alison screams Sean's name and begins to drag herself towards him but he doesn't move. There's a pile of scraggy blankets on a small camp bed that I didn't notice before and Gareth grabs one and wraps it round me and pulls the others onto Lucas. 'You're . . . you're all wet,' I stutter, so cold I can hardly get the words out.

'Yes, Merry,' he says crossly. 'You're not the only one who knows how to swim, you know.'

Over the sound of Alison sobbing over Sean's unconscious figure I can hear sirens somewhere and the sound of boats. I turn away from the disgusting sight of her and around to Lucas. His eyes are closed now and his breathing is ragged and laboured as I pull him into my arms. His head rocks back and I kiss his forehead and his cheeks, hugging him against me as tightly as I can, praying that this isn't the first and last time I ever hold my child.

34

DOWN: 5. Apart no longer (8)

LUCAS IS UNCONSCIOUS FOR THREE days and Gareth almost has to physically carry me away from the hospital each night. The nurses all loathe the sight of me I'm sure, and I can't help but harangue them constantly about when he's going to wake up. But double pneumonia and exposure is serious, and I have to wait while the antibiotics and care work to bring him back to me.

I barely even wait for Gareth to park the van at St Mary's before I'm out the door and running to the entrance. My feet could wear a groove in the floor to his room. By the time Gareth joins me with two coffees and some boring book he's reading about the SAS, I'm already ensconced in a chair, staring intently at Lucas, willing him to wake up. The nurse told me that he was awake last night, and talking to Macauley when she came, and it's taking all my self-control not to squeeze his hand too tightly in the hope it will disturb him into consciousness.

'The nurse said he was awake yesterday after you made us leave,' I tell Gareth.

'Why are you shouting?' he says and rubs his ear, that admittedly I might have just shouted a bit into.

'She was trying to wake me up,' says Lucas.

My head nearly spins off my neck I turn so quickly back to him. 'Lucas!'

He smiles weakly and moves the oxygen mask away from his mouth. 'Hello, Merry,' he says. 'Who's your friend?'

'We can discuss that later,' says Gareth while my jaw is still wagging trying to think of an answer. 'I'm going to leave you to it. I'll bring you something to eat in a bit.' He squeezes my shoulder and kisses my temple.

Lucas's eyebrows go up when he sees that, and I blush like a girl. I've been so desperate for him to wake up and now he has, I don't know what to say. We just stare at each other for an age. I'm still holding his hand.

Eventually I crack. 'Can you remember what happened? How you ended up in that bunker?' I ask.

He looks away at the wall. 'Kind of,' he says. 'Alison wanted to go over to the island on the boat. Just for something to do, really. We were on a walk and the boat was there; we were out on it the day before for a putter up to Wooton and I'd not taken it back round to the harbour yet.' His voice is scratchy and rough, and before he speaks again, he coughs. It still sounds awful, but not nearly so bad as when we found him. He holds the mask over his mouth again and breathes in and out slowly.

I pour him a drink of water from the jug on the table – hospitals must have millions of the bloody things – and help him drink some. He looks so skinny and weak.

'We went over, and walked across, and the bunker door was open. It's always shut, and chained, so kids can't get in. Mum told me to get it filled in properly, but I didn't get round to it.' He closes his eyes and coughs again. 'I went over to have a look, and the next thing I was waking up in the dark with a headache, chained to the wall. It was pitch black, I had no idea what was going on. I must have been unconscious for the whole day, or longer, I don't know.'

'So she hit you and dragged you in there? I never even knew it was there!' I manage to keep the venom I'm tasting out of my voice, but I could happily kill that traitorous snake of a woman.

'I guess so. It got a bit lighter in the daytime, enough light came in through the grates on the door to see that there was food and a cot bed with blankets and water and a bucket. She must have been stocking it up for ages when I was away at work. I had no idea. It felt like I was in there forever.' He opens his eyes again, still fever bright against the purple that underlines them in his thin face. 'I feel like such an idiot for trusting her. For falling in love with her . . .' I can hear the pain in his voice and wish with my whole heart that I could take it away.

'Sean must have been feeding her information about you, so she could pretend to be this perfect woman. And you'd only just split up with Lucy, you were vulnerable.'

'Mum must have told him we'd broken up when she was visiting him,' he murmurs. He must see my shocked face. 'I know she didn't tell you she visited him, did she?'

I shake my head.

'I guess you both had secrets.'

It's hard to meet his gaze and I feel the redness in my cheeks again.

'Would you ever have told me?' he asks softly.

'I don't know. I kept everything all locked up in my head and tried never to think about it. Sometimes I didn't even think any of it was real, that maybe I'd just imagined it all or dreamt it. Alison must have told Sean that you were adopted, she said she found a letter or something that Julia had hidden away somewhere. She liked a letter, your mum.'

We both lapse into silence and Lucas's eyelids flutter closed again, though I don't know if he's asleep or not. I just look at him, drinking in the fact that he's here, alive and breathing. Even if he decides he never wants to have anything to do with me again, at least he's safe now.

Eventually he moves his head and opens his eyes again. 'The policewoman I saw last night said that they were planning on running away together with new identities. They were going to kill me, and Alison – Kallie, I suppose I should call her – was going to sell the house and they'd live on the money. He was in deep trouble for grassing up some big names. It doesn't feel real, any of this.'

'He tried to tell me that you were the one who gave him those names. That you set the whole thing up.'

A laugh turns into another long bout of coughing, and he struggles to get his breathing back under control. 'No,' he says eventually. 'He did that all by himself. I was suspicious at the time that he was doing something stupid. I followed him down to the harbour a couple of times, asked that old gossip Peter, who he was hanging about with, who they knew. I should have spoken to him sooner, tried to stop him getting involved. I told him I would've helped him when he came out. I think finding out about me being adopted snapped something in him. I've always felt guilty about his accident, when we were kids. It was so hard to even look him in the face afterwards, to watch him give up on everything. I just wanted to help.'

'You were only eight. There's no way you could have realised what could happen. You didn't want to hurt him, did you?'

'Not like that, no. I think I thought he would just fall over and I could laugh at him. I ruined his life, Merry. This is all my fault.'

'It isn't. And you didn't. He made all those bad choices willingly. No one held a gun to *his* head.'

We look at each other for a long time before Lucas manages a weak smile. 'So, are you going to tell me who that random bloke is?'

Gareth drags me away around lunchtime because Lucas is exhausted and the nurses are looking very sternly at us. We're banned until tomorrow, and only allowed back for an hour then, and only if they say Lucas is capable. He might be conscious but he's still very poorly, so I agree without too much external fuss.

'I think they want you down the station again,' Gareth says as we're getting back in the van. 'Your Scottish detective left a message on my phone. I think you should give her the letter Julia left you. She did it for a reason, Merry.'

'I don't want to. They can't prove anything now, surely?'

'This isn't a situation that's going to go away if you ignore it. A man was murdered in that house. There will likely still be traces if they look hard enough. People are already talking.' He pulls today's copy of the *County Press* out of his driver's side door compartment and puts it on my lap before starting the engine.

Unfolding it shows a front-page picture of the tent that was in the garden and the milling people in those white paper suits. The headline screams about discovery. There's a line about the murders in Yarmouth. Nothing suggests Julia had anything to do with it, but what else would people think?

'They might not even investigate further if you do,' he goes on. 'They wouldn't even necessarily come out and say anything about Julia if they didn't think it was in the public interest. Just close the case again.'

'It's concealing evidence though, isn't it? The letter is evidence, even if it does say I wasn't involved. And I was involved. I was there when it happened. I helped cover it up. I'm guilty.'

'You're nothing of the sort. And remember the envelope says, "in the event of David returning", not "in the event of David being dug up". She wasn't stupid, Merry. She must have known what could happen and she wanted you to be safe. We're taking it tomorrow, okay? I'm not risking anything happening to you. You've been through enough.'

He keeps on at me about it until we get home. We look at the letter and he's still right. She had labelled it in such a way that I would have no idea of what was in it from the outside. And this situation is the exact reason she wrote it: because she didn't want me to suffer any more than I already have. I finally agree that we'll take it, that I'll say I forgot about it until now. But it still feels wrong.

I can't stop worrying at it the whole afternoon and into the evening. My head starts to pulse with a stress headache. Whenever I think about that night it hurts. I can't pull the pieces together; I can't cope with the horror of seeing it happen again. I can't remember.

I tell Gareth that I need to get some rest myself, an early night, the pain in my head worse than ever. I swallow some aspirin and lie down upstairs, breathing through my nose and counting in and out in the hope it will ease off and I can sleep. I'm halfway between being awake and in a dream when the firework display up at the rec starts, with screams and whistles and bangs, leaving me lurching in terror like I always do, clawing at the covers. I decide to stop trying to remember. Some things are better left buried, and I go back down to Gareth instead.

1985

I'M LATE. I SAID I'D call for Julia at seven so we can get down to the front for the fireworks, but I can't find my hairbrush and I need it because my hair is all salty and – ah ha. Under the coats on the shoe bench. Of course it is. My scalp crackles as I drag it through, and the mirror tells me I probably shouldn't have bothered, but I should at least try to not embarrass my friend occasionally.

I open the door and a cooler breeze blows through the corridor, so I pull Aunt Rosie's old shirt down from between my jackets. Three years now since she went, and I wonder when I'll stop missing her so much. Leaving all her things scattered through the house makes me feel slightly less lonely, but not much. Running across the lawn up to the big house shakes off some of my melancholy, the lawn is looking a bit tatty after the roasting summer, but it always does by this time of year. The boys have left their garden toys all scattered about and I really wish they were coming tonight but they're camping with some of Julia's other friends, making lovely memories hopefully.

The back kitchen door is open, and I dash up to it, but a noise knocks me off step, slowing my stride. I don't know what it was but all the hairs on my arms lift, and my legs feel heavy as I drag them the last few steps.

David is home.

David is home, and he has his hands around Julia's neck. Her nose is bleeding, her lip, her skin is the wrong colour and that noise, that noise I heard was her, choking.

My hands are on his arms before I even realise I've moved, pulling, but they're like iron bars. 'Stop it!' I scream, helplessly. 'Get off her!'

He backhands me in the face, and something cracks. No one has hit me since I was small, since I was small and my mum would hit me, for no other reason than I was there and she was angry. It hurts. It hurt then, it hurts now. I couldn't do anything then, but now I stand up, and I can see that he's killing her, he's killing my friend right in front of me. So I grab a knife, the biggest knife, from the block on the side and I scream again.

'Frank, stop! Stop it!'

Only he doesn't stop, and neither does the knife. It slides into his body as easy as if it were butter. The blade is gone, only the handle is left sticking out of his back, the handle and his grasping, loose fingers trying to get hold of it. He manages to get hold of it, and he tries to pull, but it wanted to go in and it doesn't want to come out. It sucks and squelches, and then there's just blood.

He turns around and looks at me, looks down at the knife, before lifting it and I see my dying written on his face, but only for a moment, because then it goes slack, grey, and he groans and falls to his knees, slipping in the blood that's everywhere now, pools and gobs of it, so much red on the white floor.

Fireworks start to pop in the distance and each one feels like a bullet as I stare at him, twitching and dying, staring up at me.

Julia coughs, tries to speak, coughs again.

'Frank,' she whispers rawly. 'Why did you call him Frank?'

This is a nightmare. This is a terror. A shimmer of unreality flickers over everything, all colour leaching away except the stains on my hands, the red-to-brown sticky lesions of his blood on my hands. 'He said he was called Frank,' I whisper back, because this is a dream, and I can be honest with her in my dreams. 'That summer. When I was sixteen.'

'Lucas is his,' she breathes, and it's not a question.

I just nod, watch my hands rubbing against Aunt Rosie's shirt. My ears are ringing. 'I'm so sorry. I'm so sorry, Julia. I'm so sorry.' Rubbing my hands. It won't come off.

'You didn't do this, Merry,' she says in her brutalised voice, crawling to me through his mess. 'This was me. I did this. This is not your fault. None of this is your fault.'

It's everywhere. It's everywhere. I don't know how I got here. How did I get here? I don't know what has happened. All I can see is blood.

35

DOWN: 35. Conclusion (3,3)

'GARETH! WHERE ARE THE WIPES!'

'The whats?'

He thinks I don't know he's hiding on his laptop upstairs. He's not doing work; he's watching documentaries about spies again. 'The wipes!'

'Kitchen,' he calls down again.

'Come on then, sweetheart, let's change this smelly bum, shall we?'

Grace dribbles out of her gummy smile and reaches for my hair again. I'll not have any left if she keeps this up. 'Leave my hair alone please, or Grandad Gareth will tell you off.' I manage to extract her little fingers and find the wipes on the worktop, which is not where they live. 'Why do you always time this for just before Daddy comes to pick you up?' I ask the baby, who looks at me like I am an idiot, and then giggles to herself.

It took some practice, but I am a dab hand at nappies and poppers and little vests now, and thankfully none of this horror show has escaped up her little back. She tries to roll over, but

I hold her gently while I wrangle her into a clean outfit. I dress her and give her a little toy to chew on, strapping her into the bouncy chair while I bag and bin the offending article and wash my hands.

Back in the front room I just watch her with the still new after five months feeling of delight I get whenever I see her, this tiny redhaired urchin. I can't resist unclipping her for another cuddle, smelling her little head and holding her closely against me until she squawks and kicks me.

The bell goes and she immediately starts pogoing on my knee, she's a clever little thing. I swing her to my hip and take her to the door. It opens to her dad, and she tries to launch herself at him through the air, but we manage a secure handover. 'Hey, baby,' he says, lifting her in the air and making her shout. 'How's my girl?' Greetings done for the most important person, I get mine. 'Hey, Merry,' he says, kissing me on the cheek. 'How's she been?'

'Gold as gold,' I tell him, deciding to forget about the pulled over drink of squash that went everywhere and the sick on Gareth's new shirt. 'How was it?'

He sighs. 'Not great. She doesn't want me to go again.'

'Did she sign it?'

'Yeah. I mean it was her idea anyway, she's not interested in Grace at all. She told me only went through the pregnancy for better treatment when she was waiting for the trial. She said she'd booked an abortion, before. She wouldn't have had her if you and Gareth hadn't been there in time.'

I want to say I don't understand how Kallie doesn't ever want to know her own baby, how she could just sign away her parental rights, but that is still a point of contention between

Lucas and I, because I am no different. He's still not happy that it took him so long to find out who I was, and that he very nearly didn't. But we're working it out. And at least he knows now that I always loved him, even if I was too scared to show it.

'Did she mention Sean?'

'I didn't ask. I really don't want to know if they're still together. They're going to have a long prison correspondence romance if they are. I just want to move on with things now.'

I can understand that, but I still worry. He's still too thin even nearly a year after the pneumonia that almost killed him, and then getting Grace. She was hard work, the little rascal barely sleeps a wink even now. But he has colour in his face and I can see how much he loves his little girl, kissing her nose even as I'm watching. I know he's been having therapy too. He's not stupid like me; he knows how to help himself get better. He won't struggle like I did, shutting himself away. I wouldn't let him anyway, not now.

'I'd better get this one back for a bath and hopefully at least a few hours' kip. She managed a four-hour stretch last night; I feel like a new man.' He laughs and boops her little nose again. 'Have you got her bag?'

'Two ticks.' I race around grabbing all her little bits and shoving them in the enormous bag that goes everywhere with her. For such a small creature, she requires a great many things. 'Here you go.'

'Thanks, Merry. I'll give you a call later, you and Gareth need to come over for dinner again soon. We'll definitely beat you at Trivial Pursuit this time.' He kisses me again and I watch them walk out and away up the path, the sunlight bouncing off Grace's head, giving her a little halo. She's got her fingers in his hair now, and I laugh to myself.

I go up the stairs and into the bedroom, where Gareth is tapping away furiously. 'Beastie gone home?' he asks, glancing at me from above the new reading glasses he's got. I like them on him, he looks like a professor or something clever.

'She has indeed, you're safe.' Grace loves Gareth, and I know he loves her too. He also needs the training, as his daughter Megan is rather heavily pregnant herself. 'What you up to?'

'Emails. A new case came in. Shropshire. I've sent you the details. Said we'd go up there next week. What's that look about?' He takes his glasses off and puts the laptop on the dresser with a wry smile.

'What look?' I fire back, grinning myself.

He laughs as I clamber on to the bed and grab his face in both my hands, swinging one leg over him so I'm sat across him. He puts his hands on my waist and slides them up underneath my shirt. I lean down and kiss him, and he kisses me back, and I thank my stars like I do every day that's it not only me who can swim.

Crossword

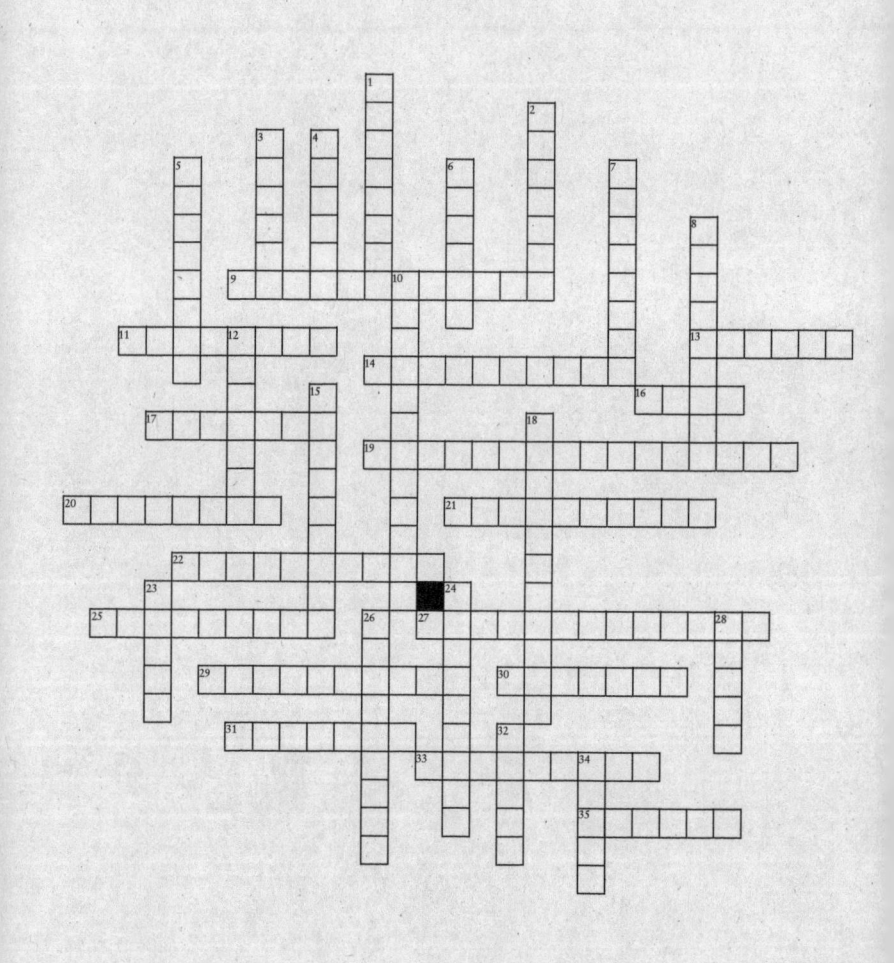

ACROSS

9. Solving step by step (12)
11. Tentative approach (8)
13. 1994 Madonna single (6)
14. In which you might find the number of the beast (10)
16. The physical practice of ancient philosophy (4)
17. False information is undesirable (3,4)
19. It wasn't me (8,8)
20. A child's toy, and another, and another, and another... (8)
21. The ways in which He works, or the ways in which she moves, perhaps (10)
22. Smaug's handiwork (10)
25. Rising water commonly associated with low-pressure (5,4)
27. One who looks out against the darkness (5,8)
29. Everything's all upside down said Tim (5,5)
30. A long support (7)
31. If Charlotte made her home in a book (3,4)
33. Who needs ethics if you can have money? (9)

DOWN

1. The lay of the upper classes, perhaps (8)
2. Yesterday or long ago, depending on the winner (7)
3. Not Father Christmas, the other type (6)
4. Air intake (that one may want to save?) (6)
5. Apart no longer (8)
6. A sleeping child, taken (6)
7. One who watches over (8)
8. A doe's vision, perhaps (9)
10. I might wear an undergarment if I weren't so scaly (12)
12. You might end up here if you steal (3,4)
15. Working undercover (9)
18. Is it really mutually assured? (11)
23. The opposite of belief (5)
24. An impossible job, even for the Greeks (9)
26. A pirate's pastime (9)
28. A red-haired sea creature on screen (5)
32. Eat something in a quick and eager way (5)
34. Does Alisha still live here? (5)
35. Conclusion (3,3)

Answers

ACROSS

9. METHODICALLY
11. OVERTURE
13. SECRET
14. REVELATION
16. YOGA
17. BAD NEWS
19. MISTAKEN IDENTITY
20. BABUSHKA
21. MYSTERIOUS
22. DESOLATION
25. STORM TIDE
27. NIGHT WATCHMAN
29. TOPSY TURVY
30. BOLSTER
31. WEB PAGE
33. MERCENARY
35. THE END

DOWN

1. LANDLORD
2. HISTORY
3. CLAUSE
4. BREATH
5. TOGETHER
6. KIDNAP
7. GUARDIAN
8. HINDSIGHT
10. INVESTIGATOR
12. THE NICK
15. ESPIONAGE
18. DESTRUCTION
23. DOUBT
24. SISYPHEAN
26. SMUGGLING
28. ARIEL
32. SCARF
34. ATTIC

Acknowledgements

And now for the hard bit – trying to remember all the wonderful people I need to thank after another publishing journey. If I've missed you out, it's not because I'm not thankful, it's because I'm incapable of making myself a note when I remember someone I should thank. But here goes.

So many thanks to my lovely editor Rachel Morrell at Black & White Publishing for seeing into the heart of this book and for being an all-round gem. Thanks also to her crew, Ali, Campbell, Tonje, Hannah and Lizzie. You're all awesome and I'm so happy you all loved Merry like I do.

Thank you to my agent Felicity Blunt and the Curtis Brown team, most especially Rosie Pierce for putting up with my very many not very to the point emails and madcap novel outlines.

Thank you to Emma Rogers for designing the most gorgeous book cover – I couldn't have imagined a better one. I love it.

Thank you to Nicky Stonehill for the PR relating to this novel and its author, it's so appreciated.

I've already dedicated this book to you, but allow me to wax lyrical in my appreciation, Liz Webb, Joanna Pritchard, Katherine Tansley and Marija Maher-Diffenthal. I would never have imagined on that first nervously sweaty day on the Faber

Academy Writing a Novel course in 2019 that five years later I would still have such good friends and readers in my corner. It isn't hyperbole to say that I wouldn't have written this novel without all your unwavering support and frankly excellent editorial ideas. You're all brilliant.

There are so many writing friends I would like to thank too, including but certainly not limited to Sophia Spiers, Sarah Leonard, Sarah Bonner, Mira Shah, Liv Matthews, Sophie Flynn and all the other gorgeous souls who agreed to have a read of this and are generally among the loveliest and most supportive people I know.

Thank you especially to the writers of the North London Writers Group, Adi, Anna, Colin, Emma, Hilary, Marianne, Neil, Rob, Rosie and Tammy. This one was in the works before I joined your hallowed ranks, but the advice and camaraderie and excellent food at our meetings are the best sort of inspiration for any writer and I wanted to include you for this book anyway!

Thank you to Jamie Humm for patiently answering my annoying questions about police procedure. Who would have thought the person I sat next to in history class thirty years ago would come in so handy now!

To my friends, you all know who you are, thank you for everything. Okay, fine, some names in no order of preference or importance . . . Anna, Ria, Lottie, Helen, Cliodhna, Kelly, Sam, Kate, Ed, Tam, Simon, Ruth – thank you for various cheerleading and drinking escapades etc, you're all awesome. Also shout out to my D&D crew, Claire, Zaheer, James, Haresh and Alvin. We may not have defeated that menace Strahd in the time it took me to conceive of, write, edit and get this book published, but I have every faith that 2024 will be our year. Or maybe 2025. Ish.

For Ash, Charlie, Jaz, Heather, Livy and any other of my elodies who might read this, thank you for being some of the funniest, wittiest, kindest, most supportive and most randomly brought together people I've ever had the good fortune to meet.

To my husband and son, Mark and Rian, thank you for putting up with me, I'm not sure anyone else would. I love you. Thanks and love as always to Mum and Dad, and especially to my sister Josie for always reading all my early scribblings and saying, 'Yeah, I like it!' You're the best.

And thank you, of course, reader. I'm still quite baffled that you even exist and that you're holding my words in your hands. I hope you liked them as much as I like you.